WHEN THE WORLD WAS YOUNG

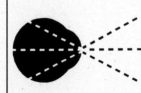

This Large Print Book carries the
Seal of Approval of N.A.V.H.

WHEN THE WORLD WAS YOUNG

ELIZABETH GAFFNEY

THORNDIKE PRESS
A part of Gale, Cengage Learning

GALE
CENGAGE Learning·

Farmington Hills, Mich • San Francisco • New York • Waterville, Maine
Meriden, Conn • Mason, Ohio • Chicago

GALE
CENGAGE Learning·

LIBRARY OF CONGRESS CATALOGING-IN-PUBLICATION DATA

Gaffney, Elizabeth.
    When the world was young / by Elizabeth Gaffney. — Large print edition.
        pages ; cm. — (Thorndike Press large print peer picks)
    ISBN 978-1-4104-7671-5 (hardcover) — ISBN 1-4104-7671-5 (hardcover)
    1. Single women—Fiction. 2. Family secrets—Fiction. 3. Household employees—Fiction. 4. World War, 1939-1945—Fiction. 5. Large type books. 6. Domestic fiction. I. Title.
PS3607.A355W54 2015
813'.6—dc23   2014041075

Published in 2015 by arrangement with Random House LLC, a Penguin Random House Company

Printed in Mexico
1 2 3 4 5 6 7 19 18 17 16 15

*For Ann Gaffney
and in memory of
Emily Boro*

CONTENTS

I
PARADE

1
RADAR

The children rejoiced.

They rollicked in the streets.

Victory! they shouted, banging on pans, climbing up streetlamps, leaping off stoops. *Victory in Japan!*

Wally Baker's mother, Stella, must have been the only person in the entire five boroughs with something else on her mind, as she set out that morning with her daughter in tow.

"Come on, darling, let's go. Pick up your feet."

But Wally couldn't stop looking around her. The sidewalks were busy, yet the people weren't going anywhere. They were celebrating — laughing, talking, crying. Halfway down the block, Wally stopped completely. She reached down, pulled up her kneesocks, and stood there, taking it all in.

On the other side of the street she saw the milkman, Sylvester, sitting on the back of his truck, which looked awfully full of milk for this time of the morning. He waved at them.

"Morning, Syl!" called her mother. "What about the milk?"

"Self-service today," he answered, reaching into the body of his truck and rising to meet them with a quart in each hand. "Take these to your mother if you're going by there, will you, Miz Baker?"

"Sure, Syl."

But instead of handing her the milk, the milkman embraced Wally's mother, and suddenly, before Stella had a chance to disengage, they were dancing. Wally found the cool, thick neck of a bottle thrust into her hands. Syl held the other bottle pressed against her mother's back. He led her out between the parked cars, and they bobbed in time to Syl singing "Happy Days Are Here Again."

Out in the street, more couples joined in.

As Syl spun her, Stella's eyes crinkled at the corners. Her red lips opened, and she laughed. *What charming nonsense,* she thought, *what madness!*

Others cheered or sang along. Cars gave way.

Then, as quickly as it started, it was over.

Wally's mother broke away from the milk-man.

"Thank you for the dance, Mr. Miller," she said, taking the milk from him and turning back to her daughter.

"Wallace? Come along now. We've got to get going."

But how could Wally go? All the neighborhood children were out. The two most popular girls from her class ran by, their fathers' air-warden helmets jouncing up and down on their small heads and American flags fluttering between their outstretched arms.

"Mother, look — that's Claire Rensselaer, in a helmet!"

"Why so it is," laughed Stella.

It was the hot end of summer vacation, but kids weren't bothering with the standard games of the season. No stickball, hop-scotch, jump rope, four square. No pushing miniature perambulators or picking up jacks. None of the usual posses of girls and boys walking toward the piers or the subway with rolled-up towels, embarking on one of the city's swimming excursions, be it dock jumping or the beach at Coney or Staten Island. They were milling about, like their parents. They were smiling, like Syl. They were waving tiny flags attached to pencils.

They were showing their glee.

Wally just wanted to be one of them.

"I don't want to go to Gigi's, Mother," Wally said, tucking her brown hair defiantly behind her ears. "I want to stay out."

The coattails of Stella Baker's blue wool suit flared. The carefully formed waves of her hair swooped forward to the edge of her jaw, then receded as she swung around.

"Darling —" She was exasperated now. "This is not a debate."

"I'm not some baby, like Georgie. I don't need to be sat for."

"Don't speak about your brother, Wally."

Stella did not want to be angry with her daughter. She didn't want to burst into tears in front of her, either. Why couldn't the child just cooperate for once? She got herself behind Wally, grasped her daughter gently but firmly by the shoulders, and guided her down the block.

"I'll just go straight out again as soon as I get there," Wally whined.

"That's between you and Loretta."

Wally and her mother had both been caught up in the morning newscast, enraptured by the idea of radio detecting and ranging, the secret technology that had improved the American fleet's ability to defend itself in the Pacific and made it far

14

more lethal to the enemy. They knew now that the sea war had been won by RADAR. RADAR had probably saved Wally's father's life many times over, without their even knowing it existed. It had been impossible to hear too much about it.

"Aren't you proud to be an American today?" her mother had asked her when the broadcast ended. But that was when they'd realized they were late.

Wally walked, but not quickly enough for her mother. She was still so busy looking at the people, thinking about RADAR and peace. Soon, she imagined, there'd be unlimited sugar and no air-raid warnings and streetlights that shone reassuringly all night, every night.

Years later, she would remind herself of the dance Stella had allowed herself that morning. She would learn that her mother had smiled at Boris the doorman when she went back home at midday, because Boris told her so, although Wally always wondered what had made him remember that smile. It was V-J Day. Hadn't positively everyone smiled at him that day? She knew Stella had ridden the elevator up to their apartment — surely setting her handbag down on the red leather bench at the back, the bench that no one but Wally ever actually sat on. She had gone to the kitchen and baked a pound cake. Wally could picture her mother eating the first slice of that cake while sitting at the enamel-topped kitchen table. Maybe it was the full bow of her lower lip, or the way she flared her nostrils, inhaling as she chewed, but Stella Baker had a beautiful way of eating. What did it mean that on that day, when she was supposed to be at work, she had gone home and baked a cake?

"Mother," Wally said, loudly enough to carry over the jubilant street noise and the clip-clip-clip of her mother's shoes. "Where was Mr. Niederman last night?"

"Pardon me?"

Wally knew it wasn't her business to keep tabs on the boarder the Bakers had taken in for the war effort, but she had a theory about him, and she couldn't let it lie.

"Where was Mr. Niederman last night? He wasn't there when I went to bed, and he wasn't there this morning."

"That's a nosy question, Wally."

"I don't think so," Wally said, coming to a halt.

"*Walk.* As a matter of fact, he went back to New Jersey for a night or two, to celebrate the holiday with his family."

"That's what he told you. But don't you think it's interesting that he vanished the

16

very night before the Allies' secret weapon was announced to the world? I think he was probably involved."

"That's quite fanciful, Wally. Now, could you walk?"

"All right, but, Mother — if he was really helping figure out RADAR, then we helped win the war, too, just by giving him a room to stay in! I'd sort of like to apologize for calling him a spy if he really was a hero after all, just like Daddy."

"Wally," said her mother, laughing, "isn't it a little late to cheer him on, now the war is over? Not to mention you still seem to think he's a liar."

"He's just mysterious. He always seemed like a spy. Right? Don't you think he seemed like a spy at first?"

"No, not to me he didn't. I always liked him."

Wally came to a complete stop. Her mother's arm stretched long before their hands separated.

Her mother certainly hadn't always liked him. At first, she hadn't even wanted him to come, and she'd been very rude to him in the beginning. When had that changed? At what point had her mother uncovered the truth? Wally stared at her mother, willing her to look her in the eye, but Stella

17

wouldn't do it. Wally knew she was hiding something.

"You always *liked* him?"

"What?" asked Stella, glancing down at her watch, then touching the corner of her lip as if to be sure no lipstick was caught in the crease.

"That's simply not true, Mother. Why would you say that?"

"Excuse me?"

"You're lying, Mother."

"Wallace, you are being impertinent!"

"Do you know his secret?"

"What makes you think he has a secret? And that's the end of the discussion."

They walked the rest of the way in silence until, at last, they were standing before the wide stoop of Wally's grandparents' brownstone.

"Go on up now. Tell Gigi and Waldo I'm running late and that I can't come in. And be a good girl today."

"Why do you have to work on the biggest holiday in the world? Everyone else has the day off."

"People are sick, and more will get sick today, just like every day. They still need caring for. You know that. Now, have a happy V-J Day, darling," she said, tousling Wally's hair and crouching to plant a kiss

18

on her daughter's cheek.

"Bye," Wally said, trudging up the stairs, disappointed, once again. For the past two years, since she returned to work, it seemed to Wally her mother had spent more time with her patients than with her daughter.

Just standing still without moving an arm, Stella waited until Wally pushed through the great double doors of her grandparents' house.

"Bye-bye," she said.

When she heard the door slam, she turned and hurried back up the street, returning the way she had come.

Inside, Wally rubbed her cheek, knowing there would be a ruby smear, then headed to the big sunny kitchen that overlooked the garden and harbor.

"Happy V-J Day!" she said to Loretta, who was washing the breakfast dishes.

"Happy V-J Day, String Bean."

Wally found Ham in the basement, feeding tiny bits of chopped apple to the ants he kept in an old five-gallon pickle jar.

"Hey, Wally."

"Come on, Ham, we've gotta get outside — there's a celebration going on."

"Like in Times Square? It was on the radio."

"Maybe not that big. Hey, let me put one in." She took a piece of apple from Ham and dropped it on top of the soil and sand, a little distance from the others. She peered through the side of the jar, watching the gleaming brown bodies of the ants as they moved along the dark tunnels that were up against the glass.

"Everyone's out in the street, you know, *gathering* — all the grown-ups and all the kids, from all the schools. I saw that bunch of guys you're friends with."

"Posse's out in force, huh? I guess we should go, too."

"Don't you *want* to?"

"Sure, I do. But, Wally, listen, I've been thinking about RADAR. Did you hear all that about RADAR on the radio this morning? How they send out signals that bounce off enemy ships and give their position away?"

"I'm pretty sure my father has RADAR on his ship."

"Probably does. I figure the ants might be using radio waves, too. We've just got to figure out how to detect them."

"That would explain why they wave their antennae at each other," mused Wally.

"Exactly!"

"We should ask Mr. Niederman. My

mother and I think he was working on RADAR all this time."

"Mr. Niederman, really? What makes you think that?"

"Because he's a mathematician, and he was excused from the draft, and he didn't enlist, but he's not sick. So we know he was doing some sort of secret stuff."

They tromped back up from the basement to the kitchen and flung open one of Loretta's vast kitchen cabinets, looking for noisemakers to take outside.

"RADAR's not the only secret project they had in the whole war, you know," Ham said.

"You just don't like him because —" Wally said, swallowing the last part of her sentence, "he's Jewish."

"You're right, I don't like him — because he always talks about me like I'm not even there. 'Are you and your friend going to the pool again today, Wally?' 'Are you and your friend going to the natural history museum?' Can't he remember my name after two years? It's just three letters."

"Aw, Ham, it's just because he's from New Jersey. He's not used to black and white people being friends. He doesn't know any better."

21

"You used to say it was because he was a Nazi."

"Well, that was before I realized he was Jewish. Anyway, he *did* help our side win the war with RADAR."

"He did *not.*"

"Did too."

"What you two squabbling about?" Loretta demanded from the other side of the cabinet door. " 'Cause you know I don't like bickering."

"Sorry, Mama."

"Sorry, Loretta."

"And as for Mr. N. from New Jersey, leave it, Ham. Let bygones be bygones."

"Yes, ma'am."

Wally came up with a copper-bottomed saucepan, and Ham found the enormous funnel his mother used to strain stock. They headed for the front door.

"Wait up now, Wally," called Loretta. She extended her arm, holding out a large wooden spoon. "You'll be needing something to bang with — and I don't want it to be a rock."

"Thanks, Loretta."

"And you, Ham, don't you lose my funnel, child."

"Awright, Mama," Ham said. Then, as they walked outside and down the steps, he proclaimed through his new megaphone, in his best Edward R. Murrow voice: "Happy V-J Day to the people of America. Last night in Times Square, record numbers assembled to celebrate the peace. This morning, in towns and cities all across the nation, even the little children have turned out in the streets, marching to express their joy."

Wally and Ham marched with the neighborhood children all morning. Shopkeepers were giving out penny candy and trinkets. Even Mr. Merganser, the grumpy, asthmatic druggist on Montague Street, had cracked open rolls of Necco wafers, cases of them it seemed, and emptied them into a great apothecary jar that he set out on a table beside his door. The children reached in, scooped up fistfuls of powdery pastel coins, then ran away again feeling as rich as if they'd gotten real money.

By midday, only about twenty kids remained — the ones with less strict mothers, or mothers who had to work, which included Wally and Ham. They were exhausted but happy. Their daddies would be coming home. Wally thought about her father, but she could only summon images from the photographs on their living room mantelpiece: the formal wedding portrait in which the train of her mother's gown was arranged in a puddle of silk before the calmly smiling couple, a snapshot of him with Georgie on his knee, the military portrait that had been taken in his crisp new uniform before he sailed away. His return was hard to imagine, it had been so long.

Claire Rensselaer, the most popular girl in Wally's class, came up and linked her arm in Wally's. Over the course of the morning, the two of them had gradually become the most enthusiastic merrymakers of the girls from their class. Once, when Ham and some of his buddies from P.S. 8 had run past, Claire asked: "You know him, right? Doesn't he work for your granny?" When Wally shrugged yes, she said, "So, go over there. Talk to him. We can't let all the big boys leave."

Wally looked at Claire, surprised she had any interest in Ham and his friends.

"It's just I think that Bobby Tomlinson is so cute, don't you?" Claire asked.

"You do?" asked Wally, in amazement, but she called out, "Hey, Ham, come on, sing with me!" and threw back her head. *O-oh, say, can you see —*"

"*What?* That's not singing, girl." Ham laughed. "You're shaming your nation!" But it had worked, somehow, because Ham and

24

his gang and then Claire and the other kids joined in.

Then it was one, and lunch was being served all across the neighborhood. The last mothers and maids started shouting names from doorways.

"Good job with the parade, Wally," said Claire. "It was super."

"Thanks," Wally said. "It's not as if I started it or anything."

"Just kept it *going,* you crazy cat, Wally Baker. See you later!"

"See you," Wally repeated, puzzled at the way the morning had gone. She was exactly the same girl she'd been the previous week at the park when Claire had called her Little Miss Professor because of her glasses and the week before at dancing class when she'd gotten her in trouble with the teacher by remarking on her dirty fingernails. Miss Baudelaire had winced in disgust, delivered a blistering lecture on the nearness of God and soap, and sent Wally to the washroom to reacquaint herself with both of them.

Now, as if God had rewarded her for scrubbing those nails, peace had broken out and Claire Rensselaer wanted, for the first time in Wally's life, to be her friend.

It wasn't to be a day of firsts, though. It was a day of lasts.

Last time she held her mother's hand and last time her mother held hers. Last time she looked in her mother's eyes and last time her mother glanced away.

"Bye," she had said, not knowing — how could she? — that with that she'd bid her mother her final farewell.

2
OLEO

The first thing people saw when they saw Wally was her knees. They were usually black (like under her nails), and often striped red and brown with scrapes and peeling scabs. The second thing they noticed — and it was a tribute to the drama of her knees that this came second — was her silver wire-rim spectacles. They had round lenses and U-shaped ear hooks, and they had made her life torture since the very first day she had gotten them, at the age of four. Without them, unfortunately, the world was a wash of unnavigable colored shapes. She needed them enough that she always wore them, but she detested the way they publicly announced her near blindness, just as her grandfather's crutches and wheelchair told everyone he'd had polio.

That summer, for her birthday, her mother had gotten Wally a gift that almost redeemed the glasses: a pair of dark green clip-ons that masked her eyes like a movie star's. The only girl in the second grade to wear glasses was about to become the only girl in the third grade — or the whole lower school, in fact — to have her own *sun*-glasses. Inside, she still felt awkward more often than not, but outside, when she put them on — click, click as the two small silver catches snapped into place — she felt grown-up and glamorous, like Hedy Lamarr lounging on a chaise beside a pool. And it wasn't just a feeling. It was scientific. Wally had spent one entire day keeping a graph of how often people smiled at her when they said hello, and it spiked when she wore the clip-ons. In fact, she had observed that more people seemed to greet her in the first place when she had the sunglasses on. They hid her eyes but made her *visible,* noticeable. Glamour, mystery — whatever power it was that the glasses gave her — she liked it.

Among the things that she didn't like about herself, in addition to her poor vision, was her name. It was a boy's name, as everyone knew, and the only other female anyone had ever heard of who shared it was some English duchess who was in the newspaper now and then because she was a Nazi sympathizer. Wally was short for Wallace, of course — it was her mother's maiden name

— but Wally's actual first name was "Beatrice." She'd been named after her great-grandmother and her great-aunt. There was even a silver cup with Beatrice engraved on it that she drank her milk from most every morning. But she had always been called by her middle name, for reasons that she didn't understand.

"Can't I please be called Bebe instead of Wally?" she'd begged her mother. "Wally is a boy's name."

But her mother just said, "Nonsense, darling. And you can't go around changing your name. I'm afraid we decided to call you Wally, and there's nothing much you can do about it."

Wally did succeed in getting her brother, who would do most anything she asked, to call her Bebe, at least when she reminded him, but that had ended when Georgie died of the whooping cough at the age of four.

She remembered life in the time of Georgie vividly. That was when everything was grand, their father had been at home, and their mother didn't work, just played with them and read to them and cooked for them and took them on excursions.

That summer of 1945 wasn't a bad summer — Wally spent her free time in the garden at her grandparents' house or swimming with Ham at the Hotel St. George's vast saltwater pool — but it wasn't the way Wally thought a summer should be. Wally still yearned for the old days, before her mother had gone to work and when she had a little brother to play with, and when summer meant they rode out to Coney Island to go to the beach at least once a week. She and Georgie each got a new tin pail and shovel every June, and they would set out with their mother in her espadrilles and large straw hat. Wally remembered listening to storybooks on the long sweaty subway ride as some of the happiest hours of her life. That had ended the year after Georgie died, when Wally's mother began her medical residency.

"You're a doctor, too, just like Gigi is and Waldo used to be?" Wally had asked when her mother first told her she was going back to work. She was boggled not to have known this key fact about her mother.

"Waldo is still a doctor, Wally. He's just on medical leave. And yes, officially I am a doctor, too, because I went to medical school, but I never did my residency, which is when you train in a hospital. That means I can't see patients on my own until I finish more training."

"Why didn't you finish it before?"

30

"I got married and had you and Georgie instead. But you're a big girl now. You don't need me so much."

Wally hadn't agreed with that, but she didn't say anything. She knew she didn't have a choice.

Her favorite time of the day was evening now, because that was when she got to walk home with her mother, as long as her mother wasn't on call overnight. Hand in hand, they would make their way home, often stopping on Montague Street to buy groceries or window-shop. It was utterly unlike their morning walks, when Wally always felt harried and rushed, and for two years straight, it was the only reliable time that Wally had her mother entirely to herself — so long as they didn't bump into some odious friend of her mother's or a tedious fellow doctor from the hospital.

On V-J Day, Wally was looking forward to that walk. She wanted to talk to her mother more about RADAR and the bomb and Mr. Niederman and how their lives would change, now the war was really over. She was a little bit afraid of asking the question that burned the hottest in her mind. Would her mother quit the hospital now that her father was coming home? Wally had heard on the radio that women who'd gone to work for the war effort were being asked to step aside so returning veterans could retake their old jobs and support their families. Somehow, she couldn't imagine her mother going back to the way she'd been before, but who knew, maybe she wouldn't have a choice.

When lunch with Waldo and Gigi was over, there were still four infinite-seeming hours before her mother would come to pick her up. Plenty of time to read some Wonder Woman, watch Ham's ants awhile, and maybe catch *Superman* with Ham and Loretta at five-fifteen. In the kitchen, Loretta stacked the dishes in the sink and ran warm water in the basin.

"We just used up the last of the oleo, String Bean. You want to help me mix up a new pound of it? And peel some potatoes? Or how 'bout some apples? And by the way, your mama called. She has some errands to do, so she can't come get you, and she asked me to please bring you home at six-thirty — which is plain ridiculous, as she knows. I can't just up and leave dinner half in the middle when your Gigi's gonna sit down and ring that bell at seven on the dot, no matter who just blew up Japan. So now I've gotta refigure my menu and turn it into a casserole that I can leave in the oven and a pie that'll be done ahead —"

"I can go home myself, Loretta. It won't be dark then."

"That's not what Miss Stella asked me to do, though, is it — send you home alone?"

It was true, Loretta always did whatever her mother asked. Loretta was loyal to Gigi, whom she'd worked for since before Wally or even Stella was born, but if Loretta loved any one person in their family, it was Stella. Wally understood it — she loved her mother best, too. Stella's smile was something one could bask in. And it almost hurt when it faded or was directed elsewhere.

It was a disappointment not to be going home till so late, but Wally was soon distracted by the chore Loretta had set her to. She opened the cabinet and took out the medium metal mixing bowl and the wooden butter paddles. She unwrapped the margarine and peered at the orangey-red powder in the see-through capsule. Wally cracked the gelatin and touched the powder with her finger, then touched her finger to her tongue. It was flavorless, like dust. She poured it out onto the greasy white block of fat and dug the paddles in, folding, whacking, scraping, and smearing until the streaks and swirls mellowed to a uniform hue almost exactly the pale shade of butter.

The absence of butter could be ameliorated by margarine, but there wasn't any way to replace a person. Wally had grown accustomed to certain gaping absences. Her father was more of a notion to her than a man, now. And then there was Georgie. There was not going to be any replacement for her brother. She missed him especially at night, the way he used to creep into her bed in the wee hours. They would snuggle and giggle till they fell back to sleep in each other's arms. But he was fading, now, even from Wally's memories. So, Georgie was dead, her father was overseas, and her mother worked slavish hours. Even Waldo, her grandfather, who was always at home, kept mostly to his own, upstairs in his sickroom or the music room, where he tinkered with models. And Gigi, her grandmother, was busy seeing her own patients. All of them were gone in some way or other, except Loretta and Ham. And oddly enough, Mr. Niederman. They were the only ones who were always where Wally expected them to be, when she expected them to be there.

Wally'd spent a lot of time with Ham since Georgie died. He'd even converted her from collecting butterflies to keeping ants. It was the summer after Georgie died that Wally had been seduced by the great, shimmering wings of a blue morpho she saw at the natural history museum and had begged for a collecting kit for her seventh birthday. For a short time, Wally had played lepidopterist, sacrificing innumerable live specimens in the name of science and mounting their tattered remains rather crookedly on a cotton-covered corkboard. She had two different butterfly books with color plates to guide her in identification and told everyone she was going to be an entomologist when she grew up. But the truth was, Wally had almost immediately developed a horror of taking six writhing legs between her fingers and forcing a miraculous creature into the killing jar. What had entranced her about her subjects was not so much their pretty wings, it turned out, but the thing the wings enabled — and the very thing the sweet vapor of ethyl acetate took away: flight.

Her final effort was going to be a classic dual mounting of *Danaus plexippus* and *Limenitis archippus:* the poisonous monarch and its non-toxic mimic, the viceroy. Wally cleaned and oiled an old picture frame she'd found in a dusty box in the cellar and asked Waldo to help her cut some shims of wood to make the frame accommodate the delicate feathered wings of her victims. She planned to put the viceroy on top because she liked it better for not being poisonous, but she had destroyed the delicate wings of three specimens in the attempt to pin them in place. Finally, she took the whole kit and stashed it out of sight in the attic. She had no taste for the hobby she'd chosen.

On a warm June day the following summer, just before she turned eight, she had wandered outside with her net, idly, without any real intention of catching anything, when Ham slammed the back door and came out to see what she was up to. His wavy dark brown hair shone with pomade, and his coppery skin glowed in the summer light.

"Hey, Ham."

"Catching anything, Wally?"

"I've seen a couple of cabbage moths."

"The little white ones, right? Caught any?"

She ignored his question. "Ham, do you really like your ants? What's so special about ants anyway?"

"Yeah, of course I like them. Hundreds, even thousands of creatures, all working together like a single mind — you got to admit, it's pretty amazing."

"Doesn't it bug you to kill them?"

"*Bug* me?" He goggled his eyes at her, teasing.

"Come on, Ham," she laughed. "Does it?"

"But I don't kill them. I keep them alive. I feed them. I help them reproduce. They live as long as they live, maybe even longer than they would in nature."

"That sounds good," Wally said. "I wish I had ants. I'm done with butterflies."

"But, ants aren't very pretty." Ham plunged his hands into the pockets of his khaki shorts. "You could get some ants of your own, you know. You just have to dig them up. Want me to help you?"

"Would you?"

"There's certainly enough to go around. C'mon, I'll show you the nest where I got mine."

Wally leaned her net against the apple tree, and they wandered back toward the fence that overlooked New York Harbor. To the south, in Buttermilk Channel, a gray warship was setting out for overseas. Wally imagined her grandfather at that moment, watching it through his binoculars from the upstairs window, scoping out as many details as possible so he could re-create them in miniature. Directly across the river was Manhattan, with its huge pointy skyscrapers. But there on Brooklyn Heights, in

Gigi and Waldo Wallace's steep backyard, Wally and Ham were apart from it all. There were worms there and plants, caterpillars and squirrels, wharf rats and feral cats, maybe a few raccoons and, of course, ants. The sounds of the city were muffled by the chirping of the crickets.

"Should we get a shovel?" Wally said.

"No, not yet. First come take a look."

3
A BALSA WOOD FLEET

Sometimes, Wally liked sleeping over at her grandparents' — the house was full of hiding places and secret cabinets, and Ham was usually there for her to play with. Other times, she chafed against the feeling of always being a guest, always having to be on her best behavior. Or felt homesick, just yearned to go back to the smaller apartment nearby where she'd grown up with two parents and her brother and their pet rabbit, Captain Nutters, and everything had been normal.

The Wallace house was one of the neighborhood's grander brownstones — a mansion — which meant it was one window wider than the scores of similar buildings that lined Columbia Heights. It had a better grade of wrought-iron railing. Inside, the details were finer: the trim mahogany, the plaster moldings more elaborate. It had five stories, including the attic with its gable windows and tiny former servants' rooms, which were now filled with the detritus of three generations. At the back of the building, a turret ascended the northwest corner, providing each floor with unparalleled views of the Brooklyn Bridge, on which Wally's own great-grandfather had labored as a young man. The story went he had arrived a penniless immigrant and narrowly escaped entombment in the caissons below before rising from the throng of Irish immigrants to become a wealthy man, the owner of a thriving stonecutting business. Her great-grandmother, his wife, had been the first woman doctor in the family, though she was said to have started out a pickpocket. There were full-size portraits of the two of them in the hallway near the music room, and Wally often tried to imagine their lives, led in the same rooms as hers, but having begun so differently.

The Harrises, for that was their name, had had three daughters, plus a staff of three, and the house had seethed with activity up until the Great War came along and the flu with it. One by one, members of the household turned a ghastly blue, for lack of oxygen, and died, until only one was left, Wally's grandmother Gigi. The stonecutting business was sold off as quickly as possible, since Gigi couldn't run it. She and Waldo had put the house on Columbia Heights up for sale as well, but there was a glut of large houses on the Heights just then, not to mention the market for them had entirely dried up — or died off, in many cases. Not to mention the sailors from the Navy Yard to the north and the riders of the several subway lines that now stopped in the district had driven off the sort of people who cared about fine parquet and walnut paneling.

It was a very good house, not the least bit derelict, only tainted by the gloom the flu had brought. Gigi and Waldo Wallace decided to return and make it their own.

Gigi, a doctor like her mother, had orchestrated the renovation of her mother's small street-level office. The waiting room, examination room, and small laboratory were more than thirty years old by then, and the finishes on the woodwork were pocked with wear. Gigi did all three rooms over in bird's-eye maple in the Art Deco style. There were settees and armchairs to match in the waiting room, upholstered in leaf-green velveteen. It went from a dark and dingy formerly elegant place to a calm, cool oasis that inspired medical and social confidence. She saw her own patients and took over most of her mother's as well. That was when she'd hired Loretta as a maid — she was just nineteen years old at the time — enabling her to expand her office hours. Patients were clamoring for appointments, and she was glad of it. She was tired of being a part-time doctor who by necessity referred pregnancies and surgical cases to her mostly male colleagues. A decade later, she had a daughter, Stella, and was the chair of her department at Long Island College Hospital.

A locked door connected the offices to the rest of the ground level: the kitchen with its great bay of sunny southwestern windows that overlooked the harbor, and the cook's rooms, where Loretta and Ham lived, consisting of a small bedroom, a bathroom, and a sitting room with an armchair and a daybed.

One story up, on the parlor floor, were the grand living and dining rooms. Up the grand staircase from there lay the music room and master bedroom, then four more bedrooms on two levels, each with its own capacious bathroom. The turret provided an additional space off the stairwell on each floor.

The front bedroom on three was the one Wally used. Her mother had grown up there. It had red and white striped wallpaper, a shelf of stuffed animals with bristly wool fur and shining glass eyes, and a doll bed with real sheets and an embroidered bedspread, all of which had been passed down from her mother. There was a bookcase full of antiquated children's books with fancy gilded leather covers and too few color plates. Again, her mother's. Whenever Wally brought her own toys or books and set them on the shelves, her grandmother returned them to her, to take home again, so as not to disrupt the order of the room with her clutter. Though she slept there at least twice a week, it was not really hers. It was a room preserved from another time, like the ones she'd seen at the Met and the Brooklyn Museum.

The top floor of the brownstone was the place Wally really felt to be hers, and so long as she didn't make messes, no one minded her using it. Two maids and a butler had lived there once. There were dressers in all three of the small bedrooms, stuffed full with stiff old leather gloves, boxes of broken paste jewelry, and the like. Old-fashioned hats and petticoats could be found in several different trunks. Her great-grandmother had been very small, she knew, because the oldest clothes in the oldest trunk nearly fit Wally already. Her great-aunts had been taller — their things hung on her like sacks. One of the closets contained nothing but black mourning garb, another held ball gowns and three white wedding dresses — Gigi's, her mother's, and her late great-aunt Bebe's. Wally loved to unbutton the canvas dress bags and look at them, but the only one of those she was officially allowed to take down from its hanger and try on was a peacock blue organza bridesmaid's dress that her mother had worn in Claire Rensselaer's parents' wedding.

"Don't worry about that hideous thing," her mother had told her after Loretta caught her trying it on one day. "I don't know why it's even still in there. It's yours."

Wally kept her comic books in the bottom two drawers of an old white painted dresser in the attic's turret room. In cold weather, she took to the window benches of the sunny turret, which was always warm like a greenhouse. Lying on her back in the sun, she lost herself in the exploits of Wonder Woman, a.k.a. Princess Diana, a.k.a. Diana Prince. In summer, when the turret was so hot as to be uninhabitable, she'd take a stack of the thin, brightly clad issues from their hiding place and plop down on the cool white tiles of the bathroom floor to read. She had the entire run of *Wonder*

Woman, beginning with the first issue in 1941 — which was before she'd even been able to read — and every issue of *Sensation Comics* that contained a Wonder Woman story. It was her grandfather Waldo who'd indulged her by buying her all the back issues when he noticed her interest in the series. He liked the idea of Wally being tough and reading comics — almost like a boy.

Wally had read each episode many times over. There was at least a month between releases, so she had plenty of time to memorize each new story. How many episodes would it take, Wally wondered, before Steve Trevor figured out who Diana Prince really was? How long before he kissed her in her human guise? Why couldn't she just tell him? Why couldn't she cast off those glasses — which she didn't even *need*? It was maddening, delightfully maddening.

On a morning in mid-July of the last year of the war, when Europe was free but kamikazes still hunted the Pacific, where her father was stationed, Wally woke early in the bedroom with the red and white wallpaper to the clanging of her alarm. She needed to be dressed and ready by seven o'clock. Downstairs, Ham would surely be rising from his bed and doing the same. At 7:07, the eclipse would begin, and they would be in position to watch it.

They stood at the ready as the minute hand of the kitchen clock hit seven, rushed outside and raised their pinhole viewers to the sky, but the sun was still obscured by the building across the street. At 7:07, nothing seemed any different, but by 7:30, there was a curious dawn-like light, despite the fact that the sun had finally risen above the roofline. Wally thought she could perceive a less than circular quality to the sun's image as cast through the pinhole, but the circle itself was so small, there was no spectacle to it.

Then Wally looked down.

"Ham! The light!"

The dappled shadows at the edges of the yard and under the apple tree had taken on a crescent shape. They trembled in the light breeze like tentative daytime moons, shivered like sequins layered on a gown, each one jostling the rest for full circularity, all of them losing, and in their loss, casting a light that was better than dawn's, rarer than dusk's, a once-in-a-lifetime kind of light.

At first they ran in circles around the tree, seeking more and more of it, wanting to see every leaf, every shadow of every leaf in the world. Then they realized that an eyeful of wonder was all they could perceive at any one time — no more — and so the two of them sat down, leaned against the trunk of the old apple tree and simply gazed out at what lay before them, the garden as it would never again be seen.

Just past 8:00 A.M., the crescents were at their crispest and most glorious, then slowly they dwindled, until by nine o'clock the world had returned to its usual state.

"Well, I've got some stuff to do before I go out and find the guys," said Ham.

"Yeah, okay, see you later," answered Wally, for once not disappointed at Ham's departure. She'd had as much of his attention as she could reasonably expect for one morning.

Together, but separate, they drifted back into the house, Ham to the basement and Wally up the staircase to the music room, where she sought out Waldo. Except for Mr. Niederman, who was not available on weekday mornings, she imagined that Waldo was the person in her family who would most appreciate news of the eclipse.

"Oh, watched the eclipse, did you? Good for you," he said, not especially interested or impressed by Wally's and Ham's early morning initiative.

As often, Waldo was deep at work painting dozens of tiny bits of balsa wood battleship gray. His polio had kept him from serving his country, and it had stopped him from practicing the profession of medicine. What it gave him was time, too much of it. The day Pearl Harbor was hit, he'd decided to memorialize the loss of the *Oklahoma* and the *Arizona* by creating models of the ships. Then, with the war under way, he'd gradually undertaken to fashion a model of every last vessel in the U.S. Navy. To that date, he'd built over a hundred models, which he'd arranged on the shelves of the music room, and even on top of the piano, which Wally had been told her mother used to play, when she was young. The piano shawl was a blue silk velvet ocean, and spread out across it were always Waldo's latest creations, or his favorites — vessels of all different classes, each one in the closest possible condition to real life. If a ship had been sunk, scuttled or hit, he broke, burned or punched holes in it accordingly, appending a small black tag indicating the manner in which the ship was lost and the number of American dead, painted meticulously in white. When the ships were overhauled and resurrected, Waldo would overhaul his models, though the casualty tags remained.

The research, construction, and demolition took up as much time as he'd ever spent on caring for patients.

"Why do you build them, Waldo?" Wally asked him once.

"Same reason you read your comics, I guess, Wally — because I can't actually set sail and fight, like your father. I'm stuck in the chair, in this house, watching the sky for planes that never come, thank God. I build them to do my part, the only way I can."

Today she asked, "Are you gonna keep doing it, now the war is over?"

"I'm not sure."

"Maybe you could give them to a museum."

"You think they're that good, do you? Well, thank you."

"You're welcome. See you later, Waldo," she said, and then she bounced out the door of the music room, where she nearly bumped into Loretta.

"Whoa, now, String Bean! Don't bowl me over."

It was Loretta, of course, who organized and maintained the attic rooms and their relics of the past, Loretta who dusted Waldo's miniature fleet once a week, Loretta who almost always knew where Wally was to

49

be found, even when Wally thought she was hidden away reading her comics in the upstairs bathroom.

Day and night, Loretta was in constant motion, keeping the house, watching the children, cooking the meals. She had been doing it for decades by then, up from the kitchen to the parlor floor, up to the bedrooms and up to the attic and then down again, down again, down again. There was a dumbwaiter, mercifully, but she still had to turn the crank to raise and lower it. She still had to go up and down to load and unload it. All that upping and downing and cranking, plus chasing after Wally and Ham, had kept her slim, but not as slim as Wally, which was why Wally called her Lima Bean and Loretta called Wally String Bean.

"Thank the Lord for that contraption," she often said as she lifted a heavy tray of dishes and glasses from the cabinet. "No one and no thing has ever helped me as much in my life. I'd marry it if I could. I just wish it went all the way up."

Loretta had lived in the house full-time for nearly twenty years, except for a brief period, during her marriage to the first Hamilton Walker, when she was there only fourteen hours a day. She'd nursed Stella through her crises — the deaths of her first fiancé and then her only son. Sometimes she wondered if the reason her own marriage had not been a success had to do with the devotion she'd given to Stella and Gigi Wallace, over the years, but they repaid it. After Hamilton Sr. left, she had sat in the attic rooms crying in an old wicker rocking chair, holding Ham, wondering why her husband had left her but relieved at least that she was not alone. The Wallaces had promised to keep her on and to allow her to keep the child with her while she worked.

Ham was her child, but truly Loretta was three times a mother — first Stella, then Ham, and now Wally, odd little Wally, who'd increasingly become her responsibility since her brother had died in the cold early days of 1943 and her mother gone back to doctoring the following summer. Same as it had been with Miz Doc Wallace, as she called Gigi, and Stella. In truth, she mothered them all, including even Doctor Waldo, since he'd gotten sick. She'd given and given of her own accord, and yes, she loved them, but many nights she'd also bitten her lip when Miz Doc asked too much: setting her some inconsequential chore at 9:00 P.M., when Ham needed putting to bed.

There was a corner of her mind that always questioned how much she gave to the Wallaces and whether her own son had gotten short shrift. But then she reminded herself that the reason she was working was Ham. Loving and caring for the Wallaces was something she did because the more she did for them, the more they would reward her, and all to the benefit of Ham, she trusted, somewhere down the line. The Wallaces had already promised to put him through college, if he went, and if she had anything to say about it, he was going to go. Loretta would make sure of that. Besides, love wasn't sold by weight, she told herself. She could love Stella and Wally for twelve, even fourteen hours a day, and even feel a kind of loyalty for Miz Doc that was close to love, without taking anything away from her son.

4
BROTHERS

The black metal stairs of the veranda had been warm on their thighs, the summer day the year before when Wally was converted from butterflies to ants. Even the dirt in the yard had smelled warm, percolating up through the grass. The soil had seemed to come alive with grubs and bugs and worms. Birds chirruped, buds swelled, and each part of nature burgeoned at its own pace, oblivious to the war being waged across the Atlantic, where another day of killing had just ended, and the far-off Pacific, where a violent new morning was about to dawn.

"Let's go, Wally. Come on. Let's go do it," Ham said, standing up.

Ham and Wally reviewed their plan one last time. Sometimes the idea of a thing was more appealing than the doing of it, Wally thought. All of a sudden, she'd rather have stayed put quietly in the shade, gazing at the harbor, scanning the gray water for

U-boat silhouettes.

"Ham, what do you think the chances are we could just, uh, find one? Or somehow attract a freshly mated queen and not have to dig one up?"

"I think they're attracted to drones, not kids. And just find one? I don't know, let me think. I would guess the odds are about one in four thousand nine hundred ninety-six."

"What?"

"They're not very good. 'Less you want to stand round-the-clock watch at that anthill the next two weeks, waiting on a nuptial flight."

"I was just asking."

"So you're ready to do it?"

"Absolutely." Wally squinted, which she thought made her look determined.

Wally got the shovel, which was slightly taller than she was, out of the little potting shed behind the house. It had been the outhouse once, her grandmother had told her, before plumbing was put in. It stood further away from the house then, of course, nearer the bluff, just above the spot in the lower yard where the big apple tree now grew. Gigi had told Wally that when they were digging the hole to put the apple tree in they found two silver teaspoons as well as some shell buttons, broken plates and bottles, and the china head of a doll.

Ham, being several years older and a whole head taller than Wally, was the one to pull the wagon out of the shed and load it. They'd done this part plenty of times before, if for a different purpose. Ham and Wally were enthusiastic tenders of the Victory Garden that had taken over the Wallaces' cliffside yard. Except for where the apple tree stood, terraced vegetable beds now covered the steep sloping lawn that connected the small upper garden behind the house to the lower yard, where the anthill was. Even the very bottom of the yard was a story above ground level, ending in a sheer drop-off, beneath which a warehouse had been built into the bluff below. The same layout of high yards atop warehouses that faced the waterfront was shared by the neighboring properties all along the bluff on either side of the Wallaces. Ihpetonga, or *high sandy cliff,* was the name the Canarsie people, who had lived there first, gave to Brooklyn Heights and its riverside cliff. Geologists called it terminal moraine, as Gigi had taught and retaught Wally till she remembered the odd term, which meant that the glaciers of the last ice age had stopped right there and gone no further before receding. Their high perch was a dumping ground for the rubble that had been scrubbed from the earth by the ice and dragged half-way across the continent, from as far away as Wisconsin.

A fence at the bottom of the yard guarded the vertical drop-off, and two of the fence posts were actually round metal chimneys that served the warehouse below. Sometimes they could hear the voices of stevedores drifting up from the pipes, and in cold weather, especially if they were sledding, they warmed themselves by huddling against the smokestacks. Wally and Ham had a theory that the warmth of the stove-pipes helped the yard's largest anthill to thrive because it overwintered better than the others. The strange, steep yard made a brilliant sledding run in January and February, when a blanket of snow smoothed over the terraced beds of the upper garden. You only had to take care not to smash into the fence at the bottom.

Gigi's was the best yard, and the best Victory Garden, on Brooklyn Heights, Wally thought. The previous summer they had harvested several bushels of tomatoes from the Wallace garden, most of which Loretta and Wally's mother had canned, plus a bushel each of potatoes and carrots, what seemed like a cartload of cabbages, and enough strawberries to make a dozen jars of jam. The apples had been plentiful as ever that fall, and during wartime not even the fallen fruit was left to rot on the ground for the wasps. Loretta used them to make apple-sauce, cooked over high heat just a little longer than the recipe said, till the sugars had slightly caramelized and given it a bittersweet edge.

This day, though, Wally and Ham's wagon wasn't piled with the usual load of produce, compost, or gardening tools. From the out-house–potting shed, they'd taken just one large shovel, two wide galvanized buckets, and a canvas tarp. From the kitchen they'd borrowed a two-quart saucepan and the metal bowl that Loretta used to convert it into a double boiler for sauces and puddings. The bottom of the pan was packed with ice the children had chipped from the block in the insulated box by the bar. There was also an old, retired pair of Wally's white kid gloves with cultured pearl buttons at the wrists and indelible black ink stains on the fingertips. Loretta had tucked them in the sewing basket with the idea of reusing the pearls or pieces of the leather for patches. Nestled safely in the tarp lay their most important piece of equipment: the battery jar, a great hollow glass block with heavy walls and an open top. Wally had found it in the basement among Waldo's dusty tools, most of them untouched since his illness, and prepared it precisely according to the instructions in the Boy Scout merit badge pamphlet Ham had given her. She'd washed it well, inside and out, filled it with clean sand and greased the rim with a blob of petroleum jelly from the pot in Waldo and Gigi's medicine cabinet.

"I'll do the digging if you want, Wally. I don't mind a bite or two."

She shook her head. The year before, Ham and a couple of his scout buddies had done everything to establish his colony, Planet Ant, in the boiler room of the brownstone. Ham had told her she was too little to help. Now Wally wanted Ham to know she was big enough, strong enough. She wanted to be sure he understood that this would be her ant colony.

"Okay, as long as you realize you're raiding their nest. You're gonna get bit."

She shrugged. "They aren't Japs. They ain't got machine guns, you know." She knew better than to say *ain't got,* but when she was with Ham, she found herself talking that way. Both of them talked properly when they were addressing Wally's mother

58

or Gigi, and more like Loretta when she was only the grown-up around. Between Ham and Wally, it didn't matter. They could talk the way they felt like talking.

"Well, no machine guns, but they can shoot formic acid." Ham grinned.

Wally didn't actually *want* to get bitten, but she did want this to be *her* colony. She also knew she wouldn't rate half as high with Ham or get as much of his attention if she acted like a girl. "I can take it," she said.

Ham adopted his newsreel announcer voice: "Here you see footage of the Battle of Columbia Heights, in which hoards of vicious guard ants opened their mandibles, snapped at human flesh, and squirted acid at the American troops." His voice rose in pitch as he reached the conclusion of his report: "But the forces of liberty will prevail here, once again, wiping the acid away, crushing the embattled venom spitters between their thumbnails and capturing the enemy queen, who will be held in captivity for the remainder of her natural-born life."

Wally smiled. This was what it was supposed to be like to have a brother, she thought.

Georgie had been younger, of course. She knew it wasn't fair to compare them.

Wally remembered pulling him in the red

wagon. She'd galloped down the sidewalk, with Georgie shouting, "Faster, faster, Wallee, faster," making wild siren noises.

"What do you want to be when you grow up, Georgie, a fireman?" she had asked him when the wagon clattered to a stop.

"No."

"A Navy captain?" she'd asked.

"A doctor."

"Oh, like Gigi and Waldo?" she'd said. She hadn't said her mother, because she hadn't known, then, that her mother was a doctor. It wasn't till Mr. Niederman came and encouraged her to go back to work that Stella began at the hospital.

"No, a *car* doctor."

"A what?"

"A car *helper*?"

"A car fixer? A mechanic?"

"Yes, that," he'd said. "A car fixer!"

"Just don't tell Mother."

Later, after their mother had bought them their gray and white Dutch rabbit, Nutters, Georgie had wanted to become a veterinarian for a while.

Captain Nutters was a daredevil with a penchant for circumnavigating the entire living room, from sofa to coffee table to armchair to side table, without ever touching the ground. Dark gray markings covered his white face like a mask and his back in a V from the nape of his neck, so that he seemed to have a gray cape flying behind him as he hurtled across the sitting area.

When Nutters had his accident, Georgie was devastated, but he didn't cry, just chewed his lip. He didn't cry when they crashed their wagon into a street tree one time, either, even though his nose bled. He had been a brave little boy.

Once, when they were out in Gigi's yard, Georgie playing soldier and Wally playing with paper dolls, Wally had deliberately clobbered him with a stick. He'd stumbled and tripped right onto her. She'd heard paper tear. Of course that wasn't grounds for clobbering. She knew that. But she'd done it.

"Hey! Quit that, you runt," she'd yelled, pushing him away to assess the damage he'd done to Eloise and Helen and their printed finery. "Look what you did!"

He'd looked at her reproachfully. It was the way he didn't cry that had turned her indignation to guilt, though the stick hadn't been all that large.

"Sorry, Georgie. But you were murdering my dolls."

"Was there a monster on my shoulder, and

you had to kill it?" he'd suggested hope-fully.

"It was actually a Nazi spy, but I got him. Are you all right?"

"Probably," he'd said, rubbing his head. "Thanks for killing him, Wallee."

"You're welcome, I guess. Come on, let's play hide-and-seek."

"I want to play tag."

"All right, tag. But for tag, we need three. Let's find Ham."

Georgie and Ham had both flatly refused to play tag, hide-and-seek, or anything else in the upstairs of Gigi's house — not in the parlors, not in the bedrooms, certainly not in the attic that Wally so loved to explore. Ham claimed to find it stuffy and boring up there, and Georgie was afraid of the two life-size portraits that hung in the parlor hall, at the top of the stairs.

"They're alive," he'd told Wally, more than once.

"They are not."

"Loretta told me," he'd said.

"She did not. That doesn't even sound like her."

"Well, Loretta said it."

"Really?" Wally had asked, wondering if that could be.

"Actually, Ham did."

That sounded more likely.

"You don't have to be afraid of them, Georgie, they're just our relatives."

"Not her — she's a mean witch. She has a pointy nose."

"No she doesn't."

"Yes she does, a pointy nose just like you, Wally."

"Humpf," she'd said, but she didn't mind. Wally liked the idea of resembling her great-grandmother, the first woman doctor in their family.

It was soon after Georgie learned to walk that Wally and Ham had first put him in the dumbwaiter. He'd agreed to let them do it in exchange for a cookie, not really understanding the terms of the agreement. He didn't mind sitting in the dark box, but he'd screamed and cried when they closed the door and Ham began to turn the crank.

"It's heavy with him in there," Ham said.

Then Georgie fell silent.

Wally's heart ran cold — had they killed him somehow, accidentally crushed or suffocated or strangled him? But when she ran upstairs to release him, there he was, very much alive, not angry or scared but smiling. His face bore a look of wonder. He was terribly pleased with himself, proud that neither of the big kids could fit where he had been. He didn't even tattle to Loretta. After that, he'd ridden in the dumbwaiter anytime the grown-ups weren't around. He hid there so reliably during hide-and-seek they didn't bother looking elsewhere anymore. When he was grumpy, he took to it for privacy. He'd given Loretta a good fright that way, more than once.

Wally and Ham still used the dumbwaiter to transport everything from egg creams with vanilla syrup to stacks of comics to contraband ant colonies. It was also a great source of imaginary objects. If ever Wally needed a weapon, say a magic lasso or a gun, she went and looked in the dumbwaiter and came back slapping her hip and letting fly bullets or coils of golden rope. Like a magic lamp, the dumbwaiter always provided — except for the one thing that Wally still somehow dreamed it would contain when she opened the door: Georgie.

When Georgie got sick, it seemed like just a cold at first. But it didn't get better, it got worse. Wally had been frightened by the eerie gasping noises that came from her brother's room. In the middle of the third night, when it reached the point that the whooping wouldn't stop, Stella came to Wally's bedside and shook her, but Wally

64

wasn't sleeping.

"Get your shoes on, Wally. I'm going to drop you off at Gigi's and then I'm taking Georgie to the hospital."

Stella walked so fast Wally had to run to keep up with her. Her grandmother and Loretta met them at the door. There was a taxi out front, and Gigi was wearing her coat. Her mother and grandmother had gone to the hospital with Georgie, and Loretta put Wally to bed in the red and white striped bedroom and sat with her, singing "Amazing Grace" until she ran out of verses and Wally still wasn't asleep. Wally drifted off at last, very late, to the droning of Loretta's voice telling the only bedtime story she ever told, a story that was always more or less the same but seemed to have a myriad possible variations — and always one to suit the business of the day, whatever the day may have brought — but which as far as Wally knew had no end, since she had never hung on long enough to hear it.

"Once, when the world was young," Loretta began, and this time, it took a comic turn, as if Loretta was trying to cheer Wally — or herself — up, "there were no grownups anywhere, because the world hadn't been there long enough for the first babies to grow up yet. Now the only problem was, the babies had to raise themselves, and so naturally by the time they were young children like yourself and Georgie, they were already spoiled rotten. They ate whatever they pleased and stayed up late every night, and there was no one to tell them it shouldn't be that way. . . ."

In the morning, Wally was pleased to wake up in the peaceful quiet of Gigi's house, no crying or whooping to take every shred of attention. It was a rarity for her, in those days, to spend a night at her grandparents' house.

But then her mother did not come home, just Gigi.

"Would you like to learn some needlepoint stitches, Wally?" her grandmother asked.

"I'm not allowed to use needles, Gigi. I don't think I'm old enough."

"Well, needlepoint needles aren't sharp, you know." It was one of the first times Wally could remember seeing her grandmother flustered.

"No, thank you. I don't think I'd like it very much. How's Georgie? Is he getting better? Is he coming home today?"

"Not today, darling, but soon."

When Stella finally came back the following day, Wally ran to her. Her mother did not kneel down to embrace her. She stood limply, her arms crossed against her chest.

"Mother, Mother!" Wally cried. "How is Georgie feeling?"

"Go play with Ham in the kitchen, Wally. Or help Loretta? I'll be there in a few minutes," her mother told her. And then she walked past Wally and into the living room to confront her own supposedly perfect and powerful physician of a mother, who had not been able to pull the strings to get the penicillin that might have saved Georgie's life.

"You're the chair of your department," Wally heard her mother shout through the door. "Don't tell me you couldn't requisition enough to treat a child, just a tiny child, twenty-eight pounds!"

"I'm an obstetrician, not a god, Stella. I can't requisition what isn't there."

"Oh, come on, Mother, none? What were you saving your allotment for, some hussy with the clap who comes into your clinic?"

"Get ahold of yourself, Stella. You know they're sending all the penicillin to the front, so men like your husband don't have to die for their country. They're filtering the stuff from the soldiers' urine, for Christ's sake, so they can reuse it."

"So now Georgie died that Rudy might live? Well, I'll tell you which one I would have —"

"Don't say another word, Stella. There wasn't any medicine there for Georgie, and I'm just as sorry as you are, but I won't listen to your accusations any longer."

Wally backed away from the door where she'd been listening and crept down to the kitchen in a fog.

"Loretta? Loretta, Mother said —"

Loretta lifted Wally in her arms, breathing in that same salty-sweet child smell that Stella had had at her age, Ham, too — and Georgie.

It was February 1943, a month after Georgie died, when the crate from Paris arrived.

"It's from your father," Stella told Wally curtly. "You open it. I'm in no mood to open presents." Her brow was tightly drawn. Her eyes avoided Wally's. Her mother was angry — not just that Georgie was dead but that their father had not somehow managed to return from the war for his son's funeral.

Inside was a real pearl necklace for Stella; a nurse costume with a hat, a white dress, and a blue cape for Wally; and, at the bottom, a great heavy book about bugs. The glossy cream-colored illustrated plates were jammed with colorful insects of every sort: ants and flies and beetles, and even spiders and scorpions, though they were not strictly insects. There were hundreds of pages of encyclopedic entries, as well — all in French.

The note on the endpaper was to Georgie, though he had been far too young to read.

To my fine son, George. Be brave and take care of your mother and sister for me while I am away. As for the bugs in this volume, some are quite wonderful, I think, and others rather frightening. Such is the way of the world!

Love,
Papa

Wally, of course, had assumed the book was for her.

How long, she wondered, did it take for a package to travel around the world, from war to peace, from ignorance to reality? Her father hadn't remembered that she was the one who was into bugs. He hadn't even known Georgie was dead when the package was sent.

Nonetheless, the book was a treasure and Wally kept it on a shelf near her bed, after extracting a promise from her mother not to give it away to charity, as she'd done with most of Georgie's possessions. It was where she first saw the startling enormity of the queen ant, in comparison to her daughters, and where she learned to identify the various butterflies and moths by the patterns of the outer as well as inner sides of their wings.

In the garden more than a year later, Ham asked Wally, "So, are you ready?"

"Yeah," she said. "They're only ants. I can take a few chomps from an ole ant."

Ham had to admit that Wally was better than the usual girl. For the most part, he didn't really think of her in terms of her age or sex or the fact that she was Miz Doc Wallace's granddaughter. She was just Wally. He did feel responsible, though. He'd given her the ant colony idea, and his mother would clobber him if he let anything happen to Wally, including getting covered in ant bites.

They decided that he would stand guard with the hose, just in case. They tested the hose nozzle and had a large bucket of water at the ready for a splash down. But Ham's main jobs, if Wally really did manage to get an ant queen and a cadre of workers into her jar, would be to babysit the colony in the Wallaces' basement and to guide Wally in maintaining it. It was clear to both of them that Stella Baker wouldn't want ants in her apartment, not even in a jar.

"She can never even know it exists," Wally had told Ham with a grin. "This whole thing has to be classified — need to know basis — and Mother definitely doesn't need to know about it."

Ham just laughed. As if Wally could keep a secret from her mother. The anthill was down at the furthest corner of Gigi and Waldo's lower yard, which you couldn't see from the house, and under a row of azalea bushes that had survived the conversion of Gigi Wallace's half acre from garden club showplace to high-yield Victory Garden only because they lay at the very edge of the yard.

The afternoon of the raid, the azaleas were rioting in several shades of pink. A golden haze of pollen and sunset sweetened the air. Women's laughter filtered down to their ears from a nearby veranda. By the birdbath in the center of the upper garden, a small swarm of insects hovered. Wally and Ham paused to watch them.

"Just midges," Ham said.

"Too bad."

What Wally would have given for a serendipitous mating flight of ants, the once-a-year emergence of fertile princess ants and male drones that gave rise to fertilized queens. If she could capture a brand-new nuptial queen, just one, that queen would populate an entire colony herself. Wally could watch it happen. And she wouldn't have to dig up a colony that already existed.

"It's too early in the season anyway, Wally. You're going have to get your colony the hard way."

"I don't mind."

Once the wagon was parked among the azaleas, Wally and Ham sat down and observed the ground around the big anthill. They quickly discerned several invisible trails that the colony's soldier ants were following. Within a few minutes, they had ascertained that one trail led back to a smaller secondary mound with a hole in it, a couple yards away from the big hill. The ants looked alike, but the ants from the two mounds did not seem to communicate with one another when their paths happened to cross. A satellite colony, perhaps. Ham said this was good because it would probably be shallower and there would be fewer ants to counterattack.

Wally tucked her dungarees into her socks, donned her gloves, and fastened elastic hair bands around her sleeves like Ham showed her. Ham stood off to the side, arms crossed, smiling a little. Then, finally, Wally took up the shovel, planted it, and jumped on the hilt, repeating this action till she'd cut a circle in the earth.

With her next thrust, she lifted a clump of earth and ants and dumped it on the tarp they'd laid out. The ants were in a frenzy, but as she transferred shovelfuls of dirt to the double boiler, the ice quickly slowed them down. She scanned the brown mass for one ant that was larger. If her colony was to live and prosper, it needed a queen. Without one, it would dwindle as the ants died off and be entirely gone in a few months' time.

Every now and then, Wally felt a sharp pinch where one of the soldiers or workers had managed to penetrate her protective gear, and she brushed herself off with sharp, swift flicks, sending the biters flying into the grass.

As the hole grew deeper and the numbers of ants dropped off, Wally became discouraged. Then she saw something so large she wondered if it might be a beetle. Did these ants keep beetle slaves? Or eat beetles?

"Ham, Ham," she said, "is that her?"

But even before he answered, she knew. She was bulbous, shiny, and enormous. All around her, attendants swarmed and nurse ants carried pale eggs the size of sesame seeds hither and thither in panic.

"Yeah, that'd be the queen all right," Ham said, clapping his hands. "You're in business, Wally."

Wally carefully dipped her shovel into the hole, lifted the queen up from the ground, and set her on the palm of her glove. She was slow enough that Wally could hold her there and look at her without her escaping.

"What a beauty," Ham said.

"We did it!"

"Naw, you did it."

Wally looked up and basked in his approval. Ham knew about bugs, cared about them. And so if Ham was impressed, that was something. Who else might care? There was Mr. Niederman, she supposed. An odd man like that might approve of studying ants. He'd taken an interest in her butterflies the previous summer, but she couldn't very well tell him. Most of what she said to him, he repeated to her mother. She wished she could tell Georgie.

While Wally pondered the people with whom she might have reveled in her conquest, the queen began to move, and now she waddled right into a hole in Wally's glove, torn by the shoveling.

"Ham!" shouted Wally. "She's gone in my glove."

74

"Don't crush her!"

Wally felt a pinch and a burning but tried not to react.

"Ham," she cried. "Help me get this glove off!"

Wally held the double boiler beneath her hand in case the queen should fall, and Ham gently tugged at the fingers of the glove. They managed to get it off and transferred the queen into the sandy terrain of the battery jar without killing her.

"All hail, Queen of Antland," said Wally.

"She got you, huh?" said Ham. "A feisty one. Antland. I like that."

Gently, gently, Wally reached out and touched the thorax of the queen mother of the future colony of Antland; then she watched the queen's attendants help her burrow into the sand, back to the safety of the dark.

5
THE WAR EFFORT

It was in the spring of 1943 that Stella Baker had opened the letter from William Niederman, Ph.D., to her husband. The grass had just grown in on Georgie's grave site. Rudy was at sea. Stella knew the Pacific Theater was a grim place to be. Every time she sorted through Rudy's mail, she thought about where he might be. Somewhere in the South China Sea, perhaps, with a torpedo from a Jap battle cruiser racing toward his ship, or a kamikaze pilot steering a plane in his direction.

Of course she recognized the name. Bill Niederman had been Rudy's college roommate. He'd been at their wedding. But he didn't live in New York, and Stella had never had more than a perfunctory conversation with him. She was alarmed to see that he was looking for a place to stay in New York for several nights a week, "for the duration" of the war. What in the world had made him think of the Wallaces? she wondered. He didn't say, just that he had been summoned to New York to work on a special project for the Navy. Apparently it was nearly impossible to find respectable lodgings for a single man in Brooklyn, these days.

Stella didn't want a stranger living in the spare bedroom, not even for the war effort. Certainly he would find something else more suitable, she thought, and wrote him a friendly apology for not being able to open her home to him. She conveyed the substance of the exchange to Rudy in her next letter, and assumed that that was that.

It was a frigid day in April of that year, with crusted patches of dirty snow clinging to the edges of everything out of doors, when the telegram arrived. Stella and Wally were eating their breakfast. Stella had been looking at the paper when the doorbell rang. She was always slightly afraid to face the new day's news. Would the description of some battle, some horror, tip her backward into the state of uncontrolled grief she had only lately escaped? What if she read one day that Rudy's ship had gone down? Then when she opened the door, things looked even worse: It was Western Union.

"Oh no. Oh damn it," she whispered, tears coming to her eyes as she signed for the telegram.

"You have a good day, ma'am," said the delivery boy as she shut the apartment door in his face.

"Mother? What is it?"

"I don't know, Wallace. Let me read it," Stella said. Then she was laughing.

"Oh, Christ. I can't believe this. *Rudy.*"

"What?" Wally asked.

"Well, Wally, a friend of your father's is going to come and stay with us for a while. Your father insists on it."

"No!" said Wally when Stella had explained who William Niederman was. "Daddy can't make us. He's not even living here anymore. I don't want a stranger to live here."

"Wally, don't make it worse than it is," her mother said. "I don't like the idea, either, but it's for the war effort, and anyhow, we haven't any choice. He can't afford suitable lodgings, what with his family living in New Jersey, and he's needed to do important work in New York. Don't you want us to win the war so your father can come home?"

He wasn't quite as Stella had remembered him. He was taller, and his silver oval glasses made him seem dignified and intelligent.

78

He had dark eyebrows, hooded eyes, and a wide smile.

"At least your husband can come home to you on weekends," Stella said to his wife, Louise, who dropped him off and stayed to dinner the first night. "Wally and I miss Rudy terribly." It wasn't particularly true, but she didn't have much to talk about with these people.

"Oh, you poor dear," said Louise. "I can't imagine how hard it must be to have your man fighting overseas."

"Louise is glad to get me out of the house," Bill Niederman said with a laugh. "This way she can have her girlfriends over to drink and play cards every night. What is it, Monday nights bridge, Tuesdays for canasta, Wednesdays mah-jongg, and poker on Fridays?"

"It's just bridge on Tuesdays, and we've been doing that for years, as you well know, Bill." Louise smiled at Stella, as if to say, *Men.*

Stella laughed, but her eyes met Bill Niederman's rather than Louise's.

At the end of the evening, Stella watched her new boarder hug his wife good-bye and deposit her into a cab bound for Pennsylvania Station.

■ ■ ■ ■

At first, Stella felt awkward with a strange man in the house — she couldn't come out of her room with rollers in her hair and she had to hide the immense sadness that always came over her in the mornings, when Wally left for school. She'd seen her husband walk up a gangway and sail off toward likely death. Her son had been rolled away on a gurney and wound up at the morgue of Long Island College Hospital. She hated good-byes.

Of course she ought to have walked her daughter to school, but taking Wally herself would have meant Stella had to change out of her dressing gown, and in those days it was still a challenge for her to get dressed in the morning, to care enough to get dressed. And so, ever since Georgie died, Wally had routinely walked to school with a classmate who lived in the building and her mother. She stepped into the elevator at 8:00 A.M. sharp, and most mornings Stella was on the verge of tears by 8:05.

She managed to hold herself together the entire first week of Bill Niederman's residence, but the second Monday morning, she hadn't the strength. She sat back down at the breakfast table and peered deeply into her coffee, not wanting the strange man across the table from her to see her face go blotchy, her nose drip tears. When it became impossible, she rose abruptly and, saying nothing, went to her room. She tried to sob quietly.

A few moments later, there was a soft knock on the door.

"Mrs. Baker," he said through the wood, "Stella — if I may —"

"I'm sorry, what is it?" she sputtered, opening the door, incredulous that he would invade her privacy to this extent.

"Please don't cry."

"It's nothing."

"Can I help?"

"I just worry about Wally leaving. I know it's crazy."

"No, it's not. And I'm sorry; I shouldn't have said not to cry." He was leaning against the doorjamb. "You probably need to cry — probably a lot more than you do. I'll leave you now, but if there's anything at all I can do . . ."

So he knew a bit more about her life than she'd told him. She imagined the letter Rudy must have written, asking Bill Niederman to look after his grieving wife. "Well thank you, but I'm afraid there isn't." She paused. "You know, no one ever says that: that it's all right to cry. I think you're right though. I need to do it."

He nodded. "Have the best day you can," he said with kindness, standing up and turning away toward his jacket and briefcase by the front door. "I'll see you tonight."

And so it became a kind of ritual, her confiding in him each morning, in the brief time between Wally's departure and his. As the weeks passed, she told him more and more. She blamed her mother for Georgie's death because she hadn't procured the medicine to save him. It was unreasonable, even Stella knew that, but he didn't judge her in return. And one morning, without really thinking about it, she confessed how much she regretted not finishing her medical training.

"Finished your training? What do you mean?" he asked.

"I'm an M.D., didn't you know? Apparently, one can't grow up Gigi and Waldo Wallace's child and not be one. But I dropped out of my internship. I never got licensed."

"Why?"

"First I married Rudy, then came Wally, and then Georgie. I couldn't very well go back and finish my internship with two children." She wasn't ready to tell him the real reason — not yet.

Stella had fallen in love with Billy Galt while she was working as an intern. He was the chief resident. It was a swift, dizzying affair. Between the wards and their evenings out at jazz clubs and charity balls, they spent nearly every waking moment together for several months.

"Of course," she said, when he proposed to her. "I was wondering when you would ask."

Everything in Stella's life seemed to be a dream, until the day they drove north to see his parents at their cottage in the Catskills and a log truck lost its load on the road ahead of them.

Stella hadn't gone a single day since without thinking of that terrible summer afternoon. She was wearing a blue silk scarf tied beneath her chin, despite the heat. She remembered how it felt, driving in the little Pierce-Arrow with the top down, wind whipping, sun beaming, her arm on his shoulder, his hand on the stick.

She never regretted that she'd let him convince her to stop at a motel on the way. It was their first time.

"Billy!" she said. "The Kozy Kabins? It

sounds so seedy."

"How can it be seedy? I've already asked you to marry me, and you've accepted."

She would always remember how Billy had undressed her, so slowly, exploring her legs from the ankles up. When he suddenly bent low and smelled her panties, she'd gasped a little in surprise. Then he reached up and took her in his arms.

"What about —" she said, when it was almost too late.

"I thought ahead," he whispered, and reached to the bedside table for a small bright blue package.

"Peacock Reservoir End?" She had laughed, then glanced shyly away.

She had never been happier in her life.

When the log hit them, she screamed. Then she saw Billy. His head was at an angle. The cream leather ran dark. His chest had been crushed against the driver's seat. She screamed till she was hoarse.

She didn't remember anything about the next few days. Gigi told her much later that they'd had to feed her Nembutal to keep her from hysterics.

She hardly moved or spoke for three weeks, even after her mother weaned her off the Nembutal. In her dreams, everyday objects loosened themselves from their moorings and cascaded down on her, torrents of lamps and books and footstools pounding against her but never quite killing her, until at last she gasped and awoke to find herself flailing at the invisible onslaught. Mostly, she stayed in her room, in her dressing gown, staring out the window at the greasy waters of the harbor and the big brown bridge to the city, eating nothing, saying nothing, growing thinner and more listless by the day. She wished she would dream of Billy himself, but she didn't. She wished such things as ghosts existed, so he could haunt her, at least, but she was disappointed there as well.

Gigi Wallace arranged that Stella be given a leave from her internship, but when a month passed with no improvement, she and Waldo began to feel further action must be taken. They sat with her, one on each side, and tried to get her attention.

"There is a clinic in Switzerland that is treating catatonia and depression with a new therapy, Stella. It has had good success," said Gigi.

"It's called electroconvulsive therapy," Waldo continued. "They stimulate your brain with electricity, Stella. Afterward, people say they feel like new again. We think it may be the right course of treatment for you, and we'd like to take you on a trip to meet some doctors and visit the clinic."

Stella seemed not to hear them, just stared straight ahead of her, but the following morning, she emerged from her room, dressed and groomed like she was going somewhere. When she walked into the kitchen, Loretta gave a shriek, as if Stella herself were an apparition.

"It's all right, Loretta. It's just me," she said quietly. "I'll be damned if I'm going to let Mother and Father send me off to have the wits shocked back into me. I can pull it together if entirely necessary. I just haven't wanted to."

"I'm glad to have you back, baby," Loretta said, and wrapped Stella in her arms.

That afternoon Stella called and got a last-minute appointment to have her hair done. When she returned from the salon, her dark waves were cropped short, like a flapper's. The following day she dressed in her blue serge suit with a gray silk shirt beneath and paid a call on Dr. Postlethwaite, the director of the Internal Medicine Department.

It was too late. He told her they'd had to find someone else in her absence. If she wanted to resume her training, she would have to start her internship over again the following year.

"Please," she had begged, but he shook his head.

If old Postlethwaite had been kinder or more flexible, she never would have married Rudy Baker, that much was certain.

She and Rudy had always known each other, it seemed. They'd learned to waltz together on Saturday mornings at the Minchon Academy of Dance, and then, when they were older, they'd danced together at various debutante and charity balls. But Stella had never paid him much mind. He was one of two dozen young men she knew equally well — by first name but not much more. And so it had seemed a simple courtesy, at first, when he came to pay condolences after Billy died. She smiled politely and said so little that he quickly left. The second time, she was annoyed. The third time she told Loretta to say she was indisposed.

"He's already sitting in the parlor with your mother. I can't turn him away."

"With my mother?"

"Mm-hmn."

"Well, let her keep him company then."

But a few nights later, he turned up at dinner. Gigi had invited him. Almost immediately after dinner, Stella found herself alone with him. Her parents still had plans for her, apparently, even if she wouldn't let them take her to Europe to have her brains addled.

"Rudy," Stella said, the next time he came. "You must forgive my mother for meddling and get back to your own life. She's trying to match us up, I'm afraid, but —"

"I've noticed."

"Well, I don't want to give you the wrong impression. I'm not looking for a boyfriend. My next step will be to get back to doctoring. I'm just taking the year off, you see."

"But the two things aren't mutually exclusive, are they? You're so lovely, Stella, you needn't hide that behind a white coat."

"I'm hardly hiding. I'm mourning."

"But anyhow, what are you going to do with yourself for all the months between now and then? Wouldn't you like to go out to the movies or dinner now and then?"

"No, thank you, Rudy, really."

"But, Stella, darling Stella, it doesn't become you to be sad like this. You should be happy. You can't be Mrs. Galt anymore, and I know that's what you wanted, but you could be Mrs. Baker. I promise it won't be so bad."

"I'd be Dr. Baker, not Mrs. Baker — if I

were to be any sort of Baker — which of course —"

"Ah, so you've taken my last name, already! So it's settled?"

"Please, Rudy, it's just too soon for me to even consider . . ."

"I promise I will make you happy."

"No one can promise that."

And yet, somehow, despite herself, after a couple of months had passed and he was still coming around, she began to step out with him. Movies, sodas, Manhattans at the Bar Bossert on Montague Street. Being with Rudy did distract her from her sadness, and after a while she began to welcome it. She found herself being happy, smiling, laughing, even dreaming again.

The first time he kissed her was startling, though. His mouth pressed too hard. His tongue probed her. She slammed her eyes shut so he wouldn't see the disappointment in them, and in a flash she was back at the Kozy Kabins, the last time a man had kissed her. She'd been thrumming then, buzzing with pleasure; she'd been seized by a feeling of urgency, a driving need to get closer to Billy, to smell his skin, to engulf him and be engulfed. His slightest grazing kiss on her cheek had set off a storm in her body. Not so with Rudy Baker, but remembering Billy's kiss, she yielded — even kissed him back.

As the nights passed, it became easier to be with Rudy, physically. He would pick her up in his car and they would drive out to City Island for a cheap romantic dinner on a barge, or go walking in the surf in the Rockaways, somewhere far away, and afterward, they would park. She taught him to kiss her more gently, and he was a willing student. By late summer, she found she looked forward to the creaking of the emergency brake when he pulled its lever. She hadn't let him take her to the backseat, not yet, but finally, on a hot night in the middle of August, he said for the umpteenth time, "What about it, Stella? Won't you marry me? You're so beautiful I think I'm going to die if you won't."

She laughed and said, "I wouldn't want that! But you know, Rudy, I think I will."

"Will . . . what?" he asked.

"Marry you."

"Oh, Stella," he said. "Darling. You won't regret it."

"I hope not."

"Come here, Stella Baker," he said, opening the passenger-side door for her.

They slid into the rear seat. The paper cups of beer they had taken out from the restaurant were still sitting on the car's roof, where they'd left them. When they sat down together, the shocks sagged and the cups rolled off the roof, spilling beer down the side of the car. They kissed, and for the first time there weren't any limits to what she would let him touch through the soft merino wool of her sweater or the chaste white cotton of her underpants. They got to the point that they were each of them madly clutching the other. She was on the verge of relenting to his plea — "Come on, Stell, we're going to get married" — when she felt a shiver of memory. It occurred to her that he was going to be able to tell that it wasn't her first time. Perhaps she should hold out till they were married, so he didn't have a chance to change his mind. But no, she didn't want to deceive him, didn't want to start out a life that way. And she didn't want to wait.

"There's something I have to tell you first, Rudy," she said.

"Tell me."

"I made love with Billy, Rudy."

He looked at her for a minute, assessing.

"How many times?"

"Rudy."

"I think I have a right to ask that of my future wife. How many times?"

"Once."

"Just once."

"Just once."

"Did he touch you like I do?"

"Rudy! He's dead. You're here. It's just us here, all right?"

"All right," he said, "you're right," and then he lowered himself over her, pressing her backward, grinding her groin with his thigh. It was unexpected, and she moaned with pleasure.

"Are you ready, Stell?"

"Yes," she said, and she was. She wanted to feel that pressure again, then the burn, the clasping, maybe even the love. "But do you have a —"

"A what?"

"You know, a — um — Peacock?"

"A *Peacock*? You mean a rubber? Why would I have a rubber? I didn't have the slightest hope in hell that you were going to say yes to me tonight."

"But, Rudy, what if —"

"Aw, come on. You're going to be Mrs. Rudyard Baker anyway. We don't need one of those things between us," he said, sliding her underwear down. First his soft fingers probed her flesh, and then he reached down to guide himself to her. She gasped as the hot thickness of his sex pushed into her.

■ ■ ■ ■

One morning after he'd been there a couple of months, Bill Niederman paused and turned to Stella before he went out the door.

"I was just wondering, what are you going to do today?" he asked.

"Oh," she said. "Well, I have a tennis match at the Racquet Club at eleven o'clock. After that, till Wally gets home, I'll read. I'm just about to finish *Pride and Prejudice.*"

"Sounds to me like you have too much time on your hands. I've been wondering, Stella — because there aren't half enough doctors, these days — why *don't* you go back to medicine?"

"What on earth, are you serious?"

"Stella, doctors are needed now, more than ever."

"Don't you think I know that? Just ask my mother. She's so busy she hardly sleeps. But it's not that easy. I'd have to do an internship and residency."

"Is it Wally? You're afraid you won't be there for her?"

"It's just, I'm not sure I'm up to the stress of it anymore. Among other things. Now, can't you leave me be, Bill? Go do your war work and let me read my novel."

"I'm just worried about you, sitting around all day. You're unhappy, having so much time to yourself. It's so obvious you were meant to do more."

She looked him in the eye, smiled and said, "Do you really think so?"

"Yes, I do," he said, taking her hand, sending thrills through her flesh.

It was not an illicit touch, but he didn't meet her eye — he didn't dare.

"Maybe you're right, Bill," she said, tremulously.

"Of course I am," he answered, which was more or less when she fell in love with him.

Before, it had been an inkling to be squelched before ever understood. Now her hunger for him was a real thing, alive and dangerous.

"Think about it," he said, grasping her other hand. And then he went to work.

Stella didn't decide that day, but Bill continued to bring it up. He left the newspaper open to articles about the shortage of medical personnel on the home front. He even tried to enlist Wally — "Wouldn't you like your mother to be a hero, too?" he asked — but Wally shook her head. Heroes were never at home, she already knew.

Nevertheless, Stella soon warmed to the

idea. Then, she started to love it. Once she'd made her mind up, the first thing she did was call her mother.

"Well, it's about time, Stella! Thank heavens you're back."

Then she called Dr. Postlethwaite — the same man who had given away Stella's place when her first crisis occurred.

"Well, well, Stella Wallace. Why don't you come down and chat with me, say a week from today?"

When the day came, she dressed carefully in her gray serge suit and a white collared shirt without frills. To Wally, she had said nothing. The appointment was during school hours, so she didn't have to know.

"Ah, Mrs. Baker," said Dr. Postlethwaite in greeting her, which she found demeaning, since she'd officially earned the title doctor when she finished medical school. She was only missing the residency.

"I'd like to resume my training, Dr. Postlethwaite. It's been a number of years, I know, but I can retake any exams you may require. I feel it's the best way I can serve my country in wartime."

Stella envisioned for an instant the stacks of books she'd had to conquer in medical school, and wasn't in fact so sure she could relearn everything, but she kept her posture perfectly straight and pursed her lips slightly, in a faint smile, projecting self-certainty where it didn't quite exist. Dr. Postlethwaite once again held her fate in his hands.

"That will hardly be necessary, I'm sure, but what about your children? Who will look after them while you're working, or on call?"

"It's just Wallace now, Dr. Postlethwaite. She's seven. And not to worry, my mother's maid can look after her when I'm working. She is extremely reliable. She raised me, after all."

"And Captain Baker agrees with your decision?"

"He does," she said, smiling more broadly now, though she had only just written to him about it and was fairly sure he wouldn't.

"Then it's settled. You can begin rotations with the new class in July. But you will have to repeat the entire internship, I'm afraid. It's been too long to carry anything over."

"I understand entirely. And I'm glad of it. I certainly need to brush up! Thank you, Dr. Postlethwaite," she said.

In the waning months of that spring, Stella took Wally out of school four separate times to go see museum exhibits and twice to take shopping trips to Manhattan. She cooked one of Wally's favorite meals almost every night of the week: meat loaf, baked salmon, Welsh rarebit, quiche Lorraine. On weekends she made her famous pound cake, carefully meting out their rations of butter and sugar the rest of the week to make it possible.

For Stella, it was like being a new mother again. Her grief for Georgie subsided into the background of days filled with Wally, and her love for her daughter bloomed. They listened to radio dramas together and laughed at the funny papers. They read Wonder Woman comics and agreed that it would have been far better if Diana Prince had been a doctor, not a nurse.

"Maybe if we write to William Marston, he'll send her back to medical school, just like you're going to do, Mother!"

"Well, it's worth a try, I guess." So they sat together and wrote a fan letter to Wally's favorite author, begging him to give the Amazon Princess a higher education.

The communion Stella Baker felt with her daughter that month melted a lump that had lived inside her since the night she'd left Wally at her mother's and raced through the icy darkness to the hospital with her only son in her arms. Even her frequent nightmares, pierced by Georgie's gasping

and whooping and the sound of sirens, subsided.

She and Bill Niederman celebrated most
evenings, that June, before she started up
again, with a nightcap on the terrace, looking out at the harbor and the dark shadows
of Manhattan's tall buildings looming
beyond. They talked war news and Wally
news, and he told her what he'd heard from
Louise about his boys' various shenanigans.
They stood closer than they would have if
anyone else had been there to watch, but
they rarely touched. Two glasses extended
for a toast, and their knuckles brushed. A
cigarette lighter's flame cupped protectively
against the breeze. His olive-toned fingertips
grazing her pale wrist. Every time it happened, she thought she would lose control
and throw herself at him, or he would take
her in his arms.

But it didn't happen.

And yet, for the first time in such a long
time she was happy, thoroughly happy. She
had a beautiful child, a renewed career, and
a man who made her feel alive — even if he
wasn't her husband and never could be.

6
THE DEPARTMENT OF MILITARY MULTIPLICATION

"Why aren't you off fighting in the war, like Daddy?" Wally asked Mr. Niederman, as soon as she got up the courage.

"I've been called to serve the country, too," he explained. It was just that rather than going to Europe or the Pacific, he was helping in Brooklyn, doing work for the men who ran the Navy Yard. He pulled his jacket tails down and briefly looked away as he said it.

"You're a math teacher, though. That's what Mother said."

"That's true, too. That's the work I was doing before the war. Now I use math to help the Navy."

Wally was dubious. As if the Navy needed math problems solved. As if math professors could possibly help fight the Japs and the Krauts from their dusty old offices. This man was sleeping in her house. What if he was a liar?

"My mother goes to the Navy Yard, sometimes. To dance with soldiers and serve tea and coffee to the workers, but I don't get why people can't fix their own tea. There's a war on, after all, and everyone's supposed to be helping out and doing all they can."

"Well, Wally, that's a good point. People definitely can fix their own tea and coffee. I think your mother does it just to be nice, because those workers are tired after building ships all day, and the sailors are about to go off and do a very difficult job, with no luxuries at all."

He was fairly reasonable. It was rare that an adult conceded a point with her. But Wally was still suspicious of him and his reasons for not going to war himself. "Maybe she should just get a job in the Department of Military Multiplication, like you have. It sounds easier."

She looked at him, waiting for his reaction. Wally wasn't sure why, but she felt a strong urge to be impudent, to challenge him.

Mr. Niederman just chuckled. "You're a pretty smart girl, you know that, Wally?"

"Well, I'm glad to hear you two have another new career lined up for me," said Stella, coming into the living room from the kitchen with a couple of highballs for herself and Mr. Niederman. "But I'm afraid I could never do Mr. Niederman's job. Now, Wally, why don't you go to your room and do some reading?"

"But, Mother, don't you think Mr. Niederman really ought to think up a better cover story than working at the Navy Yard? Didn't you tell me yourself he was working at Columbia?"

"That's enough, Wally."

"It's okay, Stella. You're right, Wally," said Mr. Niederman. "I do a strange kind of work. You see, I work for the Navy, but not on a ship, not even at the Navy Yard. Sometimes I wish I were overseas, too, facing what brave men like your dad have to face every day, instead of up at Columbia working in the, um, what did you call it? Multiplication Department."

He was a cool customer, Mr. Niederman. Oddly charming and awfully hard to pin down.

Just then there was a knock on the apartment door, and Loretta came in, carrying a casserole dish. "Shepherd's pie!" she announced.

"Loretta!" Wally called. "I was just asking Mr. Niederman what he really does for the war effort. What do you think?"

"Wally, child, what are you going on about?"

"No, it's quite all right, Loretta. It's fine. Wally here has been asking me some very insightful questions. I don't mind a bit. I think she's concerned that I have a German-sounding name. But don't worry, Wally. I'm not working for the Germans. You can count on that. The Germans don't much like my kind."

"He means he's Jewish, Wally," said Stella, quietly.

"Just like I told you," said Loretta.

"Now, tell me this, Miss Baker, how are you at your numbers? Can you solve for x?"

"I can add. I can count to at least a hundred. I don't know anything about x."

"Well, the x is what you don't know," Mr. Niederman explained. "It's what's on the other side of the equals sign. It's the answer to 'How many apples does Wally have?' in a word problem." Wally looked at him blankly. "Well, you'll be getting to it eventually. And when you do, let me know, because if I can ever help you find x — or y — Miss Baker, I'd be glad to. I'm not half bad at it, and I'd very much like the chance to prove to you that I do know my math."

Wally shrugged, unconvinced.

"I'd like for us to be friends."

"That's very generous of you, Bill," said her mother. "And thank you so much for dinner, Loretta. Tell Mother I said so. Now, Wally, chop chop, get to your homework. And don't forget to look over the spelling words for this week."

Wally was glad to go. *X* was the twenty-fourth letter, but what was the value of a letter, outside the alphabet, outside a word? She glanced at the list of words she had to memorize for the spelling quiz, then delved into the swirl and swash of words and colors, of action and danger and love that was the world of the Amazon princess known to the world as both Diana Prince and Wonder Woman.

Despite Wally's reticence, they really did seem to become friends, after that. On Friday nights, when Mr. Niederman went back home to his family for the weekends, she missed him. And Monday mornings, she was always bursting with something to tell him about. Wally spent most of one breakfast showing him the various mounting pins, tweezers, and bottles of lethal chemicals from her disused butterfly collecting set. And the varying yields from the two Victory Gardens she tended were always of interest to him; the lush beds at the

Wallace house had always outperformed the windblown planters of her family's high terrace, until a fungus crept into the beds on Columbia Heights and devastated the tomatoes there, while the terrace crop went unscathed. The amazing thing, perhaps, was that he was genuinely interested in Wally's pursuits. And unlike her mother, who ever since she'd gone back to work that July was always either at the hospital or exhausted after one of her shifts, he listened.

Over toast and juice, one August Monday, she smiled and said, "So, Mr. Niederman, guess what happened yesterday when Ham and I put an ant from his colony back on the nest where it came from?"

"A family reunion! Let me guess — it fell in line and got right back to work?"

"Nope."

"What?"

"They cut her into pieces."

And this was the great thing about Mr. Niederman: Instead of just feigning interest or expressing disgust, he said, "Really? How fascinating! Why do you think that could be? Maybe it smelled wrong."

"That's what Ham said, too — it must have smelled different after being away from the colony."

"How long did it take?"

"Not very long."

"And what did they do with the parts?"

Another morning, in late September, Wally reported to him between bites of Cream of Wheat that the tomatoes on the terrace had produced twice as many fruits per plant as the ones at the Wallaces'.

"What was different about them?"

"Well, these ones I watered in the mornings, and the ones at Gigi's always got watered later in the day."

"So we have two factors that are different: the time of watering and the place. Anything else?"

"I don't think so."

"Were they the same variety?"

"I don't know. They looked the same."

"Did you keep records of the weight and number of the fruits each plant has borne?"

"Of course not, Mr. Niederman. It's just a vegetable garden, not an experiment."

He smiled. "But it could be, if you had some graph paper and a little time to take some notes."

"I guess I could do that next year. They're already dying now."

"Yes, so next year, if we want to figure out whether the location or the watering was the decisive factor, you're going to have keep track of some more data."

"Like what?"

"Well, what about weighing the fruit when you pick it? Could you do that?"

"I'm not so sure, Mr. Niederman."

"But you kept a tally this year, of how many tomatoes you picked, didn't you?"

"Sure, Loretta and I both did. We kept a sheet pinned up near the kitchen door."

"Then how about next year, you add columns for small, medium, and large tomatoes to the tally sheet? That would be a bit more information."

"Okay."

The shocking thing to Wally was that someone other than Ham was interested in what she was doing.

The shocking thing to Stella was how Bill Niederman managed to be interested in whatever interested Wally.

The shocking thing to Bill Niederman was that he had as much enthusiasm, if not more, for his conversations with Wally as he had for weekend morning chats with his own sons, which tended toward baseball players and statistics. He was as proud of Wally as if she were his. And if it made her mother warm toward him, he certainly didn't mind. She was a gorgeous creature, Stella Baker. Who wouldn't want to be the recipient of her smiles?

7
THE WAREHOUSE

"Take me down there, Ham," Wally begged one crisp November Saturday in 1944. Her mother was on call, as she so often seemed to be now, and the two of them were out back at Gigi's. They had just watched a shipment of cargo being unloaded into the warehouse that lay beneath the Wallaces' yard.

Wally had never visited the Wallace warehouse, or the waterfront at all, for that matter, but she knew from Gigi that there were working-men there, and sailors, and that it was not a place for children. Still, she'd never been forbidden to go there, and she *was* allowed to walk to school alone, now that she was in the second grade.

It had always seemed so mysterious to Wally that there was a building within the cliff, beneath the very soil they played on and dug in, but what made her want to go down there this day was the cargo that had just been loaded into it, heavy, dusty sack after heavy, dusty sack. It was different from the usual crates and bales and barrels, and they could smell it all the way up in the yard: cocoa. Imagine there being so much of something that was rationed, so near them, beneath their very house. Just to get closer to that smell would be heavenly, but Wally imagined there was even a chance they'd come back with a sample.

Almost wordlessly — because they both knew it wouldn't be allowed if they asked — they left the house and walked several blocks south, toward the edge of the Heights where Joralemon Street led all the way down to the docks.

The heady aroma of the cocoa over-whelmed Wally even before they reached the doors of the warehouse. It was almost too rich.

"I think it's locked up, Ham."

"No, don't you see, the gate's ajar. Prob-ably someone's in there taking inventory or something, now they got all the cocoa loaded inside. Let's go look. We're just two kids, right? What can they say? And maybe they'll give us a little spillage."

"Have you been down here before?"

"Sure. Me and the guys come down here a bunch. You can always get something interesting, if you know who to ask. You just have to run up to the bar on Atlantic Avenue and bring back a growler of beer for one of the men, something like that."

"Hey you, punk!" called a voice from across the intersection. Wally looked around and was surprised how empty the street was. "What you think you're doing with that girl, huh, boy?"

Wally hardly saw the man because her eyes followed the sound of the clattering metal as he threw down his grappling hook. At least he wasn't going to use that, she was thinking when she heard Ham grunt and turned to see him fall to the pavement clutching his face and crumple into a ball. The man gave his back a desultory kick and said, "Get up!"

When Ham looked up, there was blood on his face.

"Run, girlie, run!" the man shouted to Wally. What did he mean? Was he warning her against himself?

"You get off him!" she shouted. "He's my friend." And though she was frightened, she darted forward and reached down to grab Ham's hand. "Come on, Ham," she said. "Let's get out of here."

The man looked on in apparent disgust as the children turned and ran back up the hill to the Heights together, he pulling her along to keep up with his longer stride and swifter pace. Ham's face was smeared with red. There was blood on their clasped hands, too. They were two blocks up the hill, panting, almost out of the wharf area and back to safety, when they nearly collided with Gigi Wallace in her white coat.

Gigi listened to their story with serious concern and wiped Ham's face as clean as she could with a handkerchief from her purse. Then she made a detour from her house calls to take the two of them home herself, though there was nowhere else they could possibly have gone. She did not chide them. All she said was "It's not for me to punish either of you. You'll hear it from your parents later."

"Hamilton Walker, Jr.," Loretta said, as soon as she'd handed him a dish towel stuffed with ice, "get out my sight, and don't come back into it till I've simmered down. Lord help me, I'd low the boom on you for taking her down there, child, if you hadn't been hit already."

"Come on, Mama. I didn't do anything."

"What was you even doing down there with Wally?"

"It was Wally who wanted to go."

"You just *know* better, Hamilton. You *know* how people think."

"But Wally was the one who — And nothing happened to her! She's not even in trouble."

"Just whose house you think you in, boy? Just who you think you are?" Loretta said. "When the likes of you drags Miss Wallace down to the docks, only one of you's on thin ice with me."

Wally had never heard Loretta call her Miss Wallace. It sounded like a name her mother should have been called, when she was a girl. She stood by silently, afraid of more than the man who had punched Ham. Gigi had been grim about it, too, once Ham was cleaned up — almost silent and clearly angry at both of them. Wally wondered what her mother was going to say to her.

"Sorry, Ham," Wally offered, as he rose to obey his mother. She still didn't understand why no one had called the police to go after the man.

"Just forget it. I'll see you later, Wally," Ham muttered, slouching off to his room.

"Okay, see you," Wally said.

She went to the top floor to lose herself once again in the exploits of Steve Trevor, Etta Candy, Queen Hippolyta, and Wonder Woman, but it wasn't so easy to escape reality today. If only Wonder Woman had been there, she thought, to swoop in and set things right, it would have been the longshoreman who had run away bruised and shamed.

Later that afternoon, Loretta agreed to take Wally along on her errands so she could stop in at Merganser's for the new issue of *Wonder Woman,* due out that day. Wally immediately spotted the freshly delivered bundle of Sensation Comics, wrapped in paper and tied up with twine, with the unmistakable face of Countess Draska Nishki smiling diabolically from a corner where the wrapper was peeled away.

"Oh, dear. Miss Baker. You've spotted your *Wonder Woman,* have you? I'm afraid I won't be able to unpack those today. The official sale date isn't till Sunday."

Wally imagined clocking Mr. Merganser on the jaw, binding him with the unbreakable loops of her golden lasso, and leaving him hogtied, to be found by the local authorities, while she absconded with a precious early copy of the new issue. But that level of force wasn't really necessary, she knew. Mr. Merganser was the kind of grown-up a kid could work with, she thought. She smiled at him, as endearingly as possible.

"If you don't have your scissors handy, Mr. Merganser, I could lend you my pocket-knife," she suggested.

"Your *pocketknife?* A little girl like you has a pocketknife, does she? Are you sure you ought to be carrying that around?"

"My father gave it to me," she said, though actually, she had taken it from her father's dresser drawer, without permission. Ham had promised to teach her to whittle.

She pulled it out of her dress and handed it over, still closed, to Mr. Merganser.

"What do you know," he said. "A Boy Scout knife, just like the one I've got."

To Wally's gratification, he opened the knife and used it to pop the twine on the bundle of comics, then he reached into the center of the stack, pulled out a pristine one — no dents or folds or dings in its cover — and handed it to Wally.

"That'll be ten cents, please, Miss Baker," he said.

It was funny, she thought, as she handed him her dime, how people you once thought were adversaries often turned out all right.

Once she had her comic, Wally went and found Loretta in front of Mammy's Pantry on the corner of Henry Street. She trailed Loretta as she dodged in and out of the shops on Montague Street, picking up meat at Lubetsky's, bread at Camereri Brothers, and greens further up at Esposito's.

"Afternoon, Mrs. Tiedeman." "Afternoon, Mrs. Perry." "Afternoon, Mrs. Downing," Loretta said as they passed various matrons on the street.

"Good day, Loretta," the ladies would return with benevolent condescension. "Good day, Wallace."

"Loretta," asked Wally when they were out of hearing, "how old do you have to be to be called Miss, or Missus?"

Loretta raised an eyebrow. "Good question. I suppose it all depends."

"On what?"

"Child, you are full of questions!" Loretta laughed.

Inside the shops, it was different. Mr. Lubetsky and Mr. Camereri and Mr. Esposito all called Wally Little Miss Baker, and Loretta Mrs. Walker, even as she haggled with them over pennies and ounces.

Inside Lubetsky's, Wally eavesdropped on a cluster of neighborhood ladies gossiping while they waited in line. They were talking about the druggist, Mr. Merganser, and whether he'd been exempted from the draft and why — because of bad knees or one of those *invisible* afflictions.

"Well, he's not a Christian Scientist!"

declared one, and the rest burst out laughing. Wally didn't understand what they were talking about, but there was something about an exemption for being a Jew. It had never occurred to Wally that Mr. Merganser was Jewish.

Wally didn't know exactly why, but she didn't like those women. Maybe it was because her grandmother and mother were doctors, but she thought people should help each other, not gossip and put other people down. She wished they would lower their voices.

Then she heard Loretta say her name and looked up to see her standing by the cash register, her string bag bulging with leeks, potatoes, and lettuce. Beneath the vegetables was a damp-looking brown-paper package — that must have been the meat — and under Loretta's arm was a loaf of bread in a paper sack.

"Come help me carry some of this, String Bean. And then let's get on home. It's late. Time to put dinner on."

"Am I eating at Gigi's?" Wally asked. It wouldn't exactly be a surprise, but it hadn't been the plan, that morning. Her mother had said they were going to have Welsh rarebit on toast, a meatless war-effort dinner to be sure, but one of Wally's favorites.

"Your mother called. She's going to be a little late. Do you mind having some meat loaf with us? How'd that be?"

"Fine."

That night, Wally had brushed her teeth and was almost ready to go to bed when her mother called her into the living room. She had almost begun to think she would get away without reprimand for the misadventure at the waterfront. To her surprise, Mr. Niederman was also sitting there, and rather than getting up and letting them have their discussion in private, he cleared his throat and was the first one to speak.

"Wally," he said. "Your mother asked me if I would be the one to speak to you about what happened today, because she feels she might be too upset by it."

Her mother sat with both feet flat on the floor, her eyes averted, her arms crossed against her chest.

"It was very irresponsible of you two, going and getting into trouble at the docks. Hamilton has gotten his nose broken."

"Gosh," Wally said. "I knew it was swollen up."

"Do you understand how dangerous it is down there, Wally?"

"Yes, Mr. Niederman. You don't have to

worry. We're not going back."

"But do you *really* understand? You can't go into dark storehouses or empty buildings or even movie theaters with boys. Including Ham."

"That's crazy. I always go around with Ham."

"Wally," warned her mother.

Suddenly, Wally realized what they were getting at.

"What? You mean I'm not allowed to play with Ham anymore? Because he's a Negro?"

"No, Wally, that's not what we're saying. Playing with Ham is fine. That's not the problem. But you're a young lady. You just can't put yourself in certain situations."

"What about swimming? We always go to the pool together. Is that a *situation*?"

"In fact, I don't think you should swim with Ham any longer," said Mr. Niederman, just exactly as her mother said, "Swimming is fine. Of course, you can still swim with him."

Wally looked from her mother to Mr. Niederman, but they were looking at each other, confused by their mutual contradiction.

"You know something, Mr. Niederman," she blurted out. "You're not my father. I don't have to listen to you!"

"Wallace, go to your room this instant, and stay there," said Stella. "We will discuss your behavior, and its repercussions, in the morning."

Wally turned and slammed the door behind her.

Stella put her face in her hands. "Well, that went well," she said.

"Stella," said Bill Niederman. "It's an awkward situation. I'm *not* her father. But she needed a talking-to. She can't be going down to empty warehouses with a black boy twice her age."

"But what did she hear? Me saying one thing and you saying another. What was the point of that?"

He sighed.

"You know, Bill, I can hardly believe it, but I actually miss Rudy right now."

He scooted closer to her on the couch, touched her jaw and turned her face gently toward his. "You don't mean that, do you?" He dried her cheeks with his pocket square, then slid his large fingers behind her neck and his other arm around her waist. What began as a gesture of comfort turned swiftly to a hungry embrace. It was what she had been dreaming of for months now, but she pulled away.

"Bill?"

"Yes, Stella?"

"I don't think I can do this —"

"Can't you?"

He lifted her onto his lap, eliciting a small gasp. Then he bent down, holding her close to him, touched his lips to hers, and when she opened to him, he kissed her thoroughly. She had never been so hungry for a man's flesh. Every inch of her thrilled to it.

"Maybe I can," she whispered. "But Wally — she can never know."

After a quick glance to be sure that Wally's door was closed, he carried Stella down the hall and across the threshold of her marital bedroom as if it were their honeymoon. He laid her on the bed, and she watched while he unfastened her blouse. Then she reached for his buckle and drew him to her.

In a moment, they were clasping limbs, pressing hips, rolling over, almost fighting to shed their clothes in the dark. Stella was thinking of Billy Galt when he first kissed her — Billy Galt when he took her for the first and only time at the Kozy Kabins, Billy Galt, who had died and left her alone — but then Bill Niederman grasped her shoulders and pushed her gently onto her back. He slid down and spread her legs apart and beginning at her inner thigh he moved slowly, tantalizingly inward, caressing her in a way Billy Galt had never gotten to. She was his now, Bill's, and no one else's.

Bill Niederman was visited by his own fleeting visions of another lover: Louise. Louise flaccid in the dim light of their radio dial. Louise lying on her back, receiving, and rolling away when he was done. Louise the good wife, who had borne him boys and deserved something, surely, in return, something like love, but for whom he had never felt a fraction of the passion that Stella inspired. Then Stella cried his name, shivered, and her whole body clenched around him. He exploded with pleasure like nothing he'd ever had with Louise, forgetting — for then, at least — his marriage, his mortgage, the war, his cares.

They slept lightly, but not for long, and soon after awakening, Stella found herself on her knees on the blue hooked rug in the bathroom, bracing her sweaty arms against the cool white porcelain while he thrust into her again and again. Her body was suffused with brilliance from inside her. She hadn't realized such sensations were possible. It was something ancient that had been withheld from her, till now. And now that she'd known it, her life was renewed.

She collapsed back against him, and they

clung to each other on the black and white tiles. He pulled down the bath towels from the rack to cover them and held her like no one had held her since Billy Galt. *What am I going to do?* she asked herself. *How can I possibly have done what I just did? And how can I possibly stop?*

8
NATURAL HISTORY

Stella's word prevailed in the matter of the swimming, and no particular punishment ensued for Wally or Ham. They were tentative about doing things together for a while, then life resumed as usual.

Every Saturday that winter, Wally and Ham went to the St. George pool to horse around and splash, and for Wally to attend swimming lessons. A local boy had drowned in the East River at the end of the previous summer, and even though his antics weren't anything Wally was likely to repeat, Stella was concerned that her daughter be confident in the water by the time the next summer's swimming season began.

Ham was paid a quarter by Stella every time he minded Wally at the pool or anywhere out of the house, and part of their deal was for Ham to keep this employment a secret. As far as Wally knew, swimming with her was what Ham wanted to do with his weekends.

"Tell me again about what happened to Beaver Muniere," Wally said, as they walked down the street, breath puffing white like smoke, on the way to the pool one cold Saturday morning. She'd heard it a million times, it seemed, but she always wanted to hear it again, every time they went swimming, as if Beaver's death were some talisman that would ward off any danger to themselves.

Ham hadn't been there, but he knew kids who had, which made him an expert in Wally's eyes. There was a certain debate about how exactly it had happened. Some said Beaver had been diving after a silver dollar another kid had stolen from him and thrown into the water. Others put it down to a dare — he'd been trying to stay under for a whole three and a half minutes and had grabbed on to the first thing he could to keep himself down — a rusty old milk can. The currents did the rest. Whatever the start of it, the finish was that Beaver had gotten his head jammed in that milk can. Wally shuddered at the description Ham gave of Beaver's bare heels kicking and struggling while several of the boys had tried to help free him, and then, slowly, his legs going limp in the dark gray water.

They entered the bustling hotel lobby, with its shops and subway entrance, and headed straight toward the pool entrance.

"Did Esther Williams ever wear this one?" Wally asked as she was handed one of the scratchy black woolen bathing suits that were standard issue at the pool.

"Never mind what Miss Williams wears, little missy. You won't be swimming with her," said Miss Finn, the scowling attendant who took the entry fees and handed out suits and towels. Wally and Ham had developed a supervillain persona for her: The Evil Finn had a woman's head and torso with an eel's jaws and tail, and her costume was damp black wool. She lurked in the pool after hours and devoured any guest who dared take an illicit dip.

"That's fifty cents," she croaked unnecessarily to the children, as if they weren't regulars. "And you, young man, the Negro changing area is to the left."

"Why does she have to say that every time?" Wally asked Ham, too loudly. "Don't you think she knows you by now?"

"I see a lot of people, missy, and that's the policy, so I state it. And you better mind your elders and move along."

"Come on, Wally," Ham said. "Forget it. You're gonna get us kicked out."

Ham veered to the men's locker room, Wally to the ladies'. She had seen the Negro changing area there: a cement-floored mop room with a row of stinking buckets and a small bench and several cubbies against the wall as well as a showerhead with a single knob: cold.

"Do you have to change in a mop room, Ham?" Wally asked, when they met up again, poolside.

"Naw. I don't actually *listen* to the Evil Finn. What do you take me for? Most everybody thinks I'm Puerto Rican, anyway, or Jewish. Nobody's ever said a thing, except the Evil Finn, and she ain't allowed in the men's, is she?"

"Firebomb!" shouted Ham, when he'd climbed to the top of the high dive, and dove out into the air above the water, spreading his limbs like a cross and dropping, belly flop, onto the water. "Yeowch!" he wailed when he resurfaced, and then, seeing that Wally still stood hesitating on the pool deck, he called, "Don't be a chicken, Wally. *Buc*-buc-buc-buc-*buc*!"

The other thing they did together was visit the natural history museum in Manhattan. Their first museum outing had been in the company of Gigi, who wanted to give some substance to the children's mutual interest in the insect world and had arranged a meeting with an assistant curator. She also bought them both memberships and paid Ham his usual covert fee for minding Wally.

Vernon Somersby had certainly not been expecting a seven-and-a-half- and a twelve-year-old when he opened the door to the Invertebrate Zoology Department, but Gigi Wallace was a commanding woman, and he'd given them a tour of several specimen cabinets containing Lepidoptera and Formicidae. Both of them had shown remarkable attention to the tiny details that differentiated similar species of ant and butterfly, and the young postdoctoral candidate and assistant curator was enamored. Teaching was what he'd always wanted to do, and though he hadn't been planning on teaching grammar school, he'd never had two such eager pupils. After a successful first visit, Mr. Somersby had agreed to let them visit him after school on Friday afternoons.

Each week, he had a short lesson on taxonomy or natural selection ready for them, and then he set them loose with magnifying glasses, pencils and paper, and a set of specimens. He even taught Ham to do a proper museum mounting, using some specimens of common species. Though the children were interested in ants, he decided first to focus their attention on beetles, being at once the hardiest of his specimens and the most visually arresting. How could a child who liked bugs fail to revel in a shimmering tiger beetle or a boldly striped and antlered Asian longhorn? Ants, he knew, required great attention to detail and often facility with a microscope.

"There are two principles we must start with," Mr. Somersby announced. "Classification is genealogy, and phylogeny recapitulates ontogeny. Now, what do you think that means?"

They shrugged, baffled, until he brought out a tray of weevils.

"There are more weevils than any other family of beetles. In fact, the Curculionidae make up half of all known beetles. Have you ever seen one?"

"That's a boll weevil," Ham ventured. "We studied them at school."

"Ah, the infamous cotton boll weevil. But you're a New York City boy. Have you ever seen one?"

"No, sir, I just know about 'em."

"Sometimes Loretta finds weevils in the rice," Wally said.

"Yes, unfortunately, almost all the beetles

the average person knows about are pests. But look at these —" He pulled out a second drawer and lifted a sheet of paper from on top of it, revealing a bare white surface that seemed to be studded with jewels. "These beauties are all . . . *weevils*! Let's begin by observing them. What do they have in common?"

They drew, they counted segments, they used colored pencils to reproduce the patterns on the backs of the beetles, they brought their subjects into focus under bright lights and magnifying glasses. And before they knew it, Mr. Somersby's lesson was over. The museum would be closing soon, and they had to go home.

"For next time," he said, handing each of them a small box wrapped in paper, "your homework is to draw these specimens, every barb, every hair, every spiracle. Observe the joints of the antennae! They have a number, so count them! They even have names — scapus, funicula, and clava, just to begin — but before you name them, you must see them, so look!"

"What's a spiracle, Mr. Somersby?" Wally asked, the answer to which question kept them there another quarter of an hour.

They shut the door to room 46 with its milk-glass windowpane and walked smiling, dazed, and enthusiastic down the grand, dim hallway toward the exhibit areas, where the silence of the Invertebrate Zoology Department gave way to the clatter and babble of a museum full of people. Before they left, they took time to wander beneath the blue whale and venture briefly amongst the dinosaurs.

On the way home, Wally fell asleep against Ham's shoulder, and he let her.

By the spring of 1945, Wally considered herself a junior entomologist. She couldn't wait for the warm part of the year, so she could get back out into the dirt and observe live insects, doing some of things Mr. Somersby had taught them about. The anticipation somewhat softened her disappointment that she was sleeping over at her grandparents' more than ever. At Gigi and Waldo's, she was free to go out in the backyard and explore the very first thing when she awakened, even if the air was chilly. At home, her mother would stop her from going out onto the veranda in cold weather. She didn't want to let all the cold air into the apartment.

The ants got moving earlier in the spring than Wally would have expected. By March, they were already active many days. With her green-tinted sunglasses on, what little was growing in her grandparents' lower garden seemed greener than green, making it easier to track the ants that walked in files between the scrubby blades of winter-worn grass. Wally's first discovery that spring was that there were two species of ants in the yard — or at least two. The small ones she had tentatively identified as pavement ants. The other, larger ones were the wood ants she and Ham knew so well, from whom she had stolen the queen. The raised anthill she and Ham had dug up was almost completely gone, now, but she was fairly sure that a new opening on the far side of the azaleas, closer to the chimney pipe, belonged to the same colony. Wally knew that the workers below would have chosen new larvae to elevate to royal status in the aftermath of the Antland raid, and carefully prepared the cells that would serve as the new royal nursery. Was there a new queen there already, she wondered, or did the colony have to survive without a head until summer, when the mating flights occurred?

She had a slice of Loretta's pound cake in her hand — a stolen breakfast before the usual oatmeal and eggs that Loretta would serve at 7:45 sharp — and took a few idle bites of it. Cake was not something to waste, ever, but especially not in wartime. It might just as well be made of ration coupons, all butter and eggs and sugar. Wally looked down at the cake and then up the hill anxiously, hoping Loretta wasn't watching her from the back window. She couldn't help comparing the cake to her mother's, which were so much moister, denser, and crispier at the edges — not to mention so much rarer. Plain, almond, or chocolate, it didn't matter. She'd never have fed a crumb of a cake her mother had made to an ant. But that morning, Loretta's cake was a bit dry, and Wally was feeling irritable. She decided to see if she could start a war.

She broke off bits of the soft sweet crumb and dropped them on the grass, sometimes in the path of the column of tiny brown ants, sometimes to the side, in an effort to steer the ants. Then she turned to her other side, where the big black ants predominated, and did the same thing. At first both groups of ants seemed alarmed and disoriented by the strange golden meteors that had fallen in their way. But after a few minutes, a member of each species approached a crumb Wally had laid out for it and began to carry it off. When it met a sister, it paused, and they waved their feelers at each other. Sometimes their feelers touched.

Soon columns of big black and small brown ants were marching for the treasure. Disappointingly, though, no matter how Wally tried to force them to compete, the two groups of ants ignored one another. Apparently, they were not enemies; possibly they were even allies.

In the end, she gave up warmongering and fed them all, so that the ants flowed to the crumbs like two rivers, one brown, one black. She played engineer and used twigs, dead bugs, leaves, dirt, and always more crumbs to build obstacle courses, which they roundly ignored. They always seemed to find the straightest path.

How did they find their food? she wondered. What called them to it? Smell, sight, or some other sense? And what did it mean, the way they touched? Wally put her ear close to the ground, imagining herself like King Midas, who could understand the insects. It was quiet. The grass tickled her ear, and for a moment she thought an ant had crawled up inside her head. She imagined devising a code based on the language of the ants, a code the Germans would never be able to crack.

"Wally," called Loretta out the back door. "Wally, are you out there? It's time for breakfast."

"All right, Loretta," she called back and scrambled to her feet, turning for a glance at the city before she went.

Most people said the view was best from the veranda, but Wally loved to look out between the fence posts. Straight out past the piers across the harbor stood the Woolworth Building. The Empire State Building poked up from the span of the Brooklyn Bridge, if you looked to the north. Even the great bridge itself looked close enough that it seemed to be Wally's and Wally's alone. Wally watched the silhouette of Manhattan brighten against the sky as the sun rose higher in the east. She wished she remembered what it looked like to have the city twinkle; she'd practically been a baby before the blackout.

"Wally-child, breakfast!" called Loretta, and thinking of warm oatmeal with honey and of Loretta, the one person who was always there for her, no matter what, Wally turned and walked back up the hill.

9
THE CAPE

There was a cold, sickly week that April when both Wally and Mr. Niederman came down with the grippe, and instead of shipping Wally to Gigi and Waldo's, where Waldo would be susceptible to catching her illness, and Mr. Niederman home, where he would doubtless infect his wife and children, Stella decided that the two invalids should stay home together.

"Tell me about your ants," said Mr. Niederman. "How are they doing? Is the colony still alive?"

If she had forgiven him for reprimanding her after she went to the piers with Ham — and for the most part, she had — it was because of the steadfast interest he showed in her ants.

"They're in Gigi's basement now, in a big mayonnaise jar, next to Ham's colony, Planet Ant. We talked about starting a war between them, but I feel sort of bad about letting Ham's ants just annihilate mine. He's got so many more, now, I'm pretty sure mine could never win."

Mr. Niederman nodded thoughtfully.

"But we were also thinking about sacrificing just a few workers from Planet Ant — that's Ham's colony — and adding them to Antland — that's the battery jar — and seeing what happens. That's what I want to do, so my ants can at least have a little glory."

"It sounds quite gruesome, really."

"Oh, no, it's really not. They cut each other in half and stuff, but there's hardly any blood. The type of ants we have are basically non-violent, except when they get into wars, every now and then, which they do when they're competing for territory. Some ants actually go on raids and kidnap other ants' larvae. Ham read it in *The Life of the Ant,* which Waldo gave me for Christmas — but we don't have that kind. So it may seem kind of bad. But in order to understand them, this is what we have to do."

"I see," said Mr. Niederman.

Wally thought, suddenly, of a morning not long before when she had watched Mr. Niederman quietly rise from his place at the breakfast table and capture a spider that was dangling from the overhead light. Once

135

it was safely trapped between his empty juice glass and a section of the morning paper, he had watched it for a moment as it searched the periphery of the glass for an escape route and then removed it to the terrace.

He was oddly charming, Mr. Niederman. Her mother thought so, too, apparently. For the past few weeks, they'd been going out to dinner at the Racquet Club together, and she'd even taken him to one of the Rensselaers' Friday evening gatherings. The previous weekend, they had played mixed doubles. Mr. Niederman must have been a better tennis player than her father, because they won, and Wally never remembered her mother and father winning in the old days, before her father went to war. Mr. Niederman didn't look like her father, who had thin yellow hair on his legs. When Mr. Niederman dressed up in short white pants and a V-neck tennis sweater, she could see that his legs were covered in wiry black hair. His calves were muscular and brown, at once embarrassing and compelling. Mr. Niederman's face was expressive in a way that was unlike any other man's she knew. He had penetrating, deep-set eyes, the most humorous eyebrows, and the proudest nostrils. He was tall, as tall as Waldo had been before Waldo sat down for once and for all, and very neat, but he was much less formal than Waldo or her father, when they had still gone off to offices every day in their dark suits and white shirts adorned with jewel-like ties. Mr. Niederman never wore a suit, just a jacket and pants, which she supposed was intended to contribute to his disguise as a math teacher. There was something odd about the way he'd shown up at their door two years before, without any warning, and been taken in as if he were family. He had been in her parents' wedding, but where had he been all those years in between, all of Wally's life? The truth was, she wished he'd been there, and maybe even that he had been her father. She couldn't get over the half nervous, half wonderful feeling he gave her. She imagined sometimes that he'd hypnotized or brainwashed them all, even her.

While her mother was at work, Mr. Niederman and Wally stayed in their bathrobes and puttered about the house. Mr. Niederman drank tea and read the paper in the living room. Wally did the math homework that had been left undone the day before, when she began to feel sick, and then they ate a tin of chicken soup for lunch and both took long naps. Afterward, Mr. Niederman seemed to be on the mend — he'd stopped sneezing completely — and announced that he would be going in to work the following day. Wally was hoping her fever would be high enough in the morning to keep her home one more day.

As the afternoon waned, Wally listened to the radio until the news came on, and then took a short stack of comics into her mother's room and settled on the green divan. She loved to be in her mother's room, among her mother's things, even when her mother wasn't there. But then she opened the cover of the first book on the stack, and the inky smell of the pages obliterated all awareness of the room, the divan, her mother. She herself slid away. Wally was gone. She became the story. Wally was Wonder Woman. She was even the cool, wise Queen Hippolyta. She was taken in anew by the beautiful and kind Countess Draska Nishki, at first, then outraged at how scurrilously evil she became, just as soon as she'd gained the upper hand.

The action frames spilled out from their borders — *oompf, pow, zing* — and there went the Amazon Princess, speeding through the night in her invisible plane, once again ferrying the annoying Major Trevor to the infirmary on Paradise Island.

Wally read the whole comic book, which had several other stories in it, none half as good as Wonder Woman, then read the Wonder Woman episode again. She almost had it memorized, and was unwittingly speaking the words aloud as she read. When she closed the cover, Wally realized she was draped nearly upside down across the divan, feet propped on the armrest, head dangling off the edge, braids dragging on the carpet. It was extremely comfortable, except that her hands, which she only now noticed she'd been holding up over her head, had begun to go tingly. She was just wrenching herself back to an upright posture when her eye caught sight of something in the shadows behind her mother's crisply ironed white bed skirt.

Wally had never been under her mother's bed. Never thought about it. But now she was intrigued. Kneeling down on the blue velvet carpet, she peered into the darkness. She saw her father's leather shotgun case, two dusty shoe boxes, and something else: a wide mahogany chest with little wheels underneath and fancy brass hinges. She had never seen it before, but from the lack of dust on its lid, it seemed it had been opened recently. It rolled out silently. As Wally lifted the lid, she was enveloped by the essences

139

of lavender and rose and cardamom. It was the smell her mother used to have, before the war. The box was lined with pink silk and contained the most remarkable costume Wally had ever seen.

She lifted it out and marveled at the way the sequins poured through her hands, at once heavy and fluid, like water — or money. The blue and silver-sequined cape shone not with stars, like Wonder Woman's, but with long silver triangles plunging from shoulder to hem, like daggers. The lining was electric-blue silk with blood-red piping. Wally slung the cape around herself and felt a shiver, as if some magical power had been conferred to her. The cape fastened simply at the neck with hooks. Beneath it, in the box, lay a matching dress, short with a sequined bodice and more of those spangly silver daggers on a blue field. Under the dress lay a blue and silver headband and a pair of silver high-heeled booties. It was the costume Wally would have conceived of for her mother, if her mother was a superhero.

As she slid the cape from her shoulders, she saw letters embroidered on the lining and touched the thick silver threads: "S.W." Worlds opened up in Wally's mind like accordion folds. Long-standing conundrums sorted themselves out. This discovery reconfigured her understanding of all the hours her mother spent working late on the wards, and the time she'd previously spent attending events of the Red Cross and the USO.

All those days and nights she was away, too busy for Wally — she'd been striving to make the world safe for her daughter. And the sense of withholding that Wally had sometimes felt, the sense that her mother was keeping something from her, all that made sense now, too. She'd had to keep her identity secret to protect her daughter.

Wally felt a wave of happy, simple love for her mother. Then she looked again at the initials on the cape: *S.W.* The Silver Wonder, she thought. Her mother was more than just a WAC or a WAVE or a doctor. She was Stella Wallace Baker by the light of day, and the Silver Wonder, a shining streak of justice, by night.

Wally pictured her rounding up house breakers and bank robbers, for part of her work was surely to help the police keep peace, what with so many men off at war.

Wally swirled in circles around the room, letting the cape flare out from her shoulders, dreaming she was her mother flying through the air after bad guys. When she stopped, the cape kept swinging and wrapped itself momentarily around her.

Then, before her mother could come home and catch her snooping in her super-hero box, Wally slipped off the cape and returned it neatly to the box, and the box to its hiding place under her mother's bed.

10
THE SHADOW

Wally spent the next Saturday morning helping Gigi till the soil and set out plants in the Victory Garden. It was just her, Gigi, and Waldo at the house that day. Her mother was at the hospital, and Loretta had taken Ham to Coney Island. She hoed and broke clumps while her grandmother followed her with cut-up chunks of potato, each of which she carefully placed in the softened earth with its eyes facing skyward.

Gigi Wallace didn't care about her Victory Garden the way she had her flowers, before the war, but she did enjoy getting her hands dirty.

Weekends were the best times for Gigi and her granddaughter. Unless one of her patients decided to have a baby, she could generally devote Saturday wholly to Wally, and she did. In the afternoon, when they had washed up from gardening, Gigi made them a pot of tea and got out her needlepoint basket in the hopes that she could interest her granddaughter in a hobby other than bugs.

Gigi Wallace didn't stitch bought patterns. Needlepoint was her one domestic pleasure, and as with everything else she did, she liked a challenge. She invented her patterns in her head — undulating flowers, clinging vines, whooping cranes, interlocking stars — and painted them onto the mesh. Hedges tended to grow up around her borders, sprouting flowers, whippoorwills, and thorns. What Is Home Without a Mother? might have sold better at the Women's Exchange, where she donated her work to be sold for the benefit of needy women, but she disdained mottoes, and she stitched to please herself.

"Wally, I'm going to get you started on your own square. How's that sound?"

"All right," Wally said, not too enthusiastically.

"The first thing is to get a simple design you're interested in. Let's look in some books. What about a large ant front and center and a border of little ants marching all around?"

"I don't know. Nobody would want that but me and Ham."

"Why can't it be for you?"

Gigi sat down next to Wally on the chintz sofa with her square of needlepoint. She smelled of the spicy perfumed soap they had used to scrub their hands.

"Let me show you," she said.

Wally watched her tug a string of French blue yarn in, then out, in, then out, jumping squares destined for other colors just as if she were playing checkers, and almost as fast.

"See how well this one is coming along, pumpkin? This would be a much more pleasant way to spend your weekend time — and more productive — than endlessly watching those ants of yours."

Wally seemed to consider this, then said, "Gigi, what would you think of Wonder Woman battling Countess Draska Nishki?"

Her grandmother looked up at her.

"What would I think of Wonder Woman . . . fighting whom, did you say?"

"Draska Nishki. I'd be willing to donate it to the Women's Exchange, just like you do. I'm sure a pillow with Wonder Woman on it would sell. Practically every girl would want one."

"But that's absurd, Wally."

Wally chewed her lip.

"The pattern would have to be far too complicated. You'd need red, white, and blue, plus a pink and a light blue, then black, gray, two beige tones for skin, and at least two colors for whatever the other one wears. That's eleven! Let's make one with just three colors to start. Then next time, if you want, you can do a fight between Wonder Woman and her nemesis — in Technicolor!"

"All right."

They settled on an ant after all, a black ant, with a border of off-white flowers on a green field. Wally found an engraving of a queen wood ant in the Encyclopaedia Britannica, and Gigi got out her paintbrush and ink.

The next morning, as they were prying the flesh from their grapefruit halves with the sharp spoons that Gigi kept in a special section of her silverware drawer, Stella came in to pick Wally up for church, as she'd promised when she dropped her off on Friday night.

"Wally!" she called from the front parlor. "Come here, you little heathen. I hope you're dressed and ready. Kiss your Gigi good-bye and off we go."

"But it's twenty to eleven, Mother," Wally yelled from the dining room. "I haven't finished breakfast. We have time."

"Well eat up, then," said her mother, walking into the dining room.

"Stella, come over and look at this," Gigi said.

Stella peered at the needlepoint square next to Wally's place at the table. The ant queen's head and abdomen were fully stitched. She had her front legs raised and her antennae forward as if waving curiously. The ant stood out black and three-dimensional against the white and gray squares of the backing. Wally had stayed up late into the night working on it, reloading her needle time and time again. "Wally did all the stitching. It's very good work, Stella," Gigi said.

"Quite impressive, Wally," said her mother. "It's just the subject. . . . But I'm glad you two had a good time, anyway. Well then, all right, let's go, or we'll be late!"

"Why are we going to church, Mother?" Wally asked as they went to the front hall to get her coat.

"People go to church because it's the right thing to do, Wally. And the music is beautiful." And because they are sinners, thought Stella. It would be the first time she had gone herself in months and months, and she wasn't much of a believer, but she was hoping dearly it would help her find some peace with herself, maybe even help her decide what to do about Bill Niederman.

"But we never usually go."

"And you don't usually do needlepoint, either. Maybe change is in the air."

Wally and her mother returned to the Wallaces' that evening for dinner. Stella and Gigi played cards and drank cocktails beforehand, while Loretta, Ham, and Wally sat around the kitchen table listening to *The Shadow*. There was a plate of cinnamon toast in the middle and Loretta had a bowl of beans before her, waiting to be shelled.

"Hey, Lima Bean?" Wally said.

"Yes, String Bean?" Loretta answered.

"Do you think there's any chance the bad guy's going to get away with it this time?"

It was a little script they repeated, week after week.

"Yeah, Wally," said Ham, butting in. "This week he's going to get away with it and then feed Margo Lane to some sharks, and the Shadow is gonna turn out to be a Nazi."

"Shut up, Ham Sandwich."

"Watch your mouth, Wally Baker," said Ham.

"Both of you hush," Loretta said. "Some people are trying to listen to the show."

"But, Loretta, do you think he could?"

"Nope. Not this week."

"How do you know?"

"Wally Bean. Like I always tell you, some things just ain't possible, not on radio, least-ways. Bad guys aren't allowed to win."

"Good," Wally said, and then they settled in, elbows on the Formica counter, snapping beans and occasionally munching toast.

When the program was halfway through, the Blue Coal theme song started up, and Loretta rose to put the table settings for the evening meal into the dumbwaiter. "So, Loretta?"

"Yeah, honey?" she said as she gathered the napkins and the silver.

"What do you think it takes to become a hero, like the Shadow, or even a superhero? For example, could we actually tell if one was, um, living right under our noses?"

"I guess we've got two great minds in this room."

"What do you mean?"

"Ham here's got some notions of his own about superheroes being real."

"I do not. I just said I'd like Captain America to come and rid us of that Niederman guy. It's not like I think Captain America's *real*," Ham protested.

"But there *might* be superheroes," Wally said.

"What, like Wonder Woman?"

"How do you know I was thinking of Wonder Woman? I just mean there might be some real superhero, somewhere, doing good things, someone we don't actually even know about."

"Well," Loretta said, "I don't know about that, but I got something to say about what superheroes definitely don't do. They don't bother regular people like us, or Mr. Niederman. He's a perfectly nice man, Ham."

"My mother likes him," Wally said.

"Yes, she does."

"Well, I don't," said Ham.

"I do, sort of," Wally ventured. "Loretta, can I ask you something? How can he be a Jew when he's in the Racquet Club? Everybody knows they don't let Jews or Negroes in the Racquet Club —"

Ham looked at her.

Loretta raised her eyebrows.

"Well, but it's true."

When they said nothing, she pressed on. "Isn't that what's so wrong with it? Isn't that why Gigi and Waldo aren't members anymore and are always saying Mama should really drop out, and she always says she will, except that it wouldn't be right

150

because of Daddy not being here and all
her old friends are in it and she likes to play
tennis?"

Loretta smiled her smallest smile, the one
reserved for things she had opinions about
but that were not up for discussion.

"Something like that, Wally. Just don't go
on about it in front of people, hmn? People
won't like how it sounds."

"Gigi talks about it."

"To me, your Gigi just says she doesn't
like the food in the dining room. That's
enough. I know what she means."

"I don't like it, either. Although they do
make good sundaes."

"Oh, so you do eat there?" Loretta smiled.
Wally looked down.

"And, just so you know, Wally, Mr. Niederman ain't the only Jew that goes there.
There's not a hard-and-fast rule."

"How do you know?"

"It's like this: They don't let women build
boats, generally, but look at the Navy Yard
today. When they need the women, suddenly, they let them work. At the Racquet
Club, you got to figure in the fact that it's
wartime and all the ladies' husbands is
away, and he's a good tennis player."

"My math teacher, Miss Sonnabend, is
Jewish, too, you know. It's normal to be Jew-

ish in New York."

"That's right, sugar. It's normal to be whatever you are, just regular as rain."

Suddenly, the coal ad gave way to eerie organ music.

"And now, we return to *The Shadow*. Tonight's episode: 'The Little Man Who Wasn't There.' *Who knows what evil lurks in the hearts of men? The Shadow knows.*"

Ham and Wally fell silent, staring at the radio while Loretta made a last trip to the dumbwaiter.

There was the clatter of conversation from the radio, the voice of Lamont Cranston making small talk with his friend Margo Lane, then a hair-raising shriek.

Wally traded grins with Ham, and they settled in on the wide window seat to find out who would die tonight, and how the Shadow would save the city from lurking evil.

11
THE QUEEN

It was at the end of June that Wally and Ham secretly conveyed Antland from the Wallaces' brownstone to the Bakers' apartment. As much time as she spent at her grandparents', Wally was at home more nights than not, and she wanted to be able to observe her colony. They used the wagon from Gigi's garden shed, a small wooden crate, and a large tarp, and planned the operation for a time when none of their grown-ups would be home, not even Loretta. The greatest difficulty they anticipated was explaining themselves to Boris, Wally's doorman, but even he was off sorting the mail and had hardly noticed them.

They installed the battery jar in the back of Wally's closet and covered it with a pillowcase. The ants lived peacefully inside her closet, enduring just one inspection a day, by flashlight, for two entire weeks, until the morning Wally accidentally knocked the jar over in the search for a missing shoe. None of the dirt or sand spilled out, and the ants were safe, but several of the tunnels had collapsed. To the ants, it was like an earthquake.

She gave them an extra piece of apple, reapplied the Vaseline rim that kept them contained, covered the jar with its pillowcase, and replaced it in the darkness of the closet. She knew the ants would rebuild their city. After all, she thought, they had survived being dug up and moved into a battery jar in the first place. They were tough, her ants. They would regroup and rally.

Wally spent the day with Loretta and Ham, reading her comics and poking around in the garden, but she would be going home for supper with her mother. It was Gigi's bridge night, and guests were expected at the Wallace house for cards and light supper.

"Hey, String Bean," Loretta called when the clock in the living room gonged five, "it's time for you to get on home."

"Can you walk me?"

"I've got a cake almost ready to come out of the oven, sugar."

"Please."

The timer was ticking in Loretta's jacket pocket as they walked and went off just as they got to the Bakers' apartment building. Wally pictured the cake, big and sweet and glossy and lightly browned on top, with cracks revealing the paler meat of the cake within. She wondered what she would be having for dessert. Knowing her mother, there might not be any.

Loretta turned to Boris as they entered the lobby and asked, "Miz Doc Baker home yet, Boris?"

Boris nodded.

"All right, good. Now, String Bean, that was the ten-minute warning on my nice big lemon cake. You can have a slice when you come over tomorrow, but just now, I need to hustle and take it out before it burns. So you can go up by yourself, all righty?"

"Okay, Lima Bean. See you tomorrow."

Stella's purse was on the radiator in their front hall, as usual, but Wally called "Mother?" and got no reply. Her mother must have been somewhere in the back of the apartment.

"I'm home," Wally called, but quietly, rather hoping her mother wouldn't hear. She wanted to inspect the day's progress in Antland.

Back in her room, she got out her flashlight, crept into the closet and lifted the pillowcase. Sure enough, she saw tidy new tunnels lining the glass walls of the battery jar and, in one corner, a capacious new chamber was now visible. To Wally's amazement, it wasn't just any chamber. The queen was unmistakable — fat, beautiful, and surrounded by eggs, larvae, and attendants. There must have been damage to the throne chamber in the tip-over. She hadn't been able to see it before. Wally watched for a while, and tried without much success to count the eggs and the larvae. She would have needed a lot more light to really see what was going on, but she didn't want to do any more than shine her flashlight on the ants so soon after they'd been knocked over. It would have been nice to have someone help her with the egg tally. She let her mind rest on Georgie for a moment. Of course he would have been the perfect ally in all things to do with her ant colony, but this was a time to celebrate the luck of the throne chamber being rebuilt against the glass, not to look back.

Mr. Niederman had expressed an interest in her ants just that morning, but he would still be at work, and she was so excited. That left her mother, if she wanted someone to share her ant queen with, now — the only problem being that she still hadn't told her mother the ants were living at their apartment. Wally knew that if she asked her mother to come and look at the ants, the answer would be no. She might also be angry. But what if she simply brought them forth, presented them to her mother in all their wondrousness, with the queen revealed? With the queen right there, in front of her mother's nose, she would have to look, and if she would only look, Wally was certain she would see how beautiful the queen was, how amazing the workings of her throne chamber. Together, they could watch her laying her very eggs, if they were patient enough.

Wally took a small breath, stooped and gently lifted the ant colony in her arms. She held the jar as steady as she could and slowly moved toward her mother's room — not even taking steps, for fear of disrupting the ants, but sliding down the hall in her stocking feet.

"Mother?" Wally called.

But she wasn't in the kitchen, the dining room or the parlor.

As she approached her mother's room, Wally heard a faint thump, as if something had fallen to the floor. It was odd that the door was shut.

She was going to call out again for her mother to open the door, but then she saw it was just slightly ajar. She heard her mother's voice through the crack. It sounded like she was laughing, laughing strangely. Wally pictured her sitting on the divan, reading something hilariously funny. Or could she be crying? Had something else horrible happened? Wally thought of her father on his ship somewhere in the Pacific.

"Mother?" she called again, too quietly to be heard, and stretched her toes toward the raised threshold, nudging the door open a little more, just enough for her slender self to fit through. The sound of her mother's voice grew clearer. She wasn't laughing, she was speaking to someone. Could she be talking on the phone? Was something wrong?

"Now," her mother said. "She'll be home any minute."

She was talking about Wally. Wally tightened her grip on the jar and paused to hear more. She wanted to know what her mother might say about her, when she wasn't there to hear it. But there was nothing more, just a rustling. She decided to go in.

"Mother!" she said, bumping the door the rest of the way open with her knee, "you have to see this!" She didn't want to seem tentative, as if she'd been listening at the door. "Mother, look!" Wally's eyes were on the queen's chamber. She wanted to show her mother the queen right off, before she realized what Wally had and turned away in horror.

What Wally saw when she looked up from the ants was worse than she could have imagined: her mother's face with a look of horror on it, and the thing she was horrified to see was Wally.

"Wally? Bill, it's Wally! Get off —"

"Mother? Are you all right?" What was Mr. Niederman doing, leaning over her? What was he doing in her bedroom?

"Goddammit!" said her mother.

Wally was wondering if she ought to hurl her ant colony at Mr. Niederman, who seemed to have been doing something bad, something wrong, to her mother, when suddenly the jar began to slip from her grasp.

"Mommy!" she screamed as the colony fell.

The smash of glass was like another voice in the room.

Something heavy and sharp hit Wally's ankle. Gravity had done its piece. Antland had shattered.

Afterward, she couldn't say whether Antland had begun to slip before or after she shrieked, or whether she herself had screamed because of the ants or because of her mother. It was unquestionably the first time Wally had ever heard her mother swear. Possibly all of it — the crash and the splatter of shards, the sand and the ants and the piercing of the afternoon with that terrible word and the sudden leap through the air of Bill Niederman — possibly all of it had occurred at the same instant.

The only one who hadn't made a noise was Mr. Niederman. He flew from her mother's side to hers in what seemed like an eye blink. He stood in front of Wally, shielding her mother from her view. While he reached out to Wally and touched her leg with one hand, he was doing something to his pants with the other. What was he doing?

As soon as he touched it, her ankle felt hot and strange. She felt wetness on her foot and looked to see a thin stream of blood running down her ankle. There were several spots of it on the carpet, wet and brown against the blue velvet.

Then Mr. Niederman was next to Wally. He was reaching out and pressing her ankle with his white pocket square. He was saying, "Stella! Stella. She's cut. Get a towel. A damp towel."

160

Her mother was moving as if the ants were all over her — though they couldn't have been, not that quickly. She was pulling down her skirt and grabbing at her sweater as if in a pantomime of getting dressed. Her mother had not seen the ant queen, Wally realized. Maybe she never would, maybe the ant queen was dead or lost, but Wally wished her mother would at least see the one most obvious thing before her: that Wally was hurt. She was hurt and confused, and she wanted her mother to take her in her arms.

But her mother did not look at Wally. She did not go for the towel Mr. Niederman requested. She was struggling to jam her feet into her shiny black high-heeled shoes. Wally had witnessed a thousand times the slinky way her mother donned her shoes, but now her mother's feet seemed too large, awkward somehow. She watched her mother struggle and followed her mother's eyes. That was when she saw the stockings dribbled across the back of the divan. There were so many reasons those stockings shouldn't have been there. Their long dark seams had run amok, their miraculous filminess soured to a milky stain against the green silk.

Her mother was somehow stranded without them. Just as Wally imagined the ant queen must now be stranded, outside her habitat, without her daughter-helpers. Where was she? Was she all right? And what about her precious sticky eggs, the larvae that were her future, all writhing with hope and ambition?

Wally wanted to find her — it was an emergency greater than the cut on her ankle — but her eyes were locked on her mother's empty stockings. It wasn't right that her mother had taken off her stockings. Wally felt a sick feeling and a knot in her throat and wrenched her eyes away, back to the carpet, the ants.

She pushed Mr. Niederman's hands away, dropped to her knees, and began to sort through the debris of her colony from the blue velvet carpet with her hands.

"Wally!" he said, grabbing her. "Leave that. We need to put pressure on the cut —" But she ignored him. It seemed hopeless. The mess was too great, the ants, the sand, the shattered glass. Then she felt a jab and looked down at her hand. A small shard protruded from the meat of her thumb like a glimmering porcupine spine. Wally plucked it out and watched a drop of blood bead where it had been. Meanwhile, her ants were fleeing the catastrophe. For a second, she thought she saw the one that mattered, the one that was larger than the rest, then lost her in the visual confusion of the debris on the rug. She hung her head to her chest and began to sob.

"Oh, Mommy."

"Oh my God. Wally. Sweetheart," her mother said at last, still holding the one shoe. "What a disaster."

Wally's ankle began to throb. She wanted to be taken into her mother's arms, but there was too much shattered glass between them.

Then she spotted her: the ant queen — so massive with eggs that she couldn't walk on her own, just wave her legs, and yet she was not alone after all. There were attendants all around her, striving to help her, to bear her up and carry her to safety, if safety could be had.

"There she is!" cried Wally, and she felt a surge of hope. This situation could be remedied. Wally looked around, wondering what to pick her up with, what to put her in.

Her mother's eyes followed Wally's, until she, too, saw the ant queen.

"Oh God, that one's enormous. How revolting," she said, and the black shoe went flying.

"Mommy, no!" But it was too late.

Mr. Niederman took Wally's hand and pressed it against her own ankle and the handkerchief that was soaked through with blood.

"Just hold that," he said. "I'll get a towel to wrap around it, and then we'll sweep up and we'll see if we can't save some of your ants."

"But that was the queen. She was the mother of the colony."

"I know. I'm sorry. We'll have to get you another."

Mr. Niederman was doing what her father would have done, if he hadn't been off in the Pacific, Wally thought, and she did as he told her. When he stepped out of the room to get the towel, Wally's mother finally tiptoed over through the debris and took Wally in her arms, kissing her on the top of her head.

"I'm sorry darling. I just . . . reacted. I'm sorry I killed her."

"Oh, Mommy, I wanted you to see her, to like her," Wally cried, wrapping her arms around her mother.

There were some things, she realized then, that ought not to be seen.

Wally stood still while Mr. Niederman blotted the cut with a wet towel and then wrapped her ankle in gauze. It wasn't so bad a cut, really, he said. The bleeding had slowed to an ooze.

Afterward, she watched while Mr. Niederman knelt down and used sections of old newspaper to whisk up the mess. There were black and white pictures of tanks and ships and rows of troops under review, and there, amidst the sand and shards and bewildered, doomed survivors of Antland, lay the great twisted body of the dead queen.

Wally bit her lip hard enough to taste copper but did not cry again. Her mother went out and came back with the carpet sweeper. Back and forth, back and forth it went, erasing the catastrophe better than one might have expected, if not completely.

■ ■ ■ ■

II
Fᴀɪʟ-Sᴀꜰᴇ

■ ■ ■ ■

12
RED DOOR

It was a small neighborhood. Stella kept looking behind her as she walked slowly, not wanting to draw attention to herself by rushing amidst the celebrants still cheering and marching on the afternoon of V-J Day. She had gone to work as she told Wally, but only for morning rounds. Once that was over, even she was free for the holiday. She made a detour so as not to pass her mother's house or her own building.

She had told Wally and Loretta that morning that she was on call, but it wasn't true. There was no afternoon clinic, either. It was two o'clock, and she was entirely free, free to go home and be with her daughter, to celebrate the holiday. But she had two things, two things at least, to accomplish in the hours she'd stolen.

As she walked toward the red door of Dr. Godfrey's office, she felt a familiar anxiety drape itself around her shoulders. How

often had she walked that way when Wally
and then Georgie were babies? Their lives
had seemed so full of promise, but they
were so delicate — their every fever had terrified her. She had probably taken them to
see their pediatrician too often, but she
knew enough about medicine to know every
sort of horror that could befall a child —
and then one of them had befallen Georgie.
This time, though, Wally was well. Stella's
mind was flooded with a different sort of
worry.

Every time she heard someone shout "Victory in Japan," she pictured a young mother
with narrow eyes and sallow skin — a
woman who except for the fact that they
were enemies, was like her: conflicted, grief-
stricken, filled with love for her surviving
children but resentment for her absent
soldier-husband. And then, in a flash of
light, she was gone. Burned to death. Was
the woman grateful to be relieved of her
complicated life? No. She was nothing
anymore. It was an evil way to win the war
was what Stella thought. She didn't approve
of the atom bombs they had used, but she
couldn't say that, not to anyone. Except,
perhaps, Bill.

She first heard, then saw, the parade of
children passing at the next intersection,

pot lids clanging, spoons ringing out against frying pans, tiny flags fluttering like the wings of trapped songbirds. One of them was Wally, shouting into a giant enamelware funnel. Her nut brown sinewy legs, her blue skirt just a bit short, since she'd grown so much that summer, her light brown hair gleaming, her green-lensed glasses flashing in the sun — Wally. She was so tall, now, so wonderfully gawky and yet ever so slightly glamorous, what with her glasses, her brashness. Stella flooded with love. She forgot, if only briefly, all her feelings of dread. Wally didn't see her mother, but even so, her glee was infectious. Stella wanted it for herself. What if somehow Rudy never returned? she allowed herself to think. What if she could marry Bill Niederman and bear him a child, perhaps a boy? By the time that child was born, it would be spring again, and the Victory Garden at her mother's would be plowed under, the roses and peonies replanted. Her new child would be vaccinated, vaccinated at the earliest possible age, against everything that had a vaccine. And so would Wally. But even as she dreamed, she knew it could not come true.

Before going into Dr. Godfrey's office, she lingered on the corner and watched the crowd. Wally's gang had passed, but the spontaneous, ebullient victory parade continued. She felt a sting at the edges of her eyelids as they struck up "Three cheers for the red, white, and blue." There was a sense in which she knew there was no need to bother Dr. Godfrey — she felt certain of the result already. She'd felt the same weariness, hunger, wobbliness of the soul twice already.

Watching the parade, Stella imagined the next half hour of her life. She would go to the doctor's office, and if she persuaded him to help her, she would pee in a jar. Then the doctor would send it to a lab with someone else's name — Clark, perhaps — on the label. In the morning, a technician would draw up a syringe of the yellow fluid, insert the needle in a fold of soft, furry flesh, and push the plunger, delivering a load of her waste into the system of a young white rabbit. Two weeks later, the same lab worker would slit the wee creature open and dissect its ovaries. If they were swollen, it would be true — Stella was pregnant — but either way, the rabbit would be dead.

She was dislodged from her musing by a clap on the shoulder.

"Stella, darling! Happy V-J!" It was Vera Rensselaer. "I just snapped a Kodak of our girls! Wallace and Claire seem to be getting on famously, which is a nice switch, I think. Now what are you pondering? Let me guess! How to word your telegram to Rudy? How about 'Hurry home, darling'?"

Was her smile any more arch than usual? Stella wondered.

"It'll hardly be that," Stella laughed, a little uncomfortably. "He's probably going to stay in Japan for the Reconstruction."

"Oh dear."

"Someone has to. What about Horace?"

"Still at Fort Bragg, but coming home on furlough next month."

"Lucky you, Vera," Stella said.

At the doctor's office, there was no one else in the waiting room, and no receptionist though the red door had been unlocked. Stella remained standing, wondering what she should do.

"Oh, Mrs. Baker," said the doctor, stepping through the door of the laboratory into the reception area. "Nice to see you. You know, you're one of the very few people who didn't cancel her appointment today. I felt I ought to be here anyway — you never know what children might get into, especially on a day like this."

"Isn't that the truth."

He smiled, shrugging it off. "Won't you

come in then? What can I do for you?"

"It's about Wallace," she began, as they settled into chairs in his office.

"How's her height? Has she shot up again?"

"Yes, in fact she has, but that wasn't —"

"I do think it's going to be hard going, socially, for a girl as tall as she'll be. And you want to make sure she doesn't take on a stoop, like so many tall girls do. It's neither attractive nor healthy for the spine. Probably ballet lessons would be the thing."

"Of course, I'm sure you're right. That's not really my concern today, though. I have two matters I wanted to . . . First, I'd like to see about getting Wally vaccinated. Now that the war's over, I would like to get her vaccinated against all those things we discussed: pertussis, diphtheria, tetanus, smallpox — everything there is, really." She looked down, bit her lip, thinking of every illness that might befall her child, the child that had saved her from the abyss of Billy Galt's death, the pit of her marriage to Rudy Baker. It was motherhood that had brought her back to life again. The glacier within her had begun to recede the first moment she saw her daughter, and soon her hours went by in a cascade of blissful moments, flashes of color, her lips grazing the perfect smooth skin of her baby's cheek, showering her with kisses.

Dr. Godfrey cleared his throat. "Well, there are a number of things to talk about. But I can't just order up those vaccines, Mrs. Baker. The American Academy of Pediatrics hasn't recommended the pertussis vaccine, for example. There are safety questions, adverse reactions in some cases."

"I've looked at the research. Fall is coming. I don't want to take a chance."

"Mrs. Baker —"

"*Dr.* Baker."

"I'm sorry — *Dr. Baker* — but I do think you're overreacting. What happened to George was terrible, but there's no reason to think Wally's next. He was much more susceptible, at his age. And his was the only fatal case in this area."

"But it *was* fatal. Which is why I want her vaccinated."

"It's not in the recommendations of the Academy of Pediatrics, Mrs. Baker. How can I put this? I don't agree with you on this. I'm afraid your interest in this stems from your grief, Mrs. Baker. It's not objective."

She said nothing, held her gaze. If this was hard, how was her next question going to go over?

"What does your mother think?"

"She wouldn't be in favor."

"Ah," he said, smiling kindly, then frowning slightly, as if to say, I do wish I could have helped. "You said there was something else?"

"Well, yes. There's one more thing, which is — well, it's a bit awkward for me to discuss. You wouldn't feel the need to, uh, mention anything to my mother?"

"You may speak freely, I assure you."

She blushed deeply. It was a small neighborhood. She knew people were going to talk, eventually, about the situation she was in. They knew how long Bill Niederman had been in her house, and how she and Bill had become doubles partners and frequent dinner companions. She knew people would notice if her figure changed. They would count back the number of months since Rudy had been deployed. They would be as eager to see what happened to the Baker family as they were to hear the next installments of their favorite radio plays. She had to ready herself for that, she knew. Telling Dr. Godfrey was just a practice run. *Come on, Stella,* she told herself silently. *If you can't face the pediatrician, how on earth are you going to stand up to Vera Rensselaer, or your mother?*

"I need a pregnancy test."

Dr. Godfrey looked puzzled.

Stella swallowed. "Captain Baker has not been in the country for some time, as you may know. That and my mother being so well connected to the medical community makes this all . . . very awkward for me, to say the least. I had hoped you might help me by submitting my sample to the lab under another name."

"Another name," he said evenly. "I see."

"Say, Clark," she suggested, thinking that perhaps he did not see, or would rather not. "Maybe Muriel Clark, just to keep it from being all too common?"

The situation seemed only slowly to dawn on him, but at last he said, with an expression of distaste on his features, "Yes, of course, write any name you see fit on the label in the lavatory, Mrs. Baker, and leave a specimen. You can make another appointment for two weeks from today to retrieve the results."

13
SPECIAL DELIVERY

Once the children were safely home from their parading, Loretta set off herself to the market to wheedle enough meat, butter, eggs, and sugar to make a feast, a feast that would end with a cake. She wondered how much longer they'd be using ration books. Not long, she hoped.

She planned to bake a marble pound cake. On second thought, two cakes — one to serve regally on the Wallaces' cut-glass pedestal plate, dusted with sugar, and one for the kitchen, just for Ham.

The doorbell rang while Loretta was at the market. Waldo Wallace was upstairs resting. Wally was in the yard. Ham was in the basement with his ants. He was the one who got up to answer it.

"Telegram for Mrs. Loretta Walker care of this address. Is she here?"

"That's my mother," Ham said. "I'll sign for it."

As far as Ham knew, his mother had never received a telegram before. He didn't have any idea what the telegram would say, but if there was news that concerned his mother, it concerned him, and news that came in a telegram was always bad. She protected him from things he needed to know, he'd recently begun to realize. Like the fact that the Doctors Wallace were racists who pretended to love his mother and to support him and to be open-minded about his potential — except when it came to things like allowing him into their front parlor. He was sick of being protected from the truth.

Just the week before, they'd listened to a radio play in which correspondence had been secretly steamed open, read and then resealed. The temptation was too great for him to resist. He went straight to the kitchen, lit the fire under the kettle and pulled the whistle from the spout. Then, so he could cover up his transgression, he located the jar of paste his mother used to make her scrapbooks and label the jars of jam and vegetables she put up from the Victory Garden.

He held the envelope up into the steam till the glue on the flap was moist, then sat at the kitchen table and carefully peeled it open.

■ ■ ■ ■

When Loretta walked in the back door twenty minutes later with her arms full of groceries, the steam was still gushing silently from the spout. Ham was sitting at the kitchen table, looking at his hands. The opened telegram had fluttered to the floor under the table, where Loretta couldn't see it.

"Ham?" she said, putting down her packages. "What you doing? What's happened?" She touched his shoulder, softly — a slightly risky move these days. Her boy had gotten too old to be snuggled and comforted that way by his mother, and it made her sad. He wouldn't be hers much longer, she knew.

When he failed to respond at all, just sat like a log, the concern in her voice shifted to suspicion. "Ham! What happened? What you gone and done, child? Something foolish?"

He looked up at her blankly. She had given him everything he ever got in this world. She had seemed to him to be a good mother, the perfect mother, even if she shared her love a little too much with Wally, sometimes.

But now he knew that his mother, Loretta

180

Walker, the woman who'd taught him what truth and honor and respect meant, had lied to him, and in so doing, she had stolen something from him that could never be returned.

His father.

Within him, there was a swirling sickness. He felt he would never trust another soul again. He narrowed his eyes at her and tried to make her feel his hatred, but she was his mama. When he looked at her, he couldn't help but love her. So he tossed his chin toward the door, breaking their gaze. As he felt tears flow down his cheeks, he was ashamed, and his anger returned.

"I hate you," he spat, rubbing his sleeve on his face, determined to stop crying, now and forever. Then he stood and silently walked out of the kitchen and out of the house.

Loretta was too stunned to call after him. She wished to heaven that the Wallace dinner wasn't waiting to be made. And there was Dr. Waldo, who'd be calling for his medications to be brought up to him any minute now. Not to mention Stella's asking her specially to drop Wally off at home. She wanted nothing but to chase after Ham and shake her sullen boy and make him talk to her. Then again, she told herself, she'd never catch up to him now. He was a boy of a certain age. She supposed it shouldn't be a shock to her that youthful moodiness had come over him at last.

Gingerly, wondering all the while what had put Ham into such a state, Loretta closed the door he had left ajar. Then she noticed the smell of hot metal coming from the kettle. It was over a lit burner, but the water had boiled off. She jumped up to switch off the knob, then turned in a circle, scanning the room. Ham didn't drink tea, and certainly not on hot summer days. Something was wrong. That was when she noticed the yellow form on the floor: a telegram.

DEAR MRS WALKER, she read.

I DEEPLY REGRET TO INFORM YOU THAT YOUR HUSBAND, LT. (JG) HAMILTON A. WALKER, USNR, HAS BEEN KILLED IN BATTLE ON AUGUST 12, 1945, IN THE SERVICE OF HIS COUNTRY. SINCEREST SYMPATHY IS EXTENDED TO YOU IN YOUR GREAT LOSS. WHEN FURTHER DETAILS AS TO WHETHER BODY RECOVERED AND INTERRED ARE RE-CEIVED, YOU WILL BE INFORMED.

It had been so long since Loretta had

heard from her former husband that she was surprised the news had reached her. Apparently, he still listed her as his next of kin. She thought of his handsome brown face, his wicked smiling eyes, and was overcome by silent tears. They had been truly happy for a little while, but there hadn't been much of a chance for them as a couple. He was too wild, wouldn't settle. The truth was, she hadn't heard from him for so long that she'd assumed he'd died years before.

Loretta had wanted for some time to explain the complexities of Ham's parentage to him. At first, he was too young. Then it seemed she had waited too long, and she couldn't bring herself to tell him she'd been lying all these years. Now here they were, Ham thinking wrongly that this man, his namesake, who had just died, was his father.

In fact, Loretta hadn't been able to bear a child with Hamilton. He'd left her after two years of drinking and womanizing, and by that time she hadn't been especially sorry to see him go. Then Washington and Nellie Walker, her husband's brother and his wife, had Ham, and they often asked her to watch him, which she was only too glad to do. She'd wanted a child, and Gigi Wallace was extremely tolerant, allowing her to bring the baby to work. Sometimes his parents left him for days at a time while they went off to Atlantic City or Belmont to gamble and drink. She never minded, and she hadn't minded the last time that they never came back. They were disastrous people, Washington and Nellie. She never doubted that she could do a better job with their son.

"We'll have to see how this goes, Loretta," Gigi Wallace had said, when she found out the baby was going to be permanently under Loretta's care. "He's a sweet child, but I'm not sure you can complete your duties with an infant. I never meant to hire a single mother for my maid."

Loretta managed it, though, and eventually the only remnant of Gigi Wallace's disapproval that remained was the rule that Ham must not go upstairs or be seen by guests. By the time Ham learned to talk and ask questions about his daddy, and why he didn't have one, Loretta had figured it was safe to say he was dead. She didn't go into Ham's desertion by Washington and Nellie. So the boy grew up believing that his father had died. Deceiving him wasn't anything she planned to do; it just seemed better than the alternative.

But he was her son, regardless of blood. She had raised him.

She looked at the telegram again and muttered, "You old fool, Hamilton Walker. Why'd you have to go and mess with my life now, after all this time?"

A sharp intake of breath and a few damp spots that vanished into the waffled fabric of the rose-patterned dish towel were all the wallowing Loretta allowed herself over her husband. She shook her head and rehung the dish towel over the cabinet door. It was time to get dinner started if she was to have time to stop in on Stella. Then she would see to Dr. Waldo. She simply didn't have time to go running after Ham. He was a big boy. Even if she could find him, it would serve no purpose to talk to him now, not when he was angry. As soon as he came home, she would tell him the truth.

With that, Loretta smoothed the telegram and folded it into her apron pocket, put the paste jar back in its place, then tucked the sides of her neatly waved hair behind her ears and reached into the icebox for some eggs.

14
LOUISE

"Will you be able to get home in time for the celebration tomorrow?" Bill Niederman's wife asked him over the phone. He was standing at the telephone table in the living room, Stella seated just an arm's length away.

The war was over. Hirohito had conceded defeat.

"Here's the thing, Ouise — the main work is over, but there are so many loose ends. You can only imagine."

"But if the war is over, aren't you finished, now, with the project — whatever it was? And don't they at least give you the day off to celebrate?"

He was thinking that Stella would never have called his work *whatever it was*. She'd always assumed its secrecy made it important and mysterious, never laughable.

"It's something, isn't it, Ouise? *Peace.* I'm proud to have played a small part in it."

"Can't you just take off, then, come home and celebrate? Even for the night? The boys want you, Bill, and so do I. Next weekend seems so long off."

He said he would try to get permission to leave, but the truth was, he already knew the office was going to be closed the next day. He knew he couldn't stall much longer. Now that the war was over, he wasn't going to be needed at the Columbia office anymore. He'd be expected to pick up his classes in the fall, no doubt. Everything was going back to normal.

He pictured Louise, her simple, pretty face, her simple, pretty world consisting utterly of house, garden, children, food, and him. He thought of his sons. He loved his family. It had all been enough for him, until he'd met Stella Baker.

The tangled stockings, the complex mind, the smooth, strong fingers of Stella Wallace Baker. He thought of their breakfast table conversations about her patients and war news and home-front policy. They couldn't talk about his work, but she clearly appreciated what mathematics and science could do, in ways Louise never had. Even Wally was a delight, always bursting with passion for her experiments, throwing out questions and answers.

He was surprised Wally hadn't pursued the matter of what she saw when she'd walked in on him and Stella. He was relieved, of course. But what had she seen, exactly? How much had she understood? He wished he was sure the answer was nothing. None of them had spoken of the incident aloud, not even he and Stella. It was as if Wally had merely broken a jar, which had needed cleaning up. They all went on as if nothing had happened and Mr. Niederman were just a friendly uncle figure and Stella the wife of his old friend, in whose house he happened to live.

What would his boys have done, if they'd seen him with Stella Baker? How badly would it have broken their hearts?

"So you'll call back and let me know what to tell the boys?"

He cleared his throat and thought of Hiroshima. How many soldiers' wives and families had been vaporized? How could he fail to treasure what he still had?

For Bill Niederman, there were two possible tomorrows: He could be sitting in a chair with a heart-shaped cutout at a maple dining nook in Princeton, New Jersey, with Louise and the boys playing cards; he could be a good man. Or he could stay in Brooklyn Heights with Stella and Wally, his second

188

family; he could be a happy, madly in love adulterer. Back home, he was a mathematics professor at a second-tier college. In New York, he was a scientist, a man who had helped to change the world.

For nearly two years of weekday mornings, he'd descended the elevator with the red leather bench and left Stella's building on Pierrepont Street well satisfied, primed by her caresses and conversation for the difficulties of the day ahead, then walked four short blocks to the Hotel St. George, where he'd caught the uptown IRT and ridden it to 116th and Broadway. He'd walked across the Columbia campus to the unmarked door that led into an office where a small group of mathematicians worked. They were not on the Columbia faculty. They were working for the Manhattan Project. There he had spent day after amazing day plugging away at the most important work of his life.

A new era had begun, the atomic age. This was only the start. Now that the bomb had been built, there were infinite amounts of work to be done on applications both military and industrial. He knew he would be officially released from his posting at Columbia within a week or two, same as all the others who had been called from out of state and had had to take temporary lodgings away from their families. He wondered if he was the only one who was disappointed to be going home. There was still plenty of work to be done, after all. He didn't have to go back to teaching calculus to English majors if he didn't want to. But did he have to go back to Louise? Probably. After all, it wasn't just he who was otherwise committed — Rudy Baker would be coming home, too.

He took a sip of bourbon and thought for a moment about the impact the war had had on him — it had been the greatest time of his life — and what it had done to his second and third cousins, the people his grandparents had left behind when they immigrated to America from Germany. His mother had kept in touch with several cousins until the war scattered them. Most of them were probably dead now, he knew. What sort of people were they — or had they been — brilliant or dull, faithful or philanderous, religious or secular? Did he owe them anything? Even just a devotion to his own family, to carry on their legacy?

The likelihood of his Jewish cousins surviving the war in Europe would have been greater, he knew, if America had done a year ago to Germany what it just did to

Japan. The killing factories could have been shut down that much faster. It was ironic, he knew, and somehow wrong, he felt, that the war had been so good to him. It had brought him professional, personal, and sexual satisfaction beyond anything he'd dreamed. And to think, it was Louise who had suggested, after Pearl Harbor and the call that brought him to New York, that he get in touch with Rudy Baker and his wife. "They've got some money," she'd said. "Money enough to have a place with a spare room. What can it hurt to ask?"

He did feel guilty, when he thought of her guilelessness, her lack of suspicion. And sometimes even when he thought of Rudy Baker, away on his battleship, enemy planes whining overhead. But he was in love with Stella like no one before, and there was nothing he could do about it.

They'd both known from the start that it couldn't last. In a way, that was what had allowed them to do it. But now that those magnificent, terrible bombs had gone off, it was almost at an end, and he was saddened. What he wanted, he supposed, was to wind it down happily, and possibly, just possibly, for him and Stella to dream up a plan that would let it live on in peacetime. What he didn't want was to go back home for V-J

Day. He wanted one more night of Stella, at least one.

He thought of his boys, his great, good boys. Would it do them any real harm, he asked himself, if he missed the holiday, or for that matter, if he carried on the affair awhile longer, just as long as he did it covertly? Maybe he and Stella could keep some sort of weekly rendezvous. He could always justify trips to the city, thanks to the time he'd spent at Columbia. For a second, he let himself envision a future in which they could come clean and really be together. He pictured the small, discreet wedding ceremony, Wally standing beside her mother, smiling, holding a bouquet of daisies, his sons beside him with boutonnieres on their lapels, but he knew it could never be.

Thinking of the children made him realize that he was also saddened by the prospect of losing his relationship with Wally when he left Brooklyn. Perhaps, if he played things right and everyone remained friends, Wally would still turn to him for help with math or science projects sometimes, even once her father was back at the breakfast table. It wasn't anything anyone would have called the American Dream, but it was a dream, for him, anyway.

But he had to stop thinking about some imagined future. He had to snap out of it. Louise had asked him to return. She was fearful about the atom bombs. She was exhausted by raising their boys almost alone. She wasn't strong, like Stella. He'd promised her things, including love and protection. He couldn't deny her.

He picked up the phone and called her back. Then he closed his eyes and heard himself say, "It's all right, Ouise. I just got the go-ahead from work. I can come home. I'll see you tomorrow."

"Oh, Bill, really?"

"That's what I said."

"But what's wrong? You don't sound happy," she said. "What is it?"

"Nothing, Louise. I'm just tired."

"That makes sense, Bill," Stella said when he returned to the living room and told her he had to go home for a few days.

"She begged me to come for the V-J Day celebration. I could hardly refuse, given everything."

After a pause, Stella said, "I understand."

They both glanced instinctively down the hall. Wally was supposed to be asleep, but was she? He had the *Annals of Mathematics* on his lap, a half-full highball on the side table. Stella's was nearly empty.

"I better check on her."

He watched Stella's fine legs march down the hall and go into Wally's room.

How nearly they were his, these two, he thought, and yet how completely not.

They left their drinks unfinished in the living room.

"You're not leaving for good, though, Bill?" she asked.

"We'll find a way to be together, even in peacetime," he said.

"Good, because I'm not done with you yet, Professor Niederman," she laughed softly. She thought about the appointment she had with Dr. Godfrey the next day and the burgeoning feeling she'd begun to have. What would he think when he learned he was going to be a father again? What was she going to do if he went back to his wife even so?

"Nor I you, Mrs. Baker," he said, pushing Louise from his mind, but not Rudy. There was a certain illicit pleasure to being with another man's wife.

"That's Dr. Baker, if you please." She laughed.

They went down onto the green silk divan in a careful, groping collapse. She undid her fasteners, he his belt.

"Leave the stockings?" he asked, touching where the edge of the delicate stuff met her thigh.

"Don't tear them," she said, breathing into his ear.

"I'll be careful."

He was on top for only a few moments. That was another thing about Stella — she knew what she wanted, and she liked to sit up, straddling him while he touched her thighs, raising herself up, giving him a taste, teasing him, grinding into him till he nearly burst, then retreating again, keeping him yearning till finally he lost control and capsized her onto the blue velvet carpet, where the hard floor gave them the resistance they needed to reach their exultation.

As he pushed his way through the V-J Day crowds in Penn Station the next morning, he found himself looking at his watch — ten minutes till his train left — and veering away from his track toward the Western Union counter. There was another train in thirty minutes. He'd never kept much at the Baker house, since he went home so often, and that morning before he left, he'd folded up his extra cardigan and several neckties and tucked them in his bag along with his shaving kit. He wanted to keep seeing her

— God, did he ever — but he'd decided not to go back, not that week. He needed to give himself to Louise for a while, to see if he could do the right thing and find some kind of happiness with her. He pulled a printed form from the slot in the counter and wrote the words STELLA BAKER in the space for the recipient and then the address on Pierrepont Street where he'd lived for four nights a week for the past two years. He paused before beginning to letter the message. Dear Stella? Darling? He wanted her to know that he loved her, but the voice of Louise was ringing in his ears. Everything felt different, now, with the war over, knowing he had to return to her, unless he was willing to give up his boys. Finally, he dispensed with any address at all and quickly lettered in his brief message. It was a terse form, the telegram, after all, and after the love they'd made that morning and the conversation they'd had, he knew Stella knew how passionately he felt about her. She would understand why he hadn't been able to tell her in person that he was going to stay away, at least for a while.

15
A THING OF BEAUTY

As she walked home from Dr. Godfrey's office, a feeling of hope came over her. The doctor hadn't been especially kind or accepting, but he hadn't refused her request. She had withstood his obvious judgment of her and survived. Her breath flowed easily again at last, after what had felt like a long season of worry.

Was there anyone else in America, anyone else on the side of all the Allies, who had so dreaded their winning the war? She simply did not want Rudy to come home. She thought of the way he was with her, in bed, compared to Bill. Even Billy Galt hadn't kissed the way Bill Niederman kissed, with confidence, ownership, and expectation. She thought of how Rudy hadn't come back when Georgie died. She loathed him for that. Now, come home though he might, she decided that she wouldn't let Rudy touch her. Because — she was almost sure of it — there was a child in her belly.

Bill's child.

Dr. Godfrey had said they wouldn't have the results for two weeks, but Stella had that feeling of fullness everywhere — in her hair, her breasts, all of her flesh. She couldn't know what exactly was to come, but Stella Wallace Baker, as she strode home, felt optimistic. She took a few deep breaths and savored the thrum from deep within her, a feeling of well-being not unlike the one she got from a mouthful of bourbon, just purer. The jangliness of her morning — and so much of her life — seemed far away as she pushed through the doors of her building.

"Amazing day, ain't it, Mrs. Baker," said Boris as she passed the doorman's desk on her way to the elevator, taking from him her stack of mail.

For once, she wasn't annoyed that he didn't call her Dr. Baker, not even now that she was working again. She was too busy with her dreams for a future with Bill and in the nearer term of the cake she was about to make for Wally, all cocoa and butter and sugar and eggs, and beaten together with love.

It was a puzzle yet to be worked out, how her and Bill's messy, divergent lives could be joined, but with the baby, she felt sure they would find a way. Hadn't he said as much? *We'll find a way.* Of course, it was going to be unconventional, however you sliced it, because he still had Louise, whom she knew he loved, in a way. And they didn't agree on all things. She'd learned that the morning after the bomb was dropped.

"Jesus, Bill, look at this," she'd said. "They're calling it *a thing of beauty.*"

That was the day they'd known that peace would come, but the pictures in the paper were violent.

"Oh, come on, Stella. It's the mechanism, the design, the science of it they're talking about. It's so precisely machined. That's all."

"No, here, listen to this," she'd said. "The reporter describes the blast cloud as *roiling creamy foam.*"

"I read it already."

"Well, it wasn't foam, for God's sake. It was ashes. A sixty-thousand-foot-tall tower of ashes, Bill. A whole city, women and children and all. That's how we won, not with foam."

She'd thrown down her newspaper, overturning her coffee cup. The black dregs had run slowly, like blood, toward the edge of the white enamel kitchen table, threatening to stain her light green dress.

Bill had looked at the picture of a blackened landscape and sighed. "I know, Stella, but as a result the war in the Pacific's over now. There won't be any more Americans killed."

"Bill. Don't tell me you're in favor of our having done that?"

"It's a tough question, Stella. It's complicated."

"Oh, Christ, Bill. I've figured it out. That's what you've been doing. You were on the Manhattan Project. Weren't you?"

He'd just looked at her.

"You made love to me at night after spending your days inventing a new way to kill hundreds of thousands of people at once?"

"I suppose you could think of it that way, Stella, but I don't. We were trying to win the war."

And so they had quarreled that day, but it wasn't like quarreling with Rudy, who couldn't bear for Stella to hold an opinion different from his own. When Bill had kissed her good-bye that morning, it was as juicy and tantalizing a kiss as any he'd given her in her bedroom the night before. They were adults, they were in love, they were mature enough to be able to disagree. They were complicated.

Stella was ready for complicated.

She'd decided for certain that her marriage was over. She was going to have this baby, and Rudy would never accept another man's child, so he'd be gone. Ideally, she would marry Bill, after they'd both divorced, but even if he wouldn't or couldn't leave Louise, Stella told herself she wouldn't be alone. She would have the baby. She would have Wally. She would have Loretta. She would have her family.

She began to formulate a plan. She would work at the hospital until they inevitably fired her for being pregnant. Then she'd fall back on the small trust fund she'd always had. It would be enough to get them through until she could work again. It would buy her freedom.

She laughed a little as she approached the elevator. "Yes, Boris. Right you are. What an amazing day."

The apartment was cool and breezy when she entered it. Hadn't she closed those balcony doors when she left? She stood on the threshold and looked out at the great bridge, the tall towers across the water, the warships moving out past Buttermilk Channel, and the cargo ships being unloaded at the piers. Usually, she took it all rather for

201

granted, having grown up with nearly the same view, just a few blocks down, but that day it seemed majestic.

In the kitchen, she found the window thrown wide as well, and left it that way, though there were several flies buzzing through the room. The slight breeze felt fine on her skin. They'd never had flies in the apartment before the war, she thought — before the war and all of Wally's gardening and bug-collecting projects. Then she laughed at herself, blaming the flies on war or Wally. Surely there had always been flies, even in peacetime. She hummed "Happy Days Are Here Again" and thought about dancing with the milkman that morning, as she gathered the ingredients for a pound cake, Wally's favorite chocolate marble pound cake.

A pound of flour, a pound of sugar, a pound of butter less a bit for the pan and the marbling, six eggs, a cup of milk, vanilla, salt. Beat. Pour a third of the batter in the bottom of the buttered pan. Blend the cocoa with the rest of the butter, melted, and add it to the second third of batter. Pour the chocolate batter in. On top, the final third, more plain batter. Fold, slightly, with a broad knife. Turn on the oven to 275 degrees. Bake two hours. Take out. Let cool.

Stella followed Loretta's recipe for pound cake, with two exceptions: She always put the pan in a cold oven and she always let it cool fully before she sliced it. Start from cold, go back to cold. That was the secret. She'd read about it in a women's magazine, the kind of thing she rarely picked up, but she had tried it, and found it worked. The inside always turned out miraculously moist. It was worth the wait.

Finally, when the pan was full and the cake in the oven, she washed her hands, dried them on the yellow and white checked tea towel with the black embroidered chickens pecking their way across the border.

She went to her writing table, got out several sheets of stationery, and brought them back to the kitchen, where she sat down with a cup of coffee and her fountain pen and wrote a long, crazy, hopeful letter to Bill. It was a bit of a risk, but she didn't mind taking it, just then.

She had just posted it in the mail chute in the hall when the elevator stopped at their landing.

"Telegram just arrived for you, Mrs. Baker," said Boris, when the doors opened.

"Thank you, Boris," she said and turned quickly, before she could begin to cry. Telegrams were never good news.

It was either from Rudy, with news of his transfer back to the States, or, God forbid, *about* Rudy. A wave of guilt rippled through her. She had imagined life without him. *Please, don't let that dream come true,* she thought, and her tears began to rise. She didn't wish Rudy any ill, but what if he had been killed in action? Would Wally call Bill Uncle Bill? Would he leave Louise then? Then she thought about the hundreds of other women who must be opening similar telegrams at the very same time, all across the land — for if Rudy was dead, it was likely his ship had gone down.

By the time she had the thin folded yellow sheet in her hands, she was back at the dinette table. Words had already formed in her mind before her fingers opened the paper: *We regret to inform you that your husband, Captain Rudyard Baker III of the US Navy . . .* She swallowed and flattened it out on the table before her. Her eyes leapt down the page to the signature.

It was not from some admiral, not about Rudy. Not from Rudy.

It was from Bill.

16
THE CAKE

With the great funnel in one hand and the pot and spoon in the other, Wally wandered back to her grandparents' house, wondering where Ham had got to in the end and what it must have been like to see the bombs go off from the ground.

Her mother had read an article out loud from the newspaper, the day after it happened: A seething pillar of purple fire and a mushroom cloud had flattened the city of Hiroshima. But what about the girls in those cities, girls Wally's age, girls who had seen something different, heard something — a roar, perhaps — and been vaporized? Even with Georgie so long dead and buried, even knowing girls whose fathers had been killed in action and would never return, Wally couldn't fathom the death of girls like her, or the flattening of cities — all their people, all their buildings, gone in a flash.

Someone at the parade had said the only

survivors were insects, and Wally thought about the ants of Japan and their queens, tucked safely deep in their nests, ready as ever to lay more eggs and raise new larvae, which would replace the soldier ants and foragers that didn't come back that day.

So often, in communities, there's one individual whose survival is the key to all the others'. In an ant colony, it's the queen. She is unique, but that doesn't make her irreplaceable. Wally had learned from Mr. Somersby that if the queen should die — as every queen must — a sufficiently well-established colony is prepared to bring a new one swiftly to maturity. The workers never have to know what happened to the old queen, or why. They just move forward and transform a writhing generic larva, through a special regimen of care and feeding, into the queen their colony needs — a being that can beget further life.

Wally wondered what would have happened if the Germans or the Japs had figured out the bomb first. Wally and her entire world would have died — all her secrets and all her dreams, everything she knew. How was it different from what the Germans had done, gone and gassed all those Jews?

She tried to imagine the changes that

would be coming for her. They were mostly for the better, she thought, though she knew that her Victory Garden was likely to be plowed back over in favor of camellias and roses and that Mr. Niederman would leave. Her father would return. She hoped against hope her mother would stop working.

Wally imagined Loretta would bake a cake to celebrate. She always seemed to find a way to cook what the occasion required, despite the shortages and rationing. Her mother would probably have made a cake, too, if only she weren't so busy at the hospital. Walking down the street, Wally daydreamed about the oily, moist crumbs and crispy upper edges of her mother's marble pound cake, and the places where the chocolate met the vanilla.

The rugosa roses that grew in the Wallace front yard were splendid that afternoon, sweet and spicy and splayed open wide to the buzzing bees. The sycamores scattered their patchy shadows on the ground, and in between, the paving stones basked in the sun. There were a few brown leaves from the sycamores, clustered against the curbstones. It was perfect weather, hot-in-the-sun-but-cool-in-the-shade weather, that, as long as she lived, Wally would never forget.

Nor would she forget the hazy, slightly sweet-smelling air of the evening of that day, when she and Loretta, somewhat later than intended, set out for home from Gigi and Waldo's.

"Can you hustle it up, Wally? I've got to serve Miz Doc her dinner in fifteen minutes."

Wally did as she was asked. She wanted to be home and eat dinner with her mother. She wanted to take a not-too-warm bath, have her mother scrub her dry with a great soft towel, and then slip between the smooth sheets with their yellow scalloped edges and fall obliviously to sleep.

"Evening, Miss Baker," Boris said, ignoring Loretta the way he always did, as if she didn't exist.

"Hi, Boris."

They stepped into the elevator and Wally sat down on the narrow upholstered bench at the back. Then the door slid shut, and the elevator car lurched upward.

The elevator was hot. The hall that Wally's apartment had all to itself was hot. When they got to the apartment, it was oddly stuffy. The kitchen door, which always stood open, was shut. It was eerily still.

"Why is that door shut?" Wally said.

Then a ringer sounded.

"Maybe she burned something," Loretta ventured, but the only smell was a faint one, of cake, with not the least tinge of smoke. *Could she really have baked a cake?* wondered Wally excitedly.

"Mother?" Wally called and barged right through the swinging door.

Loretta heard a thud and a clatter.

As the door snapped back on its hinges, the mirrored push plate arced across Loretta's vision. There were fragments of familiar things: Stella's hair, the checkerboard tiles, Stella's brown dress, the old ladder-back chair, Stella's pump, her stockinged toes, a dark puddle. Then the door swung shut again, cutting Loretta off from Wally and Stella. Loretta felt her blood shift. It was all wrong, the way the objects in the mirror had been arranged, how low to the floor. She didn't want Wally in that room.

On the other side of the door, Wally stood frozen, staring down at her mother. She felt like she couldn't breathe until she understood, and she couldn't understand. The door snapped open again behind her.

Loretta's hand flew to cover her mouth and nose in horror.

What she saw, that first instant, was just one shoeless foot at the end of a sprawled leg.

The nursery rhyme came unbidden: *Diddle, diddle, dumpling, my girl Stella. She knows when it's bedtime. I don't have to tell her. One shoe off, one shoe on. Diddle, diddle, dumpling, my girl Stella.*

She had sung it to Stella a thousand and one times, swooping her down and rocking her back and forth in her arms. She sang versions of it to Ham, Wally, and Georgie, too. It had always made them happy, her babies. It had made her happy, too.

She looked down and saw she held something in her own hand. Stella's shoe. The heel was brown.

"Wally, go to the living room and sit down," Loretta said. She put the shoe — a shapely organic form of molded leather, so horribly empty — down gingerly on the table and guided Wally out of the room. When she saw that the girl was sitting obediently on the couch, Loretta went to Stella. She stooped down to the floor and took her shoulder, grasped her hands, called her name into her ear, shook her, took her head in her hands, but nothing roused her. She put her fingers to her nose to see if she breathed, but her lungs were still.

The air in the kitchen was rank. Stella had soiled herself. A cup of coffee had been overturned and lay broken on the tiles. A freshly baked cake, just one slice missing, stood on the kitchen table beside a letter, written on Stella's blue stationery, and the slit-open envelope of a Western Union telegram. The batter bowls, baking powder, vanilla, and measuring things lay sticky on the counter.

The oven door gaped open, and Loretta shut it, then realized a strange thing: The oven was set to 275 degrees, but the oven was cold. The gas was on. The room was full of the silent, odorless poison that mothers warned their children against. Loretta coughed involuntarily, dashed to the window and threw it wide. As she ran to the living room to open the French doors — she had left poor Wally in danger — a sugar ant out foraging on the terrace approached the sash, surmounted it and slowly made its way toward a drip of chocolate batter on the counter.

"What's wrong?" said Wally quietly. "What's happened?"

"It's an emergency, String Bean. You need to stay out here. The air is bad in there."

"What do you mean? What about Mother? I want to go back in," Wally said, wrenching her arms from Loretta's grasp.

"No, darling. Not just now. I'm going to call the ambulance."

211

Wally turned away from Loretta and happened to spot a silver tray resting on the table near the double terrace doors. Behind the curtains, all was dim, but there, on the tray, sat a little dish of blueberries from the bush on the terrace, a glass of milk, and a small oval plate with a slice of her mother's freshly baked chocolate marble pound cake. That was when Wally first cried, when she saw her snack laid out so beautifully on that tray, though she hardly understood why.

Loretta was shaking as she returned to the kitchen. She turned away from Stella and picked up the sheet of stationery. "Dear Wally, I love you so much, and I am so proud of you —"

Loretta took a few slow breaths and wiped her cheeks. She tucked her hair behind her ears and then carefully folded the letter and slid it into her handbag. She knew Gigi wouldn't want the police to find it, not given what it said. This had to have been an accident, a horrible accident.

Then Loretta went to the phone in the small foyer. As she dialed, she could see Wally sitting quietly on the terrace, stunned.

"I need police and an ambulance," she said.

Following the operator's instructions, she went to the front door and threw it wide open, and somehow, as she did so, her eye landed on the blue rectangle of a letter wedged in the mail chute. She knew it was Stella's from the dark V of its back flap. This one had actually been mailed, but one of its corners had caught against the brass fittings, so that the letter hung there, suspended.

Who was it to? Loretta wanted to know. She needed to know. The letter might be the key. So she reached her slender hand into the slot, gouging her finger on something sharp within the chute as she did so, and pulled the letter out.

It was to William Niederman, and strangely, there was a spot of blood on the upper right corner of it, as if the stamp had been canceled. She looked at her own cut finger for a moment, and stuck it reflexively in her mouth to catch the blood.

Loretta turned to rush back to Wally, but suddenly there Wally stood in the doorway, staring at her, eyes glazed.

"Oh, Wally," said Loretta, opening her arms to the girl and listening to the sound of the elevator rising in its shaft.

While the police collected evidence, and until Gigi got there, Loretta stayed with Wally on the terrace. The air was fresh and the skyline of the city stretched across the horizon, oblivious to such small tragedies as the death of a mother.

Wally stared dumbly at the big pots of her Victory Garden, so neatly arrayed along the railing, the tomatoes tied and pruned and heavy with offspring, the blueberry bushes just recently stripped of their ripest fruits, but with any number of small greenish orbs in formation. They would ripen in September, Wally thought.

"Wally, how 'bout you eat your snack?" Loretta said.

"What?" Wally said quietly as Loretta fetched the tray.

"Your mama baked that cake for you. Eat it while it's fresh."

Wally looked at her, wide eyed. "All right."

Obediently, Wally broke off a corner and pushed it inside her lips. The cake was crisp at the crust, chocolaty and moist within, her most favorite cake in the world, but her tongue rebelled against it. She couldn't swallow, couldn't seem to keep her lips together, and the cake spewed out all over her hands and the terra-cotta tiles, as if a handful of soil from the garden pots had been scattered on the ground.

17
FINGER SANDWICHES

The last time a coffin had come down the staircase at the house on Columbia Heights, the year was 1919, and the box contained the remains of Beatrice Harris, Gigi's mother. That was when she and Waldo and their daughter, Stella, had moved into the old house, and they had needed full-time help to run it. Starting the day of Beatrice's funeral and for the next thirty-six years, Loretta had been that help.

But Stella wasn't brought back to the house, the way her grandmother had been. That was the old-fashioned way. She'd been carried away to the morgue, and then to the undertaker on Atlantic Avenue, and finally to the cemetery.

Presumably, thought Loretta, her body would be lowered into its grave any time now. She would have liked to be there to throw a clod of earth on the box and say a prayer, but of course Miz Doc and Waldo needed her at home, to get everything ready for the guests.

There were two hours before people were expected back at the house, but Loretta knew it would be less. Some people would skip the drive to Green-Wood and show up at the house early, and as soon as they arrived, they would begin to eat.

It didn't surprise her or even make her think less of the people. The heart, she believed, was strongly linked to the belly. The body expressed its need for life through the appetite, especially when it had been face-to-face with death.

And so two freshly polished silver serving trays were laid with lace doilies, and she and her friend Noreen, who usually worked for Verbena Rensselaer but had been lent out to the Wallaces for the reception, were in the process of decking them with two kinds of finger sandwiches. Loretta had punched the round ones out with an upside-down juice glass and filled them with milk-blanched Vidalia onions, minced parsley, and mayonnaise. The other sandwiches were crustless squares that showed thin green lines of watercress peeping from their buttered edges.

War or no war, Boxing Day open house, or their only daughter's funeral, whenever they opened their doors, that was what the Wallaces served at functions: onion and watercress finger sandwiches. On the serving board, a side of lightly poached salmon lurked beneath a jacket of cucumber-slice fish scales and dill sauce, its stuffed-olive eye glaring coldly at the ceiling.

"Soon's your tray's filled, Noreen," said Loretta, "could you see to setting up some eggs?"

The two women wore identical dove gray dresses, scalloped cuffs on their short sleeves, matching scallop-edged white aprons. It was the Wallace house uniform, though worn only at formal occasions.

"Press the deviling down firm and set a half a olive on top."

"Loretta, you think you invented deviled eggs, or what?"

"I'm just saying how the missus likes it."

"All right, don't fret. I'm only teasing you."

She sliced an olive in half and held the little green eyeballs with pimento pupils up to her own eyes and waggled her head back and forth.

Loretta laughed, despite herself. Noreen was only slightly older than Loretta, but after her son died at Normandy her hair had gone gray, even down to the lone

217

whisker that grew from the base of her chin. It stood out silvery against her brownness, for all the world like the barbel of a wise old cod.

Loretta wiped her eyes on her dish towel and said, "Norie, I just can't stand it. It's like my own baby died. I raised her."

"I know, Retta. It's hard," said Noreen. "Prettiest white girl in Brooklyn, and one of the nicest, and the smartest if not the most sensible, and that's because you raised her, Loretta. You can take at least half the credit. You can be proud of who she was. And you've got a right to cry. An awful thing like that, a young mother cut down, dropping dead from a bad heart."

That was the story they had broadcast. Loretta thought about all the days Miz Doc had spent at the hospital, when Stella was young, the days on end when she didn't see her mama at all, just Loretta from dawn to bedtime. They'd had a lot of fun, the two of them, making paper dolls and baking cakes and playing house, singing hymns and reading poetry and telling tall tales. Loretta had never managed to devote herself quite so fully to Ham as she had to Stella. She hadn't had the time.

"No, she had a fine heart, Stella," Loretta murmured at last.

"She was a fine woman."

"I let her down," Loretta whispered.

"Nothing you did's to blame for what happened. She was unlucky, just unlucky over and over, and her poor heart couldn't take it, so the Lord called her home, poor thing."

When the trays were all ready, the two women sat on the kitchen stools to take a load off for a moment. Loretta glanced at the clock. It wouldn't be long now till the doorbell rang.

"Norie," she said. "There's something I need to get off my chest, before I face this reception. But can you keep it to yourself?"

"You know I'm no gossip, Retta Walker."

"She never had a heart attack," Loretta said, almost whispering. "What I saw, at the apartment — She hadn't just fell over. She had shut the windows and the doors and turned the gas on. She wrote a letter."

"God have mercy on her soul."

"But, Norie," Loretta said, swallowing hard, "it was an accident. I don't think she really meant to do it."

"Well, if she wrote a letter —"

"That's not all of it, Norie. That afternoon, she called and asked me could I walk Wally over and come up to see her. I was supposed to get there a half hour before. I think she wanted talking out of it. She wanted some sense put into her. She wanted help."

"You were late?"

"I was getting dinner on for the Miz Doc," Loretta sobbed. "A person can't be in two places."

What with the craziness of the day — Hamilton Sr. turning up dead all of a sudden, and Ham running off — Loretta hadn't so much lost track of the time as given up trying to do what she had to according to the usual schedule. It had been such an exceptional day. It had seemed tolerable to get a half an hour behind, just once.

"You don't know it for sure," Noreen said, enveloping Loretta in a hug. "It's not your fault. Don't you take the blame."

"What if I'd been there earlier, Norie? I could have saved her from herself."

"We don't know that. You might have been killed, too, or the child. You don't know. Right now, you got to take care of the living. That's what matters now."

"Ham's running wild on me, too. Spent a whole night out on the street the day Stella died and came home smelling like liquor."

"Ham? He's such a good boy. What happened?"

"He found out old Hamilton Sr. got killed in action. The trouble is, I'd lied to him. I'd let him think Hamilton was his daddy, and he was already dead."

"Now that's a name I haven't heard in a while. Hamilton Walker the first. What happened to *him*?"

"Got shot down."

"Just before the peace."

"Just before the peace."

"Loretta, you have an awful lot on your plate, girl. But Ham's a good boy. He was just mad at you. Thank the Lord he came home safe."

"Naw, don't thank Him. God's turned mean, these past years."

"Don't you speak like that, Loretta Walker. Don't you say that. You'll get through this. Remember, the Lord giveth, and the Lord taketh away."

Noreen rubbed Loretta's shoulders and then turned back to her work, but Loretta just stared off into the distance, eyes shining, mind torn between worrying about Ham and wondering what would have happened if she and Wally had been on time.

18
THE NICHE

On the day of her daughter's funeral, Gigi Wallace glanced out the great double-hung parlor window at the sudden sheets of rain, glad for any cause to turn away from the platitudes of her guests, especially the uninvited one.

She had never, in all the decades of their adjacency, invited her next-door neighbor to her house, never intended to, yet here she was: great, fat Mrs. Titus Brevard, slurping sherry, snagging hors d'oeuvres and gobbling them down right along with the details of the Wallaces' tragedy. When Stella was a girl, Mrs. Brevard had always complained about the noise — as if a jump-rope song was a crime — and ever since then it had been wayward trash barrels or out-of-bounds vines creeping from the Wallaces' façade to her own brownstone's virgin walls. In '36, the Brevards had hung an enormous swastika flag in their front window, filling the lower pane. After Pearl Harbor, the flag came down, naturally, but no one had forgotten it.

"Rain *is* the most appropriate weather for a funeral, don't you think?"

Gigi ignored her, letting her eyes wander to the wide grooves of crown molding that married the red and white Chinese patterned wallpaper to the white ceiling. The plaster had begun to separate from the ceiling in the southeast corner, where the heating riser went through. A workman would have to be called in to repair it.

"And what are you going to do with young Wallace?" Mrs. Brevard pressed on. "Boarding school?"

Gigi pressed her lips together. The crowd in the parlor was becoming dense as the guests arrived.

"Children are so terribly resilient, aren't they? I'm sure she'll bounce back, as they say."

Gigi coughed and narrowed her eyes. Her hand floated up and came to rest on Waldo's mahogany cane, which stood in the nearby umbrella stand. Her fingers closed around the handle.

"It was unexpected of you to come, Mrs. Brevard," she said with a pinched smile, dreaming of brandishing the cane at the unwanted guest. "Now, you must excuse me," and with that she turned away, briefly colliding with a woman she'd never seen before, but she appeared to be with Bill Niederman. Must be the wife. *Did she know?* Gigi Wallace wondered.

"Christ, this is awful," said Bill Niederman to his wife as they made their way through the front parlor. "Why *do* these people throw such elaborate parties when people die?"

Louise looked down, shut her eyes. Georgeanna Wallace had just brushed past her, for heaven's sake.

"Bill," she whispered once Gigi was at a safe distance, "watch what you say. And it's not a *party.* It's a *reception.*"

He'd been extremely strange since they'd heard about Stella Baker's death, two nights before. She was trying to tell herself that strange was normal when a person one knew well had died. Then again, from what Bill had said, he'd hardly spoken to her most days, their schedules were so different. Apparently, he knew the daughter better than her mother. Even so, Stella Baker had been a striking woman, and Louise was beginning to be afraid that Bill had been in love with her. Why else would he behave so strangely?

"You're right. Come on, Ouise, let's go find the bar."

The truth was, Bill Niederman could hardly see straight, his head was reeling so hard. If only he'd stayed with Stella, refused Louise her wish that he come home for V-J Day. He could have called an ambulance. She would still be alive. He would have a chance to choose differently. He hated having his wife by his side in this place, and having Stella's family and friends all around simply overwhelmed him. He actually thought he might throw up. Earlier, at the church, he had been close to tears, but he'd gotten control of that. The last thing he needed now was for Louise to guess the truth.

Louise was still in the dark, he was confident, but the rest of them? Did everyone else know? He almost wished they did, so he could grieve openly, could fall down and sob and pound the ground until his knuckles bled. But now that there was no happy ending possible for him and Stella — if there ever had been — that sort of honesty would be needlessly destructive, he told himself. Indulging his emotions could only do damage — to Louise, to his boys, to Wally, to Rudy Baker, to Stella's reputation and memory. And, he admitted, to himself.

There was something uncanny about the way he and Stella had skated above the awareness of everyone, as long as the war was on. They hadn't ever touched or flirted in public, but they had been together constantly, at home and about the neighborhood. His presence was justified by his war work — not that anyone had any idea what it was — and her sacrifice in putting him up. It was all for the war effort. People were so concerned about the war effort that the two of them had gotten away with murder, so to speak, barely drawing anyone's attention. How many other sins and secrets had been papered over by the war? he wondered. How many others' lives had been changed by the strange circumstances under which they'd lived?

As he pushed through the crowd to the back parlor, Bill Niederman couldn't help but wonder if Stella had received his telegram. Was it his fault, somehow, her death? Had he broken her heart? People said it was heart failure, but that just didn't seem possible. Stella was so young and healthy. Whatever the cause, he should have been straight with her when they parted. He was sure of that now. He just hadn't known how to say it. Or should he have said something different entirely? Said, I love you. Now it was too late. The proper thing for him to do — the only thing — was vanish from the Bakers' world and go back to his wife.

He turned to see if Louise was still with him. She was, and as if from a great distance, he took in her broad lips, her pink lipstick, her brown dress, her placid expression of sympathy. She'd met Stella just that once. How smart was Louise? Did she know? He set his features into a grim expression.

"Come on Ouise, I really need that drink," he said and pushed forward toward the bar.

"Bill?" said Louise, once they were in the bar line. "Her little girl must be around here somewhere, don't you think?"

"Wally. Yes, she must be," he said, scanning the room.

Suddenly, a half-mad idea crossed his mind that Louise would meet Wally and be so charmed by her she would want to take her in and raise her as their own. He had been her de facto father for two years now, hadn't he? She could be the daughter Louise had always wanted.

As surely as he'd loved Stella, he loved Wally. And if they didn't take her, what would become of her? Her father showed no sign of returning from the Pacific. The

227

man had missed his own wife's funeral, for God's sake. He'd let a priest represent him by reading aloud from a telegram.

How long would the child be forced to live in this gloomy house with only her grandparents and the maid to raise her? Given what Stella had told him of Rudy Baker, it seemed like it might be a long time.

Bill Niederman looked for Wally in the crowd but never found her — not to say good-bye, not to say that he was sorry. He didn't find her.

Wally spent most of the reception out back, her lace-trimmed black velvet dress soaked, her white-socked toes black with mud. She and Ham had a couple of shovels, a stick, and a mayonnaise jar with the usual Vaseline around its rim. They were conscripting soldiers from the big nest for a suicide mission they'd devised.

"I can't bear to talk to any of them," said Wally, yanking off the socks that had slipped down her skinny calves and wadded up around her ankles. "Not about what happened, not about the war ending or when my father's coming home, definitely not about my mother. Actually, I can't bear to talk to any of those phony people about anything ever again. Never."

"Me neither," said Ham, thinking of his mother, who had slapped him in the face when he returned home to the Wallaces' the morning after V-J Day, his mother, to whom he was still barely talking. "Every adult I ever met was a fake. Who needs them? Let's get out of here. Let's go put some of these guys into Planet Ant's arena, see how long they last."

Wally looked back up the hill at her grand-parents' house. The yard was still wet with the sudden, heavy rain, but the sky had brightened again, and the sun was beginning to break through. Clouds of white-flies hovered and then alighted on the leaves of the Victory Garden's crops.

"Yeah, let's go," said Wally. She left her filthy socks in a tangle by the fence that overlooked the harbor. The mud of the path squelched between their toes as they walked back to the house.

"This time, no mercy," said Ham, slipping his hand into Wally's. "No big ole A-bomb. This time they're going to fight hand to hand, mouth to mouth, like Iwo Jima. They're going to be eaten alive."

The two grim-faced children wiped their feet carefully at the door, so as not to leave a trail, and then sneaked down to the boiler room with their shanghaied army.

By four, the last guest had left, and Loretta and Noreen were busy putting the house back to rights.

"But where in the world is Wally?" said Gigi Wallace. *"Wally!"* she called as she climbed up to the attic and then descended to the parlors and the ground-level kitchen. "Loretta? Noreen? Haven't the two of you been keeping an eye on Wally?"

"Yes, ma'am, Miz Doc," said Loretta, spying Wally's shoes through the glass by the terrace door. "She was outside with Ham in the garden just now. I think she was needing a break from all those people."

"But it's pouring."

"Not anymore, ma'am," said Noreen.

For dinner, the Wallaces and the Walkers ate leftover food from the reception — salmon, eggs, and tiny sandwiches — separately. Masters in the dining room, servants in the kitchen. Afterward, Wally crept silently to the room with the striped wallpaper without saying good night to anyone.

"Should we leave on the lights in the stairwell, Miz Doc?" asked Loretta, after she'd brought Gigi a fresh decanter of water for her bedside table and bid her good night. Somehow Loretta hesitated to let the house fall into darkness.

Miz Doc shook her head slightly, eyes to the carpet. "No, Loretta. That won't be necessary."

Loretta closed the door behind her.

"Good-bye, darling," she whispered as she reached up and snapped the switch.

She found her son fast asleep in his clothes on the daybed in their apartment. She threw a blanket over him and pushed a button on the switch plate, extinguishing the ceiling fixture above them. She would try to talk to him tomorrow.

All through the house, the lights were out — all but Wally's. She had no plan to fall asleep any time soon. She sat propped against her pillows with a volume of Greek mythology on her knees, occasionally sipping water from a silver julep cup marked with her mother's maiden initials. Loretta had once told her it was Stella's toothbrush cup when she was a girl, and earlier in the day, when the silver was being polished for the party, she had taken it from the breakfront drawer without asking. It must be hers now, mustn't it? She had always wanted to drink from that cup.

Wally flipped from the story of the Gray

Sisters, with their one, shared eye, to Medea, who betrayed and was betrayed in turn, and drank her tepid water. She tried not to look away from the text lest she see something that shouldn't be there. She was afraid of the shadows. She didn't want to meet her mother's spirit, the way she'd once hoped to meet Georgie's. She was afraid to sleep. It was late when Wally finally began to droop. A thread of drool dampened the illustration of Europa gathering wildflowers, just before being transformed into a cow. Wally's mind spun toward the starriness of space and back to earth, to the soil of the yard and all its sleeping bugs, its ants. Her ears rang with the sound of late cicadas and crickets from the window and with tidbits of talk overheard at the reception: *No thank you. How about that bomb? Onion sandwich, ma'am? Darling. Loved her so much. Never could stand to. What a pity. Join our foursome? But how? What a horror. What does he know? What's the use?*

Nowhere amidst the ants and the planets and the chatter did Wally encounter what she feared but yearned for: her mother. The reading light over her bed burned on until, just at dawn, the filament flashed and died.

The darkness paled, and before the sun

was fully on their nest, the ants in the Wallace yard resumed their rounds.

19
MAMMY'S PANTRY

Loretta stood at the gates of P.S. 8, waiting. The late summer air was golden with heat and dust. It was almost a week since Stella'd died, since that telegram'd arrived and thrown Ham into a fury.

Maybe if she hadn't diminished his crisis in contrast to Stella's — or really Wally's, Gigi's — he would have returned to his usual self by now. But she hadn't guessed how deep his hurt could be, and what she had thoughtlessly said had kept his rage going.

Even that morning, as he got ready for the first day of school, he had barely spoken to her and not even once looked her in the eye. There were things she needed to tell him, but he wasn't in a listening mood, on top of which she'd been hard-pressed to find a minute alone with him to insist he hear her out. All day long, she'd coped with Wally, Waldo, and Gigi Wallace in the sorry shape they were in. At night, when she was free, Ham got ready for bed in the bathroom, then climbed into his bed and rolled toward the wall, pulled the coverlet over his head and appeared to fall asleep instantaneously. Her idea in ambushing him after school was to take advantage of his deep-seated sense of manners. In public, he wouldn't dare spurn her — she hoped.

When he saw her, he scowled and looked down at the pavement, muttering, "Hi, Mama."

Better than walking the other way.

"Hi, Ham."

Both of them noticed the boys of Ham's posse wandering away together down Hicks Street, toward Fulton Ferry, casting backward glances at Ham.

"What you doing here?" he said in the flattest voice she'd ever heard from him. "I don't need to be picked up from school. I'm not Wally."

"Had to stop in at Esposito's anyways, for cabbage and carrots and a few more things." She lifted her shopping bag to show him. "It was on the way."

He did like her coleslaw, she knew.

"I need to talk to you, Ham. I want to tell you I'm sorry for what I kept from you, but I also need you to show some respect."

"Respect? You're a liar!" Ham hissed.

"You hush your mouth, Hamilton. Don't speak to me like that."

"You kept my father away from me. You told me he was dead. Now he really is dead. I don't respect you. I hate you."

It was a reasonable feeling, his rage, given what he knew, but it didn't make it any less awful. If only it were all as simple as he thought, she'd have done him a grievous wrong.

"I know you're angry, Hamilton," she said. "But when you know the whole situation, you might feel different."

"Yeah, well, you're right about one thing. I'm angry at you."

"But you're also in the dark. You got to let me talk to you."

"What is there to talk about?"

"A lot. About your parents. Ham Walker wasn't your daddy, Son. I let you believe he was, so I am a liar, but not how you think. I didn't want to tell you the real complicated truth, but now I see that I was wrong. Come on, we'll go for coffee and pancakes, and I'll tell you what you need to know."

Silence.

Finally, to her relief, he turned from the gate and began walking uphill, toward Montague Street, rather than down to the piers, where his friends had gone. She turned with him.

"Let's go get some pancakes at Mammy's, how 'bout that?"

"Awright."

Ham had changed over the summer, she noticed. His legs were so long and moved so fast, she had to strain to keep up with him. He was more of a man somehow, less of a boy. His Adam's apple had popped, his voice was lower, and his chin had grown harder, longer. His cheeks weren't just covered in peach fuzz any longer: He was close to getting a beard.

How, Loretta wondered, how could she make him understand? The only way she could see was to confess to everything in full, to tell him she wasn't his mother — not his birth mother, anyway.

At the restaurant, Mammy James unburdened Loretta of her shopping and offered condolences on Stella's death. Loretta smiled sadly. It was the only smile she'd been using lately.

"Can you give us the corner table by the kitchen, Mammy, out of the way?"

"Sure thing, honey."

When the coffee came, both of them poured in the cream.

"Awright then, Mama. Let's get down to

it," he said. "If Hamilton Walker ain't my father, then what's that make me? A bastard. And what's that make you?"

"You watch your mouth, Hamilton. You need to listen. I'll tell you everything, just like it is, if you promise to listen."

After what felt to Loretta like an eternity, he looked up at her and said, "I'm listening."

So she told him about her marriage to Hamilton, and that he'd walked out on her. Then she explained about Washington and Nellie Walker, how they had left Ham with her as a baby, gone off in search of work and never come back.

He still scowled — there was nothing welcome about this news — but he seemed genuinely interested for the first time since she'd begun.

"So you're not my mama."

I wanted you when those two fools left you behind, she wanted to shout. *I protected you from the ugly business of being black and poor, not to mention an orphan.* But the last thing she wanted to do was make him feel worse by rubbing his nose in it.

"I raised you, and I love you, and I'm the only mama you've got," she offered.

"But my own mama's out there, somewhere? She just never came back."

"I don't know why they never came back. I could never get in touch with them. I've always feared that something happened to them. They may not even be alive."

"So, any way you cut it, I'm an orphan. And you, you're just some fool do-gooder, and I'm your charity. Is that it?"

She told herself that with children you can't take things to heart. He was just a child, still, just trying on the harshness of manhood. But still, it wounded her.

"You ain't no orphan, Hamilton," she said slowly. "And I may be a fool but I'm your mama. I've cared for you since you were a baby. What more does it take to be a mother?"

To Loretta's relief, his face began to relax. If she failed at this chance to settle things, she feared he would drift away from her, and there were too many directions an angry boy could drift, few of them good.

She looked around her at the people in the restaurant, expecting them to be on tenterhooks, listening to the conversation that would shape her fate. They were eating, stirring saccharin into their coffee, wiping their lips, living their own lives. Then Mammy bustled over with two heaping plates, and set them down.

"You want the syrup, Ham?" Loretta said.

239

"Thanks, Mama." He took a forkful of pancakes and filled his mouth.

"You're welcome. Now, why don't you just ask me if you have any questions. How 'bout that?"

"What's the last thing you know about them?"

"They went off. First to Virginia, then out to California. They were looking for work, and they were supposed to send for you, but they never did. I didn't hear from them anymore, and they just didn't come back, Ham. They might have gotten into trouble of some sort. They went after trouble, those two. Drinking and drugging."

"Why you kept me in the dark all these years?"

"You were just a tiny thing, Ham, when they left. When do you think I should have told you? I couldn't figure out the right time."

"So you just taught me to call you Mama, just like that."

"No, not that simple. You used to call me Mama Lola. Somewhere along, you dropped the Lola, and I was pretty much your mama by then, anyway. I wasn't expecting them back anymore."

"Did you even try to find them?"

"Where was I gonna look? There's a whole

240

lot of country west of New York. You know what I did do? I stayed put. For you, so they could find you again if they wanted. I could have done something else with my life than be a maid, maybe. I could've gone off to nursing or typing school, but just in case they ever came back looking for you — I stayed put."

"So now you're blaming your miserable life on me?"

"My life isn't miserable, and neither is yours. All I'm saying is, I did my best, Ham."

"Do you have anything of theirs?"

"I do have a few of your mama's things — a couple trinkets, a silk scarf, some post-cards. I put them away, waiting for the time I told you about her."

"Pictures?"

"Uh-huh. I got one of them, too." Loretta thought about what he would learn when he saw the picture. Was there any point in saying it aloud, first?

A great, fat tear rolled from his cheek into his hotcakes.

"She loved you, Ham. I know she'd've come back if she could've," Loretta said, taking his hand. She couldn't stand to see him crying.

Mammy shuffled over with more coffee and refilled the cream.

They were quiet for a long moment, with just the sound of other diners at the restaurant clinking silverware on china and talking quietly amongst themselves.

Finally, Ham cut a bite of pancake with his fork and swirled it in the syrup.

"Man," he said. "Wally's ma's gone, and now I find out I'm an orphan, too."

"You're not an orphan, and neither is Wally. She's got her father, remember?" Loretta hesitated. "And you both got me."

"I wonder when he'll be back."

Loretta thought of the closet full of Japanese dolls. She wondered, too.

"I guess he knows Wally's safe where she is."

"My parents, too. I guess they knew I'd be safe with you."

"That's right, honey. You're safe with me. You always have been."

There was just one more thing she had to tell him — about his mother — and she would leave that to when they got home and she showed him Nellie's things.

20
PICNIC

Wally's father was coming home. His telegram was not specific about when, but it didn't seem to matter very greatly, not to Wally, anyhow. He'd never been there for her in any previous hour of crisis, so it seemed fitting that he would arrive late. In the end, her father was something rather technical to Wally, an essential thing she didn't bother to consider very often. He wasn't the one she wanted. The man she missed was Mr. Niederman. Why hadn't he come back, at least to say good-bye? Somehow she was afraid to ask.

When she thought of him, now, she always envisioned the smashing of Antland, her mother's empty stockings on the sofa. She wasn't sure why, but there was something wrong about that scene. If her mother had been changing, either into or out of her stockings, Mr. Niederman shouldn't have been there, should he? Unless it had some-

thing to do with the cape. Was Mr. Niederman involved in her mother's secret life as
the Silver Wonder? Had he been helping
her, somehow? In which case, where had he
been when her mother had truly needed
help, on V-J Day, when she and Loretta arrived home too late, to find her already
gone, vanquished, defeated by forces un-
known? Wally would have liked the chance
to see Mr. Niederman again. There were
questions it seemed only he could answer,
but he had vanished.

Four weeks to the day after Stella died,
Rudy Baker landed in Brooklyn. After the
appropriate naval formalities and the grant-
ing of shore leave to all but a skeleton crew
of his sailors, he left his ship and got into
the admiral's staff car. He gave the driver
the address on Columbia Heights, but then
at Fulton Ferry, he asked the man to stop,
and he got out. He wanted to walk up the
hill to the Heights by himself.

Since he'd left, his family had been cut in
half.

He came to the apartment building where
he'd lived with Stella and his children, and
slowed instinctively. Beyond the awning, he
glimpsed the figure of the doorman at his
desk. Old Boris, he thought, and considered

going up to look at the apartment. But no, there would be nothing there for him, less than nothing. The only thing left of his family was Wally. He'd had pictures, of course, but he wondered if he'd recognize the gangly nine-year-old, devoid of her old chubbiness. He wondered if he'd be able to smile when he saw her, and with that, he took out his handkerchief and blew his nose, composed his face. It was a thing he'd done countless times, without thinking about it, every time he'd had to face a body, or a body count, or to bury a sailor at sea. It was what he did in lieu of crying.

When Wally saw him, she, for one, burst into tears, then ran up to her room. Who was he, this harsh, worn-looking man? She hardly recognized him. This was her father? She wondered how many people he had killed, how many he had seen killed. He didn't seem capable of dandling a child on his knee, though she had a photograph of him doing just that, to her, on her dresser. It was one of the things she had specifically asked to be brought from the apartment when her clothes and belongings were moved to Gigi and Waldo's. The picture was taken from the back veranda by her mother, just before her father had shipped out, and showed her father and Wally on the bench beneath the big apple tree.

Even when she came down, Wally would not hug or kiss him. She did not call him Daddy but Sir. The truth was, she was slightly afraid of him.

The next day, after a strangely quiet breakfast, Wally felt a little warmer toward him. He stirred his coffee in a certain methodical way that she remembered, and then licked the spoon before he placed it back on the saucer.

"Wally," he said after Loretta had taken the plates away.

"Yes, Daddy?"

He smiled, hearing that word. "Do you think you could run and change into something a little nicer? Your church clothes?"

"Why?"

"We're going to see your mother and Georgie."

"What?" said Wally. Her heart leapt.

"At Green-Wood. Just you and me, Wally. Would you like to go buy some flowers first, and leave them there?"

Wally nodded silently. It was the first sign she'd had that her father even knew half their family was dead. She got up, went over to his chair and buried her head in his lap.

"Wally. Wally, my sweet girl. I know you

miss them. So do I. And I've missed you, you know. I've been very lonely without you."

She looked up at him. "I thought there were thousands of people on your ship, all crowded together."

"Yes, but they're a crew of rough sailors, and none of them the people I love."

It was a warm day, but she put on her black velvet dress, the same one she had muddied after the funeral, which Loretta had miraculously brought back to respectable condition.

They stopped at the flower shop across from the large stone gate of the cemetery and bought a great bouquet of black-eyed Susans and dahlias.

Rudy asked for directions to the family plot, which he had never had reason to visit before, and they walked through the beautiful parklike cemetery, up and down small hills, past majestic mausoleums, and around enormous trees. Finally, they came to the small, white stone inscribed "George Harris Baker." Stella's grave was still unmarked, except for the recently turned earth. There was just a faint haze of newly seeded grass greening the soil. He felt a sob welling up in his chest, and concealed it with a cough into his handkerchief, but Wally seemed to know he was on the verge of tears. She squeezed his hand.

"Why did they have to die, Daddy?" she asked, still clutching the paper-wrapped bunch of flowers in her other arm.

Rudy Baker thought it was the saddest question he'd ever heard.

"I don't know, Wally. I don't think there was any reason. It just happened. It was just horrible, terrible bad luck."

After they stood there, holding hands for a few minutes, he asked if she wanted to have the picnic lunch Loretta had packed for them there, by the graves, or somewhere else.

"Maybe right here, so they can kind of hear and see us, even if they really can't."

They laid out the yellow tablecloth and had chicken salad and bread and brownies on tin plates and drank lemonade from two small mason jars.

After they had eaten, Rudy Baker let his head fall between his knees, looked down at the grass, and finally let himself cry. For his fabulous wife, who had never loved him as much as he had loved her; for his beautiful son, whom he hadn't spent half enough time with while he was alive; and for his strange, curious daughter, whom he planned to abandon for a career advance, because he simply didn't think he had the strength to live in Brooklyn, in Stella's shadow, without her. He had already accepted the commission to become a rear admiral, but suddenly he dearly wished he could get out of it. How could he leave this small girl, who fancied herself so grown-up, to be raised by his in-laws and their maid? How could he choose any other role in life above that as her father?

"Daddy?" Wally said, as though reading his mind.

"Yes, Wally?"

"I love you."

"I love you, too, Wally," he said, and then he cried harder, and Wally curled up beside him and they both fell asleep in the warm sun.

When they woke, there were ants swarming over the picnic remains. As he crushed them and she brushed them away, Wally told her father about her and Ham's ants and how they'd set up their colonies. She told him she'd identified the wood ant species they had in the backyard from the insect book he'd sent to Georgie.

"Oh, I'm glad you liked that one, Wally. I suppose it arrived . . . too late for Georgie to see?" He remembered inscribing that book with words he'd imagined might be meaningful to Georgie in years to come.

"Yes," she said quietly. "It arrived afterwards."

It struck him as wrong somehow that Wally had simply appropriated the book, though of course he knew it made sense. She was the one interested in bugs, and Georgie was gone. Why shouldn't Stella have given the book to her?

"But Ham and I have both studied the pictures. And even if we don't know any French, Mr. Somersby does, so he's helped us with it."

"Now who in the world might this Mr. Somersby be?" he asked, wondering just how many people knew that his daughter had taken the maid's son for her closest friend. He would have to see what could be done about that, though in the most discreet way. It wouldn't do to get Gigi Wallace's nose out of joint, especially at this delicate time.

It was when Wally mentioned going to the natural history museum with Ham that her father's face changed back into the stiff mask of a stranger. She wasn't sure if it was because of the bugs or that he had something against her hanging around with Ham, but he seemed not to approve.

"So, how often do you and Ham go up there, Wally?"

She shrugged, as if to say she hardly knew, it was so commonplace an event.

"Every week, pretty much. Mr. Somersby says we know more than any of the science teachers who go there with their classes. Ham and I are his students."

"I see. That's quite impressive, I suppose."

They finished their lemonade in silence, and Wally's mind drifted to the graves beside them. *Dust to dust,* she thought, and began to cry silently at the thought of her mother's and brother's bodies going back to the earth. Her father was too occupied with his own ruminations to notice.

On the way home, her father was quiet, and Wally wondered if he simply had nothing to say to her. It was doubtful he was thinking about the role of bugs in the decomposition of flesh, as she was.

"Are you going to go back to work at the bank, Daddy?" she asked him at last. "Now that the war is over?"

"No, Wally. I've been meaning to tell you about my plans — for both of us."

"What will you do?"

"I'm going to stay in the Navy."

"Really? Are you going to work at the

Brooklyn Navy Yard?"

"I've been asked to stay on in Japan, Wally."

She looked at him, uncomprehending.

He hadn't meant to tell her so soon.

"I'm going to be involved in the Reconstruction. It's very important work — making sure the Japanese don't rise and become our enemies again. I'll be an admiral."

"But I don't want to go to Japan. I just started third grade!"

"I know that. You need to stay here with your friends and go to school. I understand. Japan's no place for a young girl, anyhow. That's why I'll be going back by myself, Wally. But I promise I'll send you interesting specimens of bugs — if that's what you'd prefer to dolls."

Wally couldn't believe her father was going to leave her — again — even now that her mother was dead. Did he think it was all right for a person to grow up entirely without parents? Did he even care?

"No, don't send me any bugs," she said gloomily. "Mr. Somersby already has every species ever identified. Just don't send me anything at all, because I don't want anything Japanese."

For the remaining twelve days of his leave,

Rudy Baker took care of the details required for him to go away again, indefinitely. He closed up his old apartment and arranged for the remainder of Wally's belongings to be moved to her room at the Wallace house, which was now officially hers. He signed papers conferring guardianship of his daughter on his parents-in-law. He amended his will to Wally's benefit.

Wally hardly acknowledged her father's presence.

"I don't have a father," she said when her grandmother asked her what in the world was going on. "Neither Ham nor I does. We're orphans." As a result of which she spent the rest of the day in disgrace, in her room.

When Captain Baker left again, it was without a farewell from his daughter.

At school, there were many girls with dead fathers. Verna Gage's father had died on Iwo Jima, and Karen Belham's in Alsace-Lorraine, and Rebecca Oliver's when a kamikaze plane attacked his battleship. But at least they all still had their mothers. Only Wally's *mother* had died, and only Wally's father had intentionally chosen to abandon her.

If she could have gotten away with it,

she'd have said her father was kamikazied, too, and that her mother had been torpedoed — anything to avoid the truth.

21
SUSPICIONS

Wally behaved badly at school that fall and winter, but no one criticized her. Not very much. They pitied her, rather than meting out discipline. Only once, when she called Missy Brompton and Claire Rensselaer a couple of purebred bitches, was Wally sent home early.

Gigi laughed when she heard it. "You're right, of course," she said. "Those two are just like their mothers. But don't get yourself into trouble by saying so in front of the teachers, hmn?"

So why did Gigi play cards and go to parties and dinners with them? Wally wanted to ask, but she knew it would be just another hole to climb out of. Gigi didn't like to be questioned, and certainly not to be called on her contradictions.

Loretta was stricter. If Wally came home in one of her deep gloomy moods, she was given a hug and a snack, but if she didn't buck up, she was sent up to the striped bedroom, which was now truly hers, until she could get a handle on herself.

Sometimes she slept right through dinner, but usually, after spending some time on her homework, she found herself feeling like herself again. She would seek out Ham to play checkers with, or join him in mucking around with his ants.

Wally missed Bill Niederman. She didn't understand why he'd never said good-bye to her. They had laughed at breakfast together, morning after morning, done countless calculations, developed hypotheses about pretty much everything. She wanted to tell him about the final yields from the two Victory Gardens. She wanted to ask him if he remembered certain things about her mother, like how hard she'd laughed the time he almost went to work in one brown and one black shoe, or how she had pretended to send him to his room when she caught him sneaking Wally sugar for her Cream of Wheat. But Mr. Niederman had vanished.

"I wrote to him," Wally said, holding out a two-page letter in her large, still ungainly handwriting. "And I was hoping he'd come visit, Gigi. Can you help me write the address where he lives in New Jersey?"

"I don't think that's appropriate, Wally."

"But why not?"

"He was nothing more than a temporary boarder in your house. He was in New York for the war effort, and now the war is over. Don't you see? He has his own life."

"But he was my friend —"

"Little girls don't have friendships with grown men."

"Gigi —" Wally whined.

"Yes?"

"Did he do something wrong? Or, did something happen to him, too?"

"We're not going to discuss it further. Now go and play."

When Wally asked Loretta why her grandparents didn't want her to see him, she was no more forthcoming. "I don't rightly know," she said. "I don't know what's become of him, String Bean, I don't," she said.

It was odd.

It was odder than odd.

It was suspicious.

In bed, at night, gazing at the striped wallpaper in the darkness, Wally thought about what she had seen on the green divan that time, and the cape under her mother's bed. She thought about the way Mr. Niederman had encouraged her mother to return to her job at the hospital, and she wondered if he might be the only one who really knew who her mother was, and how she really had died.

Perhaps Mr. Niederman had died, too. If he had shared some secret with her mother that no one should have known, then government agents might have come after them both.

Then again, what if Mr. Niederman himself had been her killer? It hardly seemed possible, given how kind he had been, but there was no getting around the fact that his vanishing and her mother's death had happened at the same time.

Always, in one corner of her mind, Wally kept the image of the silver-sequined costume under the bed. Even as she grew old enough to doubt them, her wartime fantasies, in which various spies or foreign agents had come up against the Silver Wonder and won, persisted. Mr. Niederman played various roles, sometimes friend, sometimes foe.

It contributed to her runaway imagination that her mother's costume was not among the things brought back in trunks to the Wallace house when the apartment was shut up.

"Mother had a beautiful silver-sequined outfit with a cape," Wally had said to Loretta when her family's apartment was emptied for once and for all, and put on the market. Various trunks and boxes and lamps and pieces of furniture were delivered to the Wallace house, but Wally knew a good deal was given away or sold as well. "It was in its own special box. Have you seen it?"

"She sure did have a lot of finery, that Stella Wallace Baker. That she did. But most of it was given away to charity, Wally. Even in this house, there wasn't room for everything."

Wally pictured the blue and silver costume drooping from a rack in a secondhand shop, its magical powers dispersed.

That whole first year after the war, Wally thought about the Silver Wonder and her unexpected defeat. She read her comics, ignored her homework and dreamed up an alternate reality in which the Silver Wonder had not died but gone deep undercover to deter the Soviet threat that had emerged so soon after the peace.

Then, in the fall, Wally's class went on an excursion to the Prospect Park Zoo, where they witnessed the spectacle of copulating monkeys. As soon as she saw that, Wally realized what she had witnessed the day Antland broke. In retrospect, there was clearly only one thing her mother and Bill Nieder-man could have been doing on that divan, and it wasn't him helping her out of her superhero costume.

As she got older, other things became clear to Wally, for example that it was very uncommon for a woman of Stella Baker's age and in her state of health to collapse and die unexpectedly on her own kitchen floor. Her childish fantasies about the Silver Wonder began to give way to a real suspicion that Gigi and Loretta were keeping something from her. Something had to have happened. Wally had a blurry recollection of the day they found her mother, including a vague mental image of her lying in a pool of dark liquid, but perhaps that was something she had imagined? She knew Loretta had protected her from seeing very much.

Wally had listened to enough radio soap operas, sitting in Gigi's sunny kitchen while Loretta peeled vegetables, to have ideas about how a healthy and attractive young woman might die. She remembered one program in which a newly married stenographer had been strangled by a halyard when she and her best friend went sailing, never guessing that her husband had forged a new alliance. Drowning was awfully popular as a way to die, in fact. There was also the girl who went rowing with her lover only to be tipped out of the boat and find herself abandoned, sinking slowly to the eelgrass below. Wally had heard about all sorts of complications that could arise between lovers. Love always ended miserably on the air, and apparently in real life, too. If her mother and Mr. Niederman had been lovers, as she now suspected, maybe he'd had something to do with her mother's death.

She had her suspicions, but as for hard evidence or actual knowledge, Wally had nothing. There was no point asking Gigi and Loretta again. They'd both made it clear they wouldn't talk about it. Her final option was Waldo.

Waldo was a daunting figure to Wally, whether he was up in the music room, doing his "work," clattering down the stairs on his crutches, or rolling around the parlor floor, though he rarely did that anymore. He'd started taking his supper on a tray upstairs.

One afternoon when she was in the fourth grade, and no one but Waldo and she was home, Wally resolved to ask him about her mother. She went up to his model-making room and parked herself on the window seat. He raised his head to look at her, smiled, looked back down at his worktable, where he kept a good supply of balsa wood, penknives, glue, and some tiny cans of gray paint. These were the things he turned to, to avoid his crutches on the one hand, and to keep him busy while sitting down on the other. Wally felt the strong yet somehow thin chemical odor of the glue in her nostrils and the pleasant, dizzy sensation that came with it. Perhaps it was the glue that kept her grandfather hunched over his projects for so many hours on end, she thought. Certainly it helped her get up the gumption to ask her question.

"Waldo, how did Mother really die?"

"What?" he said, dropping his paintbrush. "Where's this coming from?"

"Was Mr. Niederman involved?"

"*Niederman?* Bill Niederman?"

"I want to know if he did it. Because otherwise, I'm wondering if it was Mrs. Niederman. I do know a few things. I saw some things, before she died, you know. Suspicious things. And where did Mr. Niederman go, after she died? Why did he just disappear? I'm wondering if you all kept me from knowing what really happened, and that he got sent to jail for it."

"Oh, brother," Waldo muttered to himself and then turned to Wally. "No, that's nonsense. He certainly did not get sent to jail."

"So what happened then?"

"Gigi? Gigi!" he called. "I need you." Then he bellowed Loretta's name, but neither of them was in earshot. Neither of them was even home. Finally, he turned back to Wally.

"So?" she demanded.

"Wally, your mother was not murdered. I have no idea where you got that, but you need to drop it right now, before you upset your grandmother. As for Niederman, he simply went home, to his family," he said. "They lived in New Jersey, I believe."

"But why did he disappear like that?"

"He didn't disappear. He came to the funeral, Wally, he and his wife."

"I looked for him, but I never saw him."

"As I remember it, you missed most of the reception yourself," he said with a chuckle.

It amazed Wally that her grandfather remembered this and infuriated her that he laughed — as if there were room for humor in this matter, as if it were even relevant that she'd gotten her funeral clothes dirty in the yard. She glared at him.

"He also came and picked up a few of his things from your apartment. He was just an acquaintance renting a room while the war was on. It was perfectly natural for him to return home once the war ended."

"But we were close. He was part of my family. How could he just leave?"

"He certainly wasn't part of your family. Why are you so interested in him?"

Wally thought about their mornings, the way he'd helped her with her homework. She could still picture his hand gripping a yellow pencil, the black hairs on his knuckles, the small but bold, masculine handwriting so evenly spaced it looked like it was written using graph paper. Why hadn't he at least sought her out to say farewell when he came to pack his things?

"Even if he wasn't involved, I still want to know what really happened to Mother. People don't just die. There has to be a reason."

"Come here, Wally," Waldo said, and he drew her toward him and took her hands in his. "Your mother is gone. She died of natural causes. You know what I think? This isn't about your mother. It's about you. You've grown out of Wonder Woman and decided to become the next Nancy Drew. But the truth of the matter is, your mother wasn't murdered, and you can't bring her back. Dredging up the past isn't going to make you feel any better."

Finally, Wally gave in. She bent over his wheelchair, awkwardly embracing him, and after a long moment she asked softly, "Why do you build those models anyway, Waldo?"

His face softened. That was the kind of question he'd hoped to hear. Losing Stella was even harder for Wally than for the rest of them, he imagined. He sometimes wished she didn't look so much like her mother. It was a constant reminder that his daughter was gone. Then again there were moments when it brought him joy to see bits of Stella lurking in her daughter, that full mouth and those piercing eyes, even if Wally's were behind eyeglass lenses.

"Well, I'll tell you. This one is the *Indianapolis.* She delivered the Little Boy — that was the first A-bomb — to Tinian, where the *Enola Gay* took off, but she never made it back. I'm trying to get this damned gun turret on straight, see? It was here on the bow where the Nip torpedo smacked into her, on her return from Tinian. Then another one got her on the starboard side. She didn't just sink, though. It took the Navy five days to get to her. Those boys lived on for five days, in shark-infested waters. It wasn't Japs that killed them, it was the sharks. Three hundred U.S. servicemen. Now that's a drama for you. That's the kind of thing that can happen in a war. You personally help save the whole damned

world from Fascism, and then you're torpedoed, and your ship is abandoned, nobody
rescues you, and you're eaten by a godfor-
saken shark. The boys on this ship were
heroes, Wally.

"What I'm working on, when I do this,
is . . . Well, I'm not thinking about myself,
or my own sorrows. I'm getting away from
self-pity. What I'm interested in here is history. The men of the *Indianapolis* died for
all of us. I'm showing my appreciation by
documenting that. Now run along, sweet
Wally, and leave me to my battle cruiser."

22
THE TRAVELING SALESMAN PROBLEM

"Imagine a traveling salesman," said Bill Niederman to the blur of young, mostly clean-shaven faces before him. There were just a few young women and two bohemians with beards. Seventy-five potential stars, seventy-five potential dropouts. His job at the outset of each semester was to make them believe that advanced math was exciting, and hard as he might try, he knew from long exposure to college students that it wouldn't work for at least half of any given classroom.

"Or imagine a bread delivery truck. Or an Army quartermaster's unit. Take anyone who has to make a trip with many stops, and for whom fuel and time are of the essence. The question is how you determine the most efficient route between those stops. Well, I'll tell you, that problem is still waiting to be solved. If we had worked out a simple formula for solving it, millions of gallons of gasoline could have been saved in the war. Rationing might not even have been necessary. Just imagine how much more quickly we might have defeated the Axis and how many lives might not have been lost. Now, turn to page twenty-three. We'll begin by reviewing the basics. Who can tell me what a differential equation is?"

For Bill Niederman, returning to Rutgers after his wartime post at Columbia had been less a disappointment than a relief. Of course, he wouldn't have minded being transferred to Los Alamos, especially after Stella, but he hadn't been of such great importance. The problems he'd been working on had been solved at least once before he'd even seen them. He was just a safety, really, a backup, because they certainly weren't going to trust any essential calculation to a single man. He'd known that, more or less, all along, but still, that work had given him such energy, such a sense of power and purpose. He had believed in himself and America and the power of the weapon they were working toward to save the world from evil.

Then Stella had said, just a few days before her death, "Oh, Christ, Bill. I've figured it out. You were on the Manhattan Project. Weren't you?"

He'd been so proud, all along — and especially after the bombs were dropped. They had ended the war! Ended the war with their minds, saving the lives of countless thousands of American soldiers. He'd been so proud until he looked at her, and then something sank down inside him and he saw the other side: They had unleashed a terrible force on the world. In the years since, he had gotten used to this unpatriotic feeling of shame, but he'd never become inured to it.

"You made love to me at night after spending your days inventing a new way to kill hundreds of thousands of people at once?" she had said.

Of course he knew Stella was the odd one — *everyone* cheered the bombing of Japan, in spite of the civilian casualties — but a part of him agreed with her. She was like a Siren: He couldn't help but agree with everything she said or did. Something in him withered and was paralyzed when she died. He was left alive but somehow incapable of joy.

Back in New Jersey, he was rigorous to the point of being ruthless with his students. When his grading and class preparation were done, he spent his time working on the old mathematical puzzle that he always used to lead his first lecture of the year: the Traveling Salesman Problem.

How do you win a war? he had asked himself, time and again, since the war had ended. By killing hundreds of thousands of people. But that was a very bad means. He'd been trained to worry about means; he'd been trained to solve problems. There must be a better way. At some point it had dawned on him that solving the Salesman Problem was the alternate route to victory, the peaceful way to win the war that he'd been dreaming of ever since Stella died. If only routing and logistics had been the things that the best minds of all the great nations had bent their heads over, instead of mass destruction, the war could have ended far sooner, with far fewer casualties. Everyone knew that campaigns and even wars had been *lost* because of insufficient matériel, so why couldn't a war actually be won in a corollary manner — by the wise apportionment of fuel through perfectly efficient routing? Maybe it could have been. If only they'd tried.

He wasn't sure if it was working on the Manhattan Project that had turned him into a pacifist or having Stella, the only woman he'd ever really loved, disapprove of that work. All he knew was that he'd been a happy warmonger once, and now he was a deeply unhappy believer in peace.

Life with Louise in New Jersey couldn't have been more different from the whirlwind of his war years with Stella. It was simple, predictable, and utterly uncontroversial. Without his weekdays in Manhattan and Brooklyn, it was sometimes boring, but he supposed boring was good for the children. As it turned out, his life was mostly about the children. Doing homework with them, going to their games and concerts. Sol played clarinet with some talent, and Gus, the younger one, was a math whiz, like his father, and an athlete, like his mother. Bill transformed himself from a mostly absent father to a prototypical suburban dad: groundskeeper of the family lawn and griller of the weekend beef. Sundays, he passed from morning to dusk on the fields at the county park, throwing baseballs or cheering his boys on, if a bit more sedately than most of the other men, while Louise used her day off to play paddle tennis.

He was grateful, every now and then, that his children and their lives were so far from Wally Baker's. He didn't want to think about her, because when he did, he missed her, and he knew he had no right to meddle in her or Rudy's life, both of which must certainly be complicated enough already.

He'd seen Rudy Baker, once, from the corner of his eye, at the Harvard Club, still dressed in Navy blue. Seen him and then ducked into a bathroom to avoid being seen himself. He was afraid, he supposed, of inadvertently showing his grief. He was also concerned about what Rudy might do. He didn't know how much Rudy or the Wallaces knew, but it seemed safer to keep his distance. Eventually, he actually gave up the Harvard Club because of it.

"But, Bill," Louise complained, a few years after everything had happened, when she wanted to eat there before they saw the new hit show *Kiss Me, Kate,* "how could you? You're a Harvard man! I always liked it there. Now we have to go to some restaurant."

"Never mind, Louise," he told her. "There are plenty of places to eat in New York. It wasn't worth the dues, to use it once or twice a year."

Louise still wanted a third child, a girl, but certain things must occur, after all, to create a pregnancy. And anyway, the boys were in middle school, he reminded her. The gap would be too great.

One day in the winter of 1949, Louise gave up her little notion of having a daughter and went in for a tubal ligation. She was hoping that Bill would return to her, and to her bed, if he didn't fear having another child. When the surgeon encountered a sizable fibroid, it fell to Bill to give the go-ahead to remove it. One thing led to another, as things do, and the couple of anticipated snips became a hysterectomy.

It was hard for Louise, naturally. She wasn't yet forty. It changed her, in more than just one way. Afterward, she didn't crave her husband's affections so much anymore, which came as a relief to both of them.

23
THE ANT LION

"It's lunacy! Who would build a highway on the edge of a cliff?" bellowed Waldo when the city announced its plans to put a cantilevered thoroughfare right through their and the adjoining properties, obliterating gardens and warehouses alike.

He shouted about it at the meeting of the city council, which he attended despite all the white marble stairs he had to ascend on his crutches. "There's plenty of flat terrain nearby!" He grumbled about it at the dinner table to Gigi and Wally and in the kitchen to Loretta, but there was nothing he could do to stop it.

Gigi hissed and fumed about it rather than bellowed, but she was equally up in arms. Her father had bought the lot on the Heights so that he and her mother would always have a view of the bridge he'd helped to build. When she was a child, he'd told her the bridge was a remedy for his soul:

Seeing its height uplifted him when he felt low, and remembering the men who'd died in its construction humbled him whenever he began to feel proud.

"I'll be damned if I'll let the very people I've doctored for all these years take my view from me," she told Loretta, "or spoil it with a highway and all the racket a highway makes."

They felt righteous in their claim to their own land, but the vast majority of Brooklynites, whose yards were smaller affairs, overhung by wash lines on screeching pulleys, had no sympathy for Gigi Wallace and her terraced garden. Everyone, it turned out, was for the Brooklyn-Queens Connecting Highway but the Wallaces and a few other families whose yards were similarly condemned. It simply wasn't a local matter, the argument went; it was about the metropolis, its connection to the rest of the state, the nation. The city would have its new highway at the cost of Gigi's apple tree and Wally's stomping ground. The public would get a promenade built on top of the triple-cantilevered structure — bottom level for the northbound cars, center for the south, and the upper one paved with asphalt octagons and fenced in by wrought-iron railings for the strolling pleasure of lovers and ladies with prams. The Wallaces would get only the right to select the plantings in the narrow strip of parkland that separated their remaining patch of yard from the new structure.

The day it happened was hazy and warm. The Wallaces watched out the rear windows as men with a crane and wrecking ball came and, with a few well-placed blows, collapsed the bottom of the hill. The old fence and its stovepipe post went down. The lawn fell out from under the things that had been left upon it: a peeling green wheelbarrow, an old wooden bench, and a perfectly good hoe that Wally had meant to bring up to the toolshed. The Wallaces' backyard had always been hollow after all. The soil fell into the cavernous vaults of the warehouse below, which had been emptied of coffee and cocoa the month before. The coffee would be going to New Jersey, now, the cocoa to Red Hook. All the yards along Columbia Heights went down like that, one after another, in a span of just a few weeks. Then a new set of earthmoving vehicles came to shape and buttress the cliffside.

The ants of the nest that had spawned both Planet Ant and Antland were mostly out foraging. They wouldn't find their ways home. Their nursery was scattered, their ungainly queen was briefly stranded on a gnarled, uptwisting azalea root, then snatched up by a robin pecking amongst the debris.

As Gigi watched her beloved yard destroyed, she thought of Stella standing at the fence in the lower yard, looking out, dreaming, just as she herself had done as a girl and then a young woman. She imagined her parents standing there for the very first time, looking north past the newly planted azaleas, which must have been tiny, then, and out at the bridge. She and two sisters had been wooed on the bench beneath the apple tree, and Stella, she knew, had first kissed Billy Galt amongst those azaleas. She had come back up the hill glowing and after he left had told her mother all about it. Billy Galt had been such a catch for her. She had been so happy. And they were closer, then, mother and daughter, before all of Stella's troubles.

It had been the beginning of Stella's end, when that young man died, Gigi thought. She'd never quite gotten beyond it, never been as glorious or happy again. Gigi had tried too hard to force her out of her grief, and Stella had hated her for that, for what Stella saw as her lack of sympathy — but Stella had been wrong. Gigi understood loss, she just had a different way of managing it. She wished she'd been able to convey some of her strength to Stella, then, and in the decade after. She asked herself what she could have done differently, to change Stella's fate, and wondered for the thousandth time what the final straw had been for Stella, that V-J Day. As Wally stood beside her, silently weeping over the destruction, Gigi Wallace renewed her resolve to keep her granddaughter from ever knowing how her mother had died. She would protect this abandoned girl from her mother's mistake if it was the last thing she did.

They were on the verge of a different era, it seemed to Gigi, a less gracious time. America had won the war, and she and Waldo had outlived their own daughter. For what? To see the world fall apart. From the Communists in Russia to her own backyard, it seemed everywhere, now, there was trouble and encroachment.

Wally and Ham stood scowling at the edge of the work zone and watched their world dwindle. They didn't actually see it, when the ants were scattered, when the tunnels collapsed, when the queen was eaten and the eggs and larvae crushed. They couldn't get anywhere close enough, what with the backhoes, cranes, and dozers, and the men in their coveralls waving flags and yelling, and the clouds of dust rising up. But they knew.

"I hope they get bitten," said Ham.

"To the ants, they're alien invaders. No worse than we were," Wally said doubtfully, looking out at the construction workers.

"But we never killed the whole colony," said Ham.

"In a way you could say we sort of saved it. Planet Ant's ants are the only survivors," Wally said.

"Their whole society has been annihilated," Ham intoned. "All that remains are the ants who were abducted long ago and taken away in the strange glass spaceship. Now, these survivors will set forth to explore the universe and establish a new home world."

Wally laughed. "You want to set them free, plant them out here in the yard after all the construction is done?"

"We could. We're their gods."

"Or the superheroes that helped them to survive."

"Yeah, *superheroes.* But, Wally, have you ever thought about how we've never gotten mating flights or new queens being born in our colonies? We might have a queen, and she might lay eggs, but a real colony produces several queens every spring."

"So what does that mean?" asked Wally.

"If you look at it in the long term, they're still goners. Their line will die out."

"Maybe a few workers carrying larvae will manage to establish a new nest, raise a new queen. Right?"

"Yeah, maybe. And maybe Wonder Woman's real."

Wally's face fell. She didn't like it when Ham teased her.

For a minute Ham thought he'd made Wally cry, but then she broke out laughing. She knew there was no Wonder Woman, after all. That was the good thing about Wally, he thought: She acted like a sissy sometimes — she was just a girl after all — but overall, she was pretty tough.

Wally and Ham boarded the uptown IRT together, bound for West Seventy-Ninth Street, and walked east, to the museum.

The light was on in room 46.

Ham knocked, and they heard Dr. Somersby — who had now received his doctorate — clear his throat, then call for them to come in.

"Good, good, it's my favorite pupils! You're going to be fascinated by what I've got for you two, today."

"Army ants?" asked Ham. He was always begging for Dr. Somersby to teach them about army ants.

"No, no, nothing as sensational as that."

"Dr. Somersby, they dug up the part of my yard where the black ants' nest was. They're putting in a highway," Wally said.

"Oh dear. What a pity, but I must say it's fitting. Today we're not going to examine ants but ant predators. Not people, bulldozers, ant-eaters, or even chimpanzees, mind you, but other insects that manage to invade ant nests without detection, which is quite a feat."

"Why don't the sentries fight them off and remove them?"

"Why indeed. But let's start at the beginning, shall we? We'll look at *Myrmecophila acervorum* and *Myrmecophila oregonensis* — two ant crickets — highly specialized creatures to be sure. I also have some ant lions, otherwise known as doodlebugs, for you. Interesting behavior *and* morphology. Some of these fellows have mandibles the size of earwig pincers! If we have time I may show you one or two mimetic spiders that resemble but do not actually prey on ants. Now, let's take a look."

He took from his pocket an index card,

which had a series of numbers and letters printed neatly across it, and he consulted it as he moved between the specimen storage drawers, eventually pulling out five wide wooden trays and setting them on the large lab table by the room's southern window, where he did most of his taxonomical work, because good light was so essential.

"Ant crickets manage to live and reproduce inside ant colonies, preying on eggs and even feasting on regurgitated pap begged from their hosts. Now how do you suppose these critters pull that off?"

He gestured to a row of tiny, plump mounted crickets with long, downward-swooping antennae, urging, "Take a close look at the first one — *Myrmecophila acervorum!*" and handing Ham a large magnifying glass.

"Can we put one under the microscope?" asked Ham, after a few minutes of quiet observation. "Maybe the similarities are in the details."

"Good thinking, yes, very good. But first let Wallace take a look at it with the glass, won't you, son?"

Wally took off her glasses and huffed on them, then polished the lenses on the hem of her dress.

"Maybe it's something we can't see, like

282

smell," she said, at last, having been completely unable to discern anything the least bit antlike about the cricket.

"It's something we can't readily see, that much you both have right. It's behavior. It's the way the cricket moves and even how it feels to the ants it parasitizes, when they touch. They beg regurgitated food from foragers, quite successfully. The damnedest thing you ever saw, really. Listen to this — from the *Mittelungen der Schweizerischen entomologischen Gesellschaft.*" At this point he snatched up an earmarked copy of a densely printed journal and began to read to the children in rapid-fire German, pausing only when Wally started to giggle.

"What's that, did that strike you as funny, somehow?"

"Dr. Somersby . . ."

"Oh, dear. Of course you two don't speak German. But you must learn it, you know, the bad business of war notwithstanding. It's still the most essential language for advanced scholarship. Are you taking it in school, I hope?"

"I'm taking French," Wally said.

"Me too," said Ham, "but my mother was German." He thought of the picture Loretta had given him of his mother, of her light hair and eyes.

"Is that so?" asked Dr. Somersby.

"I never knew her."

Dr. Somersby reached for another reference work, then let his hand drop. It was in German as well. Instead he told them, without further quotations, about how the ant lion hunted with a trap leaving marks in the sand that were easy for human eyes to spot but eluded the notice of the ants they preyed on. He went over the various ways the ant cricket mimics the movements and behaviors of various ant species. He brought out the curious mimetic spider. He drew a breath, amazed and gratified that the two children, so different, so young, had sat still for so long.

"If you're not tired of ant predators," he continued, "I'd like to introduce you to the art of documenting what you are seeing." He set each child up with a specimen. Wally chose the ant lion and Ham the ant cricket. Then he gave them each several sheets of paper and a fine-tipped ink pen.

"Don't worry about size or accuracy at first, but try to include every feature you can perceive. Every detail is essential! If you miss something, your work is useless — it might as well be a different species — because it may create confusion in your mind, or the mind of anyone who sees what you've drawn."

"So, can we draw now?" asked Ham.

Dr. Somersby smiled. "By all means. Draw. I'll be right here if you have any questions."

Wally brought her renderings to Dr. Somersby as soon as they were recognizably insects, seeking praise and instruction, but Ham held his drawing board at an angle that hid his work, and kept at it for over an hour, often hardly seeming to move his fingers for minutes on end. That's how fine the strokes of his pen were.

"Well, what have you got there, Ham?" asked Dr. Somersby, at last.

"Nothing, it's not finished," muttered Ham, avoiding eye contact, except with his subject.

He tried to put it away without letting Wally or Dr. Somersby see, at the end, but Vernon Somersby was too curious to allow that.

"Come on, Dr. S., leave me alone," protested Ham as the picture was gently pried from his hands and the covering sheet of vellum lifted by Dr. Somersby. What Vernon Somersby and Wally saw was unexpected: an ant lion so meticulously rendered, so accurate in its line, proportion, and detail that Dr. Somersby's jaw slackened. It could have been published in a taxonomical guide. He himself had never had much skill at rendering his subjects, though he'd long used drawing as a tool to teach aspiring entomologists.

"Well," said Dr. Somersby, quietly. "You may have found your calling, young man. This is exquisite."

"Yeah, I don't know," said Ham. "It's just a picture of a creepy crawly. It's not even really finished. No big deal."

But clearly it was. The ungainly ant cricket looked capable of leaping from the paper as Ham had drawn it.

"That's so beautiful, Ham. It's a lot more beautiful that the ant cricket itself."

"Well, that's not hard. It's a bloated little tick of a thing, don't you think? I like the ant lion better — his whole jaw looks like some kind of evil lawn mower."

"Yeah." Wally laughed. Ham seemed to see the insects so much more clearly than she did.

"But honestly, Wally," he said. "I like yours. It's not exactly perfect anatomy, but it's cute."

She smiled, grateful for his kindness, wishing she were better than cute.

After that, it was the main thing they both came for, really: the beautiful light, the quiet, dry room, the calm reassuring drone of Dr. Somersby, and the scratching of their pens on paper. Wally's insects were careful and crowded and not quite to scale. She worked almost too hard to include every part she'd been taught was there, every last detail she was able to notice, and the overall effect was not one of likeness. Ham's illustrations were in another class entirely.

Dr. Somersby appreciated Wally's interest in entomology, but she was just a girl, and he didn't expect her to persist with it. He had begun to have higher hopes for Ham. His drawing skill was based upon exquisite observational ability, and it was the sort of thing that got a young man in the door — that and a talent for exotic travel and cataloging the resulting collections, of course. Ham being a Negro boy and the son of a maid, he wasn't likely to get many of the latter sorts of opportunities, but Vernon Somersby determined to make sure he prospered in the field nonetheless.

24
MOTHBALLS

One morning in the summer before seventh grade, Wally awoke to a horrible embarrassment of stained sheets and underwear that she couldn't conceal from Loretta, despite considerable efforts with shampoo and a nailbrush in the bathroom that adjoined her room. Loretta told Gigi, despite Wally's pleas for privacy, and Gigi decided it was time for Wally to move on from her bugs and tomboyish ways.

She signed Wally up for dancing lessons and, worse yet, began trying to interest her in medicine. Gigi, it turned out, had powerful notions about Wally following the family tradition.

"Come spend a day on the wards with me," Gigi encouraged.

"No, thank you, Gigi," Wally said, as politely as she could.

"Would you like to observe a surgical procedure?" Gigi offered, as if it were a tantalizing opportunity, but Wally demurred.

"Wally, it is your likely profession. I must urge you to take some interest," Gigi finally said. "Once school begins again, you won't have time."

So Wally reluctantly accompanied her grandmother to work the following day, instead of going uptown to work on the pencil sketch of a wood ant soldier that she was creating under Dr. Somersby's tutelage.

"Can you tell Dr. S. I'm sorry, and I'll be back next week?" Wally asked Ham, as though her contribution were essential to the museum's functioning.

"I don't think he'll mind, Wally," Ham said, not mentioning that if she wasn't going to the museum, neither was he. "I just wish Miz Doc wanted to take me to the hospital instead of you. I'd like to see what she does."

Wally found the building and its laboratories and even some of its patients interesting, at first, but she had to gulp down her revulsion at the sight of the very first patient's oozing sores. Like Waldo's, the bedridden old gentleman's legs were useless thanks to polio, and the weight of his own flesh against the footrest of his wheelchair had broken down the skin on the backs of his heels and the sides of his feet.

Gigi and a nurse worked together to scrape the wounds clean, irrigate them, and treat them with a medicated salve. There was a smell of meat. Wally stood as far back as her grandmother would let her.

"His circulation is very poor," Gigi told her out in the hall, once the patient was bandaged and transferred back to his bed for elevation of his limbs. "If we can't keep the pressure off those spots, they won't heal, and he'll lose his foot or the whole lower leg before long."

"Is that going to happen to Waldo?" Wally asked quietly.

"Of course not! First of all, he still has some mobility, and second of all, he has the best of care. Everyone in our household understands the importance of frequently changing his position. We won't *let* it happen."

Wally pictured Waldo, hunched over in his wheelchair for hours on end at his ship models, and wondered.

She felt awkward around Waldo afterward, as if she'd seen a glimpse of his fate, and it was a terrible one.

After the hospital visit, Gigi wanted Wally to sign up for the hospital's volunteer program, and Wally tried it for a couple of Saturdays that fall, but she felt embarrassed in the red and white striped blouse. She didn't especially mind handing out books to sick people, but the most important function of the volunteers was to cheer the patients up, and Wally didn't know what to say to encourage them. Their groans and their gas, their uneaten trays of dinner and their half-open hospital gowns were all too much for her. She glanced away just when she should have been helping out, or being kind.

Finally, she told the nurse supervisor that she needed the time for her studies and brought the news home to Gigi after the fact.

"What? How could you quit something so half in the middle? It's irresponsible. I am just terribly disappointed," Gigi said.

Wally hung her head because she thought it would look better, but she wasn't sorry.

"Aren't there doctors who don't see patients?" she asked. "Scientists? Researchers? Could I help out with something like that?" she asked hopefully, not wanting to disappoint her grandmother but praying to be spared further specimens of human misery.

But what Wally really wanted was to be left to her own devices. What she did in her free time was study ants. Her notebooks from school were full of drawings of ants. What she had to say, if her grandmother offered her a penny for her thoughts, was some curious fact about some species or other of ants. Where she wanted to be was on the subway, headed for the natural history museum and its ants. Gigi pointed out to Wally how all the women in their family — from her own mother, Beatrice, to Gigi herself, to Stella — had been doctors.

"There's such a thing as a doctor of entomology, too, you know," Wally said.

After a while, Gigi Wallace gave up a bit on guiding Wally's career. She simply didn't understand about the bugs or the comics. She'd raised — or helped Loretta to raise — Stella, a radiantly feminine daughter who was not a tomboy in the least. She herself had had only sisters, and all of them had been the dolls-and-tea-parties sort. Practicing a profession was one thing — she knew many thought it masculine — but it didn't give her any experience with how to handle a tomboy. She was, for better or worse, a doctor first, not a natural mother or grandmother. She'd loved the children in her life most when they grew older (the more's the pity that Georgie hadn't gotten a chance to, she often thought). Till then, she decided, Loretta was surely better company for Wally.

And in truth, Wally was so grown-up — thirteen already! — and so busy with school and her bug studies up at the natural history that she didn't really need her grandmother. The child went through a dollar in dimes some weeks — the fare had gone up — just riding the subway to and fro. And that wasn't counting Ham's fares, or the fifty cents a day Gigi paid him to escort Wally up and back.

Wally still had a lot of questions about her mother, but there was no one left to ask. She'd long since exhausted the attic's more obvious storage places, and now took every chance she got to root around in the cellar and various closets' upper shelves. She was hoping to come across some sort of evidence. Evidence of what? she often wondered. It wasn't just the mystery of her mother's early death but her whole life that Wally craved to understand. Where had she worn that sequined cape and dress? Had she ever kept a diary? What about her letters? Wally wanted anything that would make her mother real to her, whole to her, something more than just a fleeting series of images — Stella dancing, Stella laughing, Stella angry, Stella crying, Stella impatient with Wally, once again.

For Wally, then, the old champagne crate at the back of the closet near the music room was a find. It held some ancient ledgers and two black-paged scrapbooks with photos and yellowed clippings, and among them was a picture of her mother, so young, at a party.

She was wearing it.

The cape's glitter showed white against a darker background, as if her mother were somehow electrified. Her face was perfectly in focus. Perfect in every way. Her escort was a young man Wally had never seen before, but it was clear they were hand in hand. It was captioned, "Miss Stella Wallace, last year a Brooklyn Junior League debutante and this year a Long Island College medical student, steps out on the arm of Dr. William Galt, first-year resident and native of Great Neck, Long Island."

Who was William Galt? Wally wondered.

As before, she turned to Waldo for information. Loretta might have been inclined to dole out more details, but she would have gone straight to Gigi and told her Wally was snooping.

There he was, as usual, dressed in one of his elegant silk dressing gowns — the burgundy paisley with the black shawl collar — and a pair of pajama bottoms. He continued to build his model warships to exacting detail up in the music room, and to destroy them just as they had been destroyed in action, despite the fact that he'd been less well, the past few months, chest rattling and sweat coming quickly to his forehead when he tried to walk. He couldn't seem to shake a case of what he somewhat bitterly called the rolling pneumonia. He smelled more of liniments now than of the Brylcreem that used to be his signature. Wally knew Loretta had to lift the once formidable Waldo into and out of his chair these days. She'd heard Loretta say to Gigi that he couldn't dress himself that morning. She pictured Loretta coaxing his limp limbs into the beautiful pajamas, gently easing his aimless fish feet into their velvet slippers with the little ribbons sewn onto the backs of them by Loretta, so they'd stay on. Wally felt a horror, suddenly, that Waldo, too, was going to die. His breath was just a little too shallow, too fast, Wally thought.

"How are you today, Waldo? Are you all right?"

"Damn the polio, damn the pneumonia, I can't cough!" he growled. "Call Loretta to bring me some tea, will you, Wally?"

After Loretta had carried up a tray, Wally asked, "What are you working on, Waldo?"

That usually got him talking, but this time he just gestured at the boat. Wasn't it obvious?

"So, it's a PT boat?"

"Apparently."

"Waldo, I wanted to ask you another question about Mother —"

"I was afraid of that. Can't you please let me be?"

"No, not about how she *died.* Just something about when she was young. I found an old album, and there was a picture of her looking so, so glamorous. She was with a man. William Galt. Who's *William Galt?*"

Waldo began to hawk. Wally heard the phlegm bubble inside him, and waited for that sound of clearance, the moment when the cough had ejected the obstacle to the breath.

"Waldo?"

"Christ almighty, Wallace," he blurted at last, depositing a mouthful of sputum into his handkerchief as he spoke, "where do you come up with these questions?"

"I don't know. I was just wondering. She looked so happy. Was William Galt her boyfriend, *before?* Before Daddy?"

"Ask your grandmother. Leave me out of it."

She didn't ask Gigi, of course. First of all,

Gigi was out, at the clinic, but more important, Wally knew she'd never get any information out of her. Gigi did not believe in allowing her to wallow in the past.

She went to Loretta, who was there, just across the hall, tackling the problem of Waldo's walk-in closet. Not that his closet was messy. Waldo's shoes and suits were immaculately arranged, with dust cloths thrown over them, as if they were merely out of season, but truth was, they had languished since he became ill. Even so, even when a man never wore his clothes, once a year cleaning wasn't enough. She knew it, but she hadn't acted on it. Then the previous day she had swatted a tan, feathery bug that left a mark against the wall, and she'd known she was too late.

"Loretta," Wally said, "can I ask you about Mother? I wanted to know more about her when she was a young woman. I found some old pictures."

"Found old pictures, did you? Then you must've been digging, child, because I know there ain't no old pictures of Stella setting out."

"I was just looking in some old trunks and crates."

Loretta put her hand on her hip and raised her eyebrows. "Wally, Wally, Wally. What we going to do with you, Wally?"

"Come on, Loretta. Tell me. Tell me about William Galt."

"Tell you what: You help me work this closet over for moths, and while we work, we'll just talk? How 'bout that?"

Armed with brushes, a laundry sack, a garbage pail, and the Electrolux, Loretta and Wally went looking for infestation and found it in the form of long silken tubes clinging to several of Waldo's suit lapels, crumbly bits of digested wool in his pants cuffs, and a few live caterpillars still working their way through fabric.

"Now I got you, you bugger," Loretta exclaimed, popping one between her fingers.

"So that picture I saw was when my mother came out?" Wally began.

"Hold tight, I got another one here!"

The tiny moths were mightier than all of history, it seemed. Wally couldn't get Loretta away from them.

"Oh, Lord," she said, every time she found more webbing or a crusty spot that turned to a hole when she touched it. "Ruined!" There must have been a whiff of sweat in every jacket lining, crumbs lodged in every cuff, a stain on every lapel.

"It seems like they always eat away the fronts of things, too, like they want to ruin them," Wally observed. "Why does that make sense?"

"Well," Loretta answered, "the front is where people spill food on theyselves. It's the food that attracts the moths."

"Where do they come from, the moths?"

"Where do *ants* come from? And how do the ants always find the sugar? I don't know. *Nature.* It's their nature. I thought that's what you're going to find out for me, one of these days, with all that science that you do. Isn't that right?"

Wally shrugged and fell silent, and it was only then that, as Loretta bagged a riddled cashmere sweater, she finally talked.

"Your mother was in love with that boy, Billy Galt. She was going to marry him. But he died. That's who he is."

Wally looked at her, silently asking her to go on, but Loretta wouldn't say any more.

"Does all that have anything to do with, with Mother dying?"

"No, Wally, it ain't got nothing to do with that. It's not anything but ancient history. Now, go read your comic books or play with your ants, or something else useful, awright, sugar?"

In the morning, Loretta returned to the closet and took out every remaining undam-

299

aged piece of clothing and either brushed it well or put it aside for washing in hot water. She scrubbed down the walls and the floors and the drawers and strewed them with cedar chips and mothballs.

The following day, she turned with apprehension to Gigi's wardrobe. There was one bad drawer, in it two irremediable paisley scarves that had probably been brought back from their honeymoon in India, Loretta thought. Beautiful things that Gigi Wallace had barely worn, but apparently just enough to take a scent upon them, a smudge of hair oil or jam: bait. And so Loretta sanitized the closet in its entirety, brushing and washing, ironing and steaming. It was a good week before she was finished putting everything back together and the last folded and ironed items had been tucked away in tissue paper and lavender.

Then she thought again and decided you couldn't win a war if you were going to get fussy about fumes, so she went out to Woolworth's and bought a half dozen more boxes of mothballs, too.

That night, Waldo had to be moved to the hospital. He simply couldn't catch his breath. They didn't put him back in the iron lung, but there were suctioning procedures that were necessary. It wasn't a terribly long stay, just a fortnight, but he came back weaker.

25
A CALLING

Waldo's pneumonia lingered all through the winter of 1950. It acted up again the following spring, in a long, fearful bout that demanded another hospitalization. On Sundays, Wally went to visit him, but she had trouble focusing her gaze. He had a tube going up into his nose, which was horrible enough that she couldn't look him in the face. She mostly kept her eyes to the floor. There were so many things she didn't want to catch sight of, but worst was the vat attached to the wall behind his bed by a shining chrome bracket: a calibrated jar of blood and mucus. She wondered if Georgie had been hooked up to something like that when he was sick, and if it was really the death sentence it looked like. Wally swallowed and smiled, stared at the linoleum, left quickly. There was really no point visiting the sick if your distress at their illness made them feel worse, she thought, but Gigi disagreed. She insisted that Wally go at least once a week.

Even back home, Waldo required occasional suction with hoses and black rubber bulbs. He just couldn't cough it up the way a person ought to. There were nurses to help in the mornings, but they weren't always there when he needed them. Gigi did it. Loretta did it. Wally assisted them now and then by taking the bedpan away, holding her breath and closing her eyes. She wished she could have closed her ears so as not to hear the sloshing.

Wally was surprised at how much Ham helped, too. In fact, he wanted to help with exactly everything she wanted to avoid. It wasn't that he loved Waldo so much. It wasn't just about helping his mother or sparing Wally the ordeal. It wasn't just some Boy Scoutly virtue, assumed for the purpose of earning badges. He seemed to find meaning in doing the things that others found hard.

That summer, when Ham was about to be a senior and Wally was going into eighth grade, Waldo died. People said it must have been a relief to him. He hadn't been able to do much but suffer that last half year. Wally felt an ache, a hollowness, but she didn't cry much. It seemed to her if she started, she'd never stop, so she made very sure not to.

"Hamilton," Gigi said, the day after the funeral, "would you do something for me? Would you take a morning this week and clear out the music room? Throw out all the models, the wood and supplies, all that? I can't bear to see it anymore."

Ham nodded and said, "Yes, ma'am, Miz Doc," the way he always did when she asked something of him, but when he undertook the project, he didn't throw the models away. He carefully wrapped and labeled and boxed them and carried them up to the attic, where he found room among the old trunks and crates of unwanted dishes and gray felt bags of rattling tarnished silver plate.

To everyone's surprise but possibly Ham's — because he had sat with and talked with Waldo so much more than anyone in that last period — Waldo had made a codicil to his will at the end, stipulating that money be set aside to pay for Ham to attend medical school, should he choose to.

"That's such a good idea," said Wally, when she heard about it, from Ham. "I hadn't thought about needing to pay for school."

"He was a good man," said Loretta, when Gigi told her. "Bless his soul."

"But it wasn't necessary, as you must know. I've always told you I will provide a college education for Hamilton."

"Of course. But bless him anyway. It shows he had faith in Ham going far. Medical school's a long way off, but the fact Doc Wallace set it out like that, it gives Ham something to aspire to."

"Do you want to be a doctor, Hamilton?" Gigi asked him. "I hadn't been aware, although I am grateful you were such an attentive nurse this past year."

"I don't know," said Ham. "I'm not too sure about that. I did talk to Dr. Waldo about it a couple of times, and I think he wanted me to. I've also been talking to Dr. Somersby. He wants me to apply to college and study biology."

"Well, either way, I suppose a bug man and a people person both start out with the same background." Gigi smiled. "It's all about life."

Ham stopped going to the museum with Wally that year. She was finally deemed old enough to ride the subway alone, and when offered the choice, Ham elected to spend more time with his cronies, sitting on

305

stoops, smoking cigarettes and sometimes more. For the last year, Ham'd been going with Wally mostly for the pocket money. He also dropped out of scouting. He had earned the badges required for him to make Eagle Scout, but instead of beginning the service project that would complete the requirements, he quit.

Now, when Ham drew, he didn't draw bugs or animals; he drew warships, warplanes, and sometimes frightening dragons with their snouts engulfed in smoke and flames. He didn't have much time for Wally. Wally was the ant nut, now, not him. Without her to feed Planet Ant, it would have died out.

What Ham Walker was thinking a great deal about, in those days, was his father. He thought about the real father he had never known and the uncle who might have been his adoptive father, if he'd stayed. But he'd left Loretta alone with Ham instead, and went fifteen years without so much as writing or calling, much less coming back to visit him. Ham thought about the stupidity of being shot down by a Jap just before the armistice. On several afternoons, when no one was at the Wallace house but him, he spent hours on end calling various long-distance operators and asking for listings for Washington Walker. His real father. There was no reason to assume he was dead. Twice, he'd been put through to numbers — one somewhere in Oregon, one in Baltimore — but he hadn't been able to speak when the phone was answered. Neither voice had sounded like a father, not that he knew what that might sound like. He'd pressed his finger down on the button before he said something foolish.

And then one day, before anyone had a chance to talk him out of it, he went and signed certain papers.

"There's boys dying in the service, still, you know," his mother shouted. "Off in the middle of nowhere, in Asia. How you know you won't be stationed there?"

"I guess I probably will be, Mama."

There was all the danger and none of the glory of the war in Europe. Loretta, the Wallaces, Dr. Somersby, and Wally all argued, shouted, and begged him not to go, but it was too late. He had a month before his eighteenth birthday, five weeks before he was due to board a train for Fort Bragg.

The day before he left, Wally wouldn't come out of her room.

She hadn't cried that hard when her mother died. Not for lack of feeling then, but she was older now. She knew better what loss was.

Ham came up and banged on the door, but the old lock held fast.

Instead of saying good-bye, Wally shouted, "I hate you," through the keyhole, not knowing if she'd ever see him again. Or even if she did, whether he would be the same person.

■ ■ ■ ■

III
PHEROMONES

■ ■ ■ ■

26
LETTERS

"Dear Mr. Niederman," Wally began. She was fourteen years old, and nearly half her life had passed since he vanished — along with her mother — but she still wondered about him. Nothing anyone had ever said about her mother's death added up, and sometimes she imagined that Bill Niederman really was the x, the mysterious factor that would solve the equation, if only she could figure it out. "I believe that you are a murderer."

She smeared the blue ink and tore the page in half.

Dear Mr. Niederman,
Where did you go, when my mother died, and why didn't you ever

Fold, tear.

Dear —

Just as she was about to draw the first stroke of the *M,* she lifted her pen, thought a minute, and lowered it again, a whole different letter in mind.

Dear Ham,
Since you left, I have been feeding the last survivors of Planet Ant, even though you never asked me to. I guess you just figured I would. You probably didn't expect Loretta to do it. I would like to know why you decided to join the army. Why would you want to shoot people and get shot at instead of staying here with your family, which includes me, I think. There aren't exactly Nazis over there in Korea, are there? I am not so upset about Communists as some people. They seem to me to have similar ideas to ants. I wouldn't want to be one, but I'm not afraid of them. So Ham, I am quite mad at you. And worried. Although my father made it through all of WWII without getting killed, you might not be as lucky since you are not on a battleship. Which would really stink. So don't get killed, okay?

Love,
Wally

That one she folded in thirds and tucked in an envelope. Loretta had the military address written down in Gigi's telephone book, she knew. Wally slid the metal pointer on the cover to the letter *H* and pushed the lever, causing the lid to pop open, revealing the entries for *H* through *J*. When she'd addressed her envelope, she went back to the table and attacked another sheet of paper.

Dear Mr. Niederman,
I believe that you must know things about my mother that no one else does, as you were an adult who lived with us up to the day she died.

Tear.
"What you wasting all that paper on, Wally?" Loretta called from the kitchen.
"Just trying to write letters, and sometimes they come out stupid."
"Who you writing to?"
"Just Ham."
Loretta looked at her.
"And, um, Mr. Niederman."
"What? Why you want to write him?"
Wally shrugged. "Well, I was thinking of writing Ham, first, and it made me think of Mr. Niederman because they both just left, without warning. I want to write them both

313

and ask them why. So I wrote Ham. That was pretty easy. Not so easy to write Mr. Niederman, though, because I was only little, then, when I knew him. I want Mr. Niederman to tell me more about Mother. He was friends with her. He knew her better than I did. It's not fair. I'm old enough to ask him questions if I want."

"So why you keep tearing them up?"

"It doesn't seem quite right, no matter what I say. And I don't really have his address. How much does it cost to send a letter to Korea, anyway, Loretta?"

"It's not extra, like that, when you send a letter to the Army. Let's just go get you a regular stamp. That's all you need."

The afternoon light in the Wallace kitchen was as bright as ever, in those first weeks after Ham's battalion shipped out to Seoul, but the gloom of Wally and Loretta made it seem like evening. The light came in and glanced off the oilcloth table cover, but the chickens and blue-bells didn't shine like they used to. As fall descended, the sun slid lower in the sky. It seemed to rain all the time. After school, Wally came in and found the house dim. She had to turn on the lights to do her homework.

One afternoon, she was craning over her lab notebook, carefully plotting the results of an experiment she had done at school. They were determining the melting point of naphthalene. The report wasn't due for several days, but Wally adored using the lab book, with its graph paper and carbon sheets. She would sketch her equipment, draw her methods in the form of a flow-chart, or diagram the relevant molecules, generally adding whatever visual element she could to embellish the reports.

Loretta watched Wally work as she leaned into her rag. Was the porcelain of the sink getting older and more porous, or was it just her? she wondered, and then turned on the radio. The first sound to play was the dull thunder of big guns, and she jumped. Wally and Loretta still listened to the mystery shows and soap operas, and avoided the news. Loretta feared the war reports every single time one came on, even though she didn't know enough about where Ham actually was to know if the bad news might turn out to be *her* bad news.

"Lima Bean," said Wally, "switch over to NBC so we can hear *The Saint* instead. Isn't it almost time?"

"Sure is," said Loretta, her hand already on the dial, and static replaced the guns.

Wally continued her visits to Dr. Somersby

at the natural history museum, and grew more serious about entomology when she entered high school. She skipped joining the art club and glee club in favor of spending two afternoons a week at the museum. Over vacations and on holidays, she spent even more time there, and Dr. Somersby put her to work on real projects, alongside actual college and graduate students. The museum could have used a dozen or more young entomologists to identify, catalog, and mount the tens of thousands of unsorted field specimens that lay waiting in crates in the storage area, and Wally had become a reliable member of his team.

In school, Wally thrived in chemistry, then aced biology and her math classes. Her grandmother was pleased. She was receiving the proper foundation to go into medicine. In the fall of her ninth-grade year, she suddenly grew tall, like her father, and her face began to resemble her mother's, not that she saw that herself. It was the others — the people who'd known Stella — who found the resemblance so uncanny.

Planet Ant's queen stopped laying eggs that winter and died. The colony began to wither, and Wally didn't bother to try to repopulate it. By the end of the school year, the only ants she had much to do with were the dead ones in Dr. Somersby's collections.

Through it all, she never stopped thinking about what had happened to her mother, never stopped missing her. Once a year, on or close to the day her mother had died, she ritually sorted through every trunk in her grandparents' attic and combed through the contents of each dresser drawer. She'd never found a proper answer to the question *why,* not even the shadow of a clue, and she no longer really expected to find anything, but she still did it. She was driven to, as if by the circling of the earth around the sun.

Then, that anniversary, she found a hand-written card stuck in the crack in the back of a drawer:

William B. Niederman
Department of Mathematics
Rutgers University
New Brunswick, New Jersey

She remembered his strong blocky hand-writing, and all the sudden she remembered him vividly. She went for a piece of stationery and a pen.

"Dear Mr. Niederman," she wrote,

You might remember me from the year 1945, when you lived in Brooklyn, at my house, with me and my mother. I am fifteen years old now, and I have some questions I would like to ask you about my mother and that time. Please write me back and let me know if we could meet or if you would agree to correspond with me.

Sincerely,
Wallace Baker

She almost set her letter on the silver tray where outgoing mail awaited the postman, then decided against it and slipped the letter into her bag. She could mail it from the box on the corner just as well. Gigi or Loretta was all too likely to flip through the envelopes on that tray before giving them to the mailman, mostly just to check that all the letters were properly addressed and stamped, but that name, that address might raise a red flag.

Wally kept the letter in her bag for weeks, then months, eventually turning it into a bookmark for her physics textbook and covering the back of it with jottings and notes. She wrote Ham often, and mailed those letters, but the letter to Mr. Niederman had been only an exercise, she realized. She actually had nothing to say to him, no idea what to ask.

■ ■ ■ ■

And then, somewhere south of the Thirty-Eighth Parallel, a shell exploded, and thirty or forty died. A Jeep happened to shield Ham, so all he got was a legful of shrapnel, but he watched his friends fly into the air before him. He lay on a gurney beside a fellow private named Milo Twombley, whose guts were rent, and he listened to him die.

The telegram Loretta received contained very little information. It was the envelope itself that caused the shriek Loretta let out when the messenger delivered it. Wally and Loretta were both in tears as Loretta slit it open. Loretta was already thinking about her scrapbook as she unfolded the message, about the page she would create, memorializing her son.

But then the telegram itself said something so much smaller: It said, "leg wound" and "stable" and "transferred to a military hospital in Kanoaka, Japan." It was the best news they could have gotten. So Loretta *would* create a page, but a page devoted to a Purple Heart.

Ham wrote to Wally about it, while he was convalescing, and though considerable portions of the six-page letter were blacked out, the description of what happened after the explosion was not. The way it worked, he explained, was this: You got a dose of morphine, enough to last four hours. If you were still alive when someone got back around to looking at you, you could have another. Except that somehow, if you were going to die for sure, you were so low in the triage that you never got your second dose. That was what happened to his friend Twombley. "They were ugly, his last few hours, after his first and only shot of morphine wore off. Twombley was a lousy hand at poker, which was fine with me. He was also one of the three men in our platoon who never said the word *nigger.* I would have given a lot to be able to stop his pain. I wished I still had the second ampoule of morphine that I got. I'd rather Twombley'd had it, but it didn't work that way. By the time I came around to noticing anything again, Twombley was just slack, dead."

Ham was at the hospital in Japan for a month and would be eligible for an honorable discharge a short time after that. They were all waiting to hear when he'd be home when Loretta received a long letter from him, which she read aloud to Gigi and Wally at the kitchen table.

Ham had signed on to be trained as a

medic and to do another tour of duty. In subsequent letters, he described his training, most of it on the battlefield, and included considerably too much detail for Wally and Loretta. His first field surgery was the disarticulation of the elbow of a peasant woman whose forearm had been shattered by a grenade.

"This don't make sense," said Loretta. "Doesn't sound like him."

"It sort of does to me," Wally said.

"What do you know?" said Gigi, smiling. "He's been bitten by the bug."

"But he's staying in the combat zone. It's awful. It's not regular medicine. What good is that gonna do him?"

"It's medicine, all right. Combat medicine, so of course there's more trauma, more surgery."

"They're not even calling it a war yet," Wally said.

"What's the difference between killing people and killing people?" Loretta asked.

"Ham's saving people, not killing them," said Wally.

"That's right. And we'll pop him straight into medical school when he returns, Loretta," said Gigi. "Don't you worry."

"I don't know what's he doing, staying over there, when he doesn't have to," muttered Loretta. "Fool boy."

"He's found a calling, Loretta. He's going to make something of himself. This will end well, Loretta. I know it will."

"It might, Miz Doc. It might not."

You idiot was all that Wally could think. *How could you, Ham? You idiot.*

27
UPTOWN / DOWNTOWN

It wasn't until Wally was a senior, already looking forward to her freshman year at Barnard College, that her father, now a rear admiral, came home for good.

To Wally, he felt more like a stranger than a father. He wore strange little socks with toes around the house and wanted rice with every meal.

"I'm sure he's done great good over there, really," Gigi Wallace said to Wally and Loretta in the kitchen the night of his first dinner back, after the admiral had retired to the third floor, where he would be staying until he set up his new apartment. "After all, they're not our enemies anymore."

Wally couldn't think of anything nice to say, so she held her tongue, but it sure seemed to her he cared more about Japan than his daughter. There had been biennial visits since 1945, about a month apiece, which amounted to five months' time together across a decade. It was simply not enough to make her feel he was a part of her family. She didn't know him, and she didn't need him. To Wally, his long absence had made him obsolete.

He was still stuck in the lingering concerns of World War II, but she was more worried about what had gone on under United Nations auspices in Korea. Since Wally and Loretta had begun following the news of Korea, Wally'd found she had strong opinions about the news. She didn't understand why Ham — or any American — had had to risk his life for the sake of another country. It wasn't as if the Communists posed the same threat the Nazis had. Loretta disapproved of her stance. She said it was unpatriotic, but Wally had come increasingly to question the point of the conflict. In the meantime, Ham had been stationed in Germany, a comparatively plum posting, but even so, if Wally could have traded in her father's homecoming for Ham's, she would have, in a trice.

That her father was taking a job with the UN and planned to live up near the new headquarters on the East River made it even harder for her to reconnect with him.

"You're going to work in that monstrosity of a building?" was what she said when he announced his new job over cocktails at the Wallace house at the end of the first week he was back. "It's the UN's fault Ham nearly died in Korea!"

"What's happened to you while I was away, Wally? Did you join the Communist Party? Don't you know you can get arrested for that?"

"Of course I'm not a Communist. I'm in favor of *peace.* Maybe you've never heard of it."

"I've spent the last decade of my life trying to keep the peace, young lady."

Wally just shrugged.

Her father left soon after, claiming weariness, but he returned the following day, interested in some sort of rapprochement. He'd collected a good amount of Japanese art, which he was eager to show off, but Wally wasn't interested. Then he tried to get her to move in with him, in his new apartment.

"I've rented a great place, Wally. It's a penthouse in Tudor City. Why don't you come live there with me? We can get to know each other again."

"No thanks, Daddy. This is where I live."

"I know it is, and I understand. You probably think I wouldn't take proper care of you. Not compared to Gigi and Loretta. Right?"

"That's right, Daddy," she said, looking at her knees. "I don't think you would."

Registration at Barnard took place in an enormous hall. There, amongst hundreds of almost identically dressed girls, with their smooth, curled-under hair and their knee-length skirts and their cardigans, Wally hurried from departmental table to departmental table, hoping to find places in all the elective courses she wanted to take. The required freshman courses would fill her schedule fairly tightly, but she had received permission ahead of time to enroll in a premedical curriculum, including biology, calculus, and German. No one but Dr. Somersby and Wally had to know that the medical schools' prerequisites were identical to those an aspiring entomologist would need to get into graduate school in zoology.

Every line she stood on, every table she stopped at, it seemed there was one particular young woman directly in front of Wally. She had bobbed hair and wasn't quite a carbon copy of the others: Her sweater seemed to be hand crocheted, and a black scarf graced her neck in lieu of the usual pearls. Her name, Wally overheard her say, was Mallory Sellers.

When she saw over the other girl's shoulder that they were going to be taking the same biology lab section as well as the same lecture, Wally decided to introduce herself.

"Maybe we can be lab partners," she suggested. "We seem to be taking the same program."

"Wallace Baker is it? I noticed you following me. Are you planning to be a doctor, too?"

"No, though my grandmother's planning on it. I'm actually interested in studying bugs."

"How revolting. Maybe it will lead you into medicine of the tropics?"

"I hope not."

"Well, I'd be glad to be partners with you, if they let us pick. It was nice to meet you. I'll see you in class."

Wally had planned never to spend a single night in the room her father had set up for her, but by October she was swamped with schoolwork and exhausted by the long commute from Brooklyn. She realized that living in midtown would shorten her time on the train each day by half, and decided to capitulate. She would stay with her father weeknights, then return to Brooklyn for the weekends.

Wally's best hours were spent in the study of life: She and Mallory dissected a fetal pig together. They quizzed each other on the steps of the Krebs cycle and identified various cell types under the microscope. Wally had also arranged to get course credit for the work she still did with Dr. Somersby, both in his collections at the museum and out in the field, on trips to several colonies he was studying in the Hudson Highlands and on Long Island. Her schedule was so busy that some weekends she didn't make it home to Brooklyn at all, and she didn't miss the house on Columbia Heights as much as she'd expected to. There was a new feeling she had — of independence — that flourished in Manhattan, whereas being in Brooklyn made her feel like a girl. Her father managed not to rub in the reversal. He was just glad to see more of her, and finally to learn a bit about the woman his small daughter had turned into.

On weekend evenings, Wally would venture out with Mallory and a couple of other new friends. They went to famous little bars with sawdust on the floor in the West Village and smoky basements in Harlem where black and white and Latin men sat together and played wild jazz. They listened to folk singers and poets perform from atop tall stools in the middle of crowded cafés. Other nights, they drank Chianti from straw-wrapped bottles in Little Italy and stayed out till dawn talking about their childhoods.

By the beginning of the spring semester, Wally's hair had grown longer than was fashionable, and she and Mallory had both bought berets, though only Wally would actually wear hers. At all the places she went with Mallory, there were men who sought her company — straitlaced ones in blue button-downs and pretentious ones in black turtlenecks and every sort in between. She had her mother's face and smile, after all. But Wally was singularly uninterested in romance. She declined their offers automatically, and those who persisted she drove away with a lengthy set piece on a study she had done with Dr. Somersby on ant colony behaviors.

"Yesterday, I spent most of the morning gluing colored markers to the backs of workers. We'll be tracking their wanderings in response to seven different food and threat stimuli. Out of sixty individuals, there are eight soldiers and fifty-two foragers . . ." If that wasn't boring enough, she described the process of grinding the ants up with her tiny mortar and pestle and attempting to analyze their chemistry.

"Why don't you just tell them something regular, like 'My grandmother watches me like a hawk'?" asked Loretta, when Wally was back home on Sunday.

"But that would encourage them to take me out and get me home early and try to get me to introduce them to Gigi, which is the last thing I want! And it would be a lie. You want me to lie?"

"Of course not, String Bean. I'm just saying," said Loretta.

The fact was, Gigi didn't watch her at all.

Living weekdays at her father's was almost like having her own apartment, because her father was always busy, either at work or having dinner with diplomats, and neither he nor Gigi was ever quite sure which place she planned to spend Friday nights. If she did see him when she came in, he wasn't likely to smell the wine on her breath or notice the smoke in her hair. He'd been out on the town himself, after all.

"Mallory," Wally said, one lazy Saturday morning when the admiral was out of town on some official business and her friend had slept over at the Tudor City apartment, "there's something I've never told you about my family." She'd had a dream the night before that she and her mother and Mr.

Niederman lived in her father's apartment. In the dream, Mr. Niederman had been her father. It was a happy dream, the kind that only turns disturbing when the dreamer awakes and perceives its great distance from reality.

"What is it?"

"Before my mother died, I think she was having an affair."

"But didn't she die when you were a baby? How do you know?"

"Not a baby. I was nine."

"Did you *know*?"

"I didn't, exactly. I didn't understand, but I saw some things I shouldn't."

"Well, I can hardly believe it. Your father is so handsome and distinguished."

"He was gone."

"But he was fighting in the war!"

"I know. She was fairly outrageous, I think. Anyway, I've been thinking about the man she was with. I think he must have been in love with her. And I'm pretty sure he knows more about her death than my father, who wasn't even in the country when it happened."

"Your poor father. I can't believe he never remarried. I think he seems very romantic."

"He doesn't have time to remarry. He's too busy."

"So who was the other man? Do you remember him?"

"Yes, I was pretty good friends with him. His name was Bill Niederman, and he was a math professor from New Jersey who was in the city doing some kind of war work. My mother and I thought it was RADAR, but we never knew for sure."

"Oh, that's right — RADAR. So what happened to him?"

"I'm not sure. He just left at the end of the war, when my mother died."

"Have you ever thought about tracking him down? He must have stories, remember things. You could learn a lot about your mother that way."

"I don't know," Wally said. It was such old business, and there were so many current things to distract her: acrobat ants in the Hudson Highlands, the *Tractatus Logico-Philosophicus,* adenosine triphosphate, deoxyribonucleic acid, Shakespeare's *Antony and Cleopatra.* And of course, she had no idea what she'd actually say to him. There were questions she could ask, but she was rather afraid to hear the answers.

And then one day, while Wally was studying at the library at Columbia, she looked up from her books and saw a young man staring at her. The library wasn't very crowded, but he pulled out the chair right next to hers and sat down. He set an enormous art book on the table and opened it, seemingly at random, then just looked at her until she turned to look back at him. He smiled, and she returned a small, discouraging smile, just polite enough.

Wally could see that the book contained reproductions of the work of Dürer. She recognized the image of a brown rabbit. Her grandmother had sent her a postcard of that same painting when she and Waldo traveled to Europe, years before, back when Wally and Georgie had had Nutters. Wally still had the card in her desk drawer, in a small bundle with the few other letters she'd received as a girl. Then the man began turning the pages, flipping past various versions of Christ and a slew of important personages, not so much browsing, she thought, as in search of some particular image.

Wally turned back to her books as well and tried to focus, but now she was distracted by his presence. Why had he sat so close to her? She found herself stealing glances. He reminded her oddly of Mr. Niederman. He was dark haired, and his lips were full and shapely. His hair was a little long, a little wild, compared to that of the other young men around them, and he was wearing blue jeans. Who was he? she wondered. What was his major?

After a half an hour, Wally couldn't bear it anymore and began to pack up her books. She would find another table in another room. She had an exam coming up at the end of the week, and she needed to concentrate on her work. She hadn't noticed till then that a note on a folded sheet of legal paper lay on top of her stack of books.

Will you have a coffee with me?

— Leo

Leo.

She turned to him, planning to smile consolingly, politely, and shake her head, but when she saw his strong jaw and hooded eyes a quiver went through her chest.

She took a breath.

"All right," she whispered, in spite of herself. She wasn't sure when she'd been so thrilled. "When?"

"Now?" he mouthed.

Leo. Over thick china coffee cups in a booth at a Greek diner, he told her he had graduated from Columbia the year before but still used the library to look at the art books. She told him that she'd grown up in

Brooklyn, with her grandparents — and why. It seemed like a big thing to divulge, and yet it rolled off her tongue without Wally even second-guessing herself. He was somehow just easy to talk to, Leo. After an hour and a half, he paid for the coffee and Wally wrote her number down on a paper napkin. Then she got on the subway and went to Brooklyn. She was supposed to be staying at her father's that night, but her head was in such a swirl, and the first person she wanted to tell about it was Loretta.

Leo lived on Jane Street in a studio apartment, and he invited her there on the very second date, to see his paintings — huge cityscapes with thick streaks of ultramarine and burnt umber and every shade of black. They were strange, she thought, strange and wonderfully compelling. Then, without any impropriety on his part, to her relief — for it had been a bit of a risk, going to his apartment — he suggested they go out to Chumley's and see what was happening.

When Leo wasn't painting, she learned, he worked in the art department at an ad firm so big it was known only by its initials, laying out ads for dishwashers and transatlantic cruise lines. Among the perfect things about him were that he had never even been to Brooklyn Heights and that he had opposed the war in Korea, too.

One evening a few weeks later, they sat hand in hand in Washington Square Park alongside Mallory and her latest boyfriend, passing around a brown-bagged fifth of rye and listening to a band called the Weavers sing "America the Beautiful" and "If I Had a Hammer."

"Wally Baker," he murmured into her ear, "would you marry me?"

Wally felt a thrill of the sort she'd never experienced, and a fleeting terror. She hardly knew him. She turned to Mallory, swaying to Pete Seeger's banjo beside her, as if this were a question her friend could better answer than she, but Mallory hadn't heard.

"Don't be silly, Leo," she said, squeezing his hand.

"No," he urged, "I mean it. Marry me."

"I'm not even sure I believe in marriage," she said, trying to turn it into a joke. "I believe in peace and justice — and science," she said.

"I couldn't agree more," he said, smiling broadly, nothing daunted. "And I like art, too, of course. So let's not get married after all, at least not yet. How about you just be my girl?"

"That I can do," she said, relieved.

It was like having Ham back in her life again, she sometimes thought — someone who truly understood her and cared about the things she did. She thought his paintings were powerful — at once violent and beautiful, somehow. He'd passed the ant test and the Gigi and Loretta tests — though he hadn't met the admiral. Later that night they went back to his apartment and necked on a drop cloth at the foot of one of his paintings. Wally was giddy with the heady aura of the linseed oil and solvents and the vibrations of the colors and the yearning of their flesh. She hungered for more as they strained against the limits of their underclothes — that was when she fell, for certain, in love with him.

"Leo," she whispered. "I think I'm in love with you."

He smiled, amazed to hear it, even though he knew it already.

"But don't start up asking me again, you know, to marry you. I might marry you someday, but I don't want to get engaged. Not till after college, at least."

"I'll wait," he said.

"But the thing is, I don't want to wait for

everything. To — *you know.* Do you?" she asked.

"You're asking *me*?" He laughed. "Not if you don't."

"But not tonight. We need to get —"

"I know. I'll take care of it," he said. "Don't worry."

That semester, Wally didn't study for exams. She studied Leo.

She skipped her bio lectures and got the notes from Mallory. She wrote her English I papers the night before they were due and didn't mind the Cs.

She and Leo spent days wandering Greenwich Village and visiting the Metropolitan Museum, drinking coffee and peering nose to nose at tiny gilded reliquaries, kissing amongst the beatniks and the statuary and armor. She became interested in art, especially in his art.

One day, when she went back to his apartment with him, there was a red and green Indian sari strung up with wire and artists' clips, separating off his sleeping area. In front of it, there sat his one lumpy armchair and his easel with a freshly gessoed canvas.

"Redecorating?" she asked as she sat in his armchair.

"Would you mind if I painted you, Wally?"

"Me? I thought you did urban land-scapes."

"I do."

"Well, okay. You mean now?"

"Yes."

"You don't want me to get naked? I'll freeze," she said.

"No, you don't have to. Just sit."

He painted for an hour that day but wouldn't show it to her, and then again for several other sittings. When he decided he was finished, she walked around and looked at it for the first time. The painting was strange to her — which wasn't a surprise, since all his work had an eerie quality. But this was something beyond. It wasn't a like-ness really, but it captured something alarm-ing to her. She did and didn't recognize herself. It seemed to Wally that Leo had painted her mother.

"Do you like it? It's still just a sketch."

"I'm not sure. Do you mind if I don't?"

"It's okay. You're still my muse. Now, come over here," he said, and she came. He slid his hands beneath the ribbed hem of her sweater and his fingers sent quivers through her flesh. The sun pushed through the unwashed windowpanes, illuminating clouds of motes and making the air itself seem to glow. They collapsed on the daybed, and kissed. He was over her, but not heavy upon her. She reached up and slid her hand between the buttons of his shirt. She'd never felt stranger or more excited than when he flipped her, somehow, so that she was on top, straddling him.

"You be in charge today, okay?" he said.

"Yes." She smiled, happier than she remembered having been in years.

28
CHEMISTRY

During her sophomore year, Wally was listed as the sixth coauthor on a paper for the natural history museum's science bulletin about the changing foraging habits of a wood-ant colony situated on the edge of a new housing development in Nassau County, Long Island.

"You are brilliant and amazing, Wally Baker," Leo said.

Wally laughed and said, "You should really date Dr. Somersby, if you think I'm so amazing. I just helped."

"No thanks. I like your glasses a lot better than his."

"That's great, Wally," said her father when she gave him a copy of the article. "Good job there." But then he placed it neatly on his desk, on a stack of mail he never looked at. "And what about your social life? Any other young men you like at school or the lab these days?" The admiral had been fairly unimpressed by Leo when he met him one Sunday for brunch. Neither his beatnik way nor his less than rock-solid financial outlook made him seem a long-term prospect for Wally.

She flushed and glared at him. "No, it's just Leo, Daddy. We're serious."

"Good for you, darling," Loretta said when Wally showed her name — Baker, B. — in the author listing for the paper. "Not that I could make heads or tails of what you're doing."

Gigi was the only one who actually sat down and read the article, beginning to end.

"Wallace," she said. "You know what amazes me? That all those hours you spent watching ants in the grass actually came to something. Congratulations."

The person who might have been most interested in the article was Ham. Wally had no idea how much of her correspondence actually reached him — he almost never wrote back — but she decided to send him an actual tear sheet of the paper anyway, enclosing a long rambling letter all about her work with Dr. Somersby. She didn't mention Leo.

"The thing that's remarkable," she wrote, "is that the colony seems to have been innately adaptable to this new way of being.

In just one year and a couple of generations of workers, under the same queen, the colony changed dramatically. The ratio of soldiers to foragers decreased and the foraging habits evolved to suit the new environment."

She didn't expect to hear back. He was in the Army, not off on some extended holiday. That's what she told herself. But amazingly, two months after she sent the paper to him, an answer arrived. He asked questions about their methods and theories, and described a column of leaf-cutter ants he'd seen in Korea carrying chunks of plant matter many times their size. "Just like us — you wouldn't believe the size of the packs we had to haul when we marched," he wrote. "They were massive. I miss you, and a life in which there is time to think about why bugs do the things they do. They've got the usual roaches here, but the bugs in Korea were too much even for me. Mostly I just tried to kill as many mosquitoes as I could — I don't know if the itch or the malaria was worse — and to ignore the weevils in our food. And patch up the guys when they got shot at, keep them alive so the gooks could take another crack at them."

He had killed people, over there, Wally knew, and now he wrote to her in depth about the first time — the horror of seeing a human body fly away through the air, shredded by his gunfire. How he couldn't fall asleep for days afterward, kept jerking awake, imagining his own death — in an ambush, in a pitched battle, by firing squad. After that first letter, they kept coming, and he often made brief mentions of death punctuating the dailiness of his life during the war: "We marched and marched, day in day out, God knows where we were going. . . . I shot an old man one day on a raid, just by accident, but for him. . . . My feet were so cracked they bled. We all had what we called the jungle fungus between our toes. . . . One morning I threw a grenade into a hut where we believed the enemy was hiding. Afterward, I noticed a pair of tiny pants laid out to dry on a rock. Some pots. A family lived there. Were they our enemy? Maybe."

She thought of Ham killing weevils in his food before he ate it. She thought of him raising a gun and killing a human being. She thought of some North Korean bullet flying through the air toward him, trying to end his life as he stopped to bind a wounded comrade's gaping flesh. Wally could feel the effort he'd expended to find some way of responding that respected the work she was doing as well as to chronicle his life for her, and it meant the world to her. She couldn't believe how different their lives had become, and she was terrified that she would never see him again. He was her best friend.

She thought about sharing the letters with Leo, and she almost did. But there was a fear in her that Leo would deride Ham as a tool of the military, would condemn him for the horrors he'd committed and had faced. For the fact that he had reenlisted despite it all. She folded the letters back into their envelopes and kept them in her desk drawer tucked into the bundle of all the other letters she'd received in her life.

The spring semester soon began, and Wally's studies became more intense. In addition to taking biochem at Columbia, she was invited to work on a new study on ant communication with Dr. Somersby and a professor of entomology from Columbia called Milan Pottmeisel. They were focusing on the secretions of the newly identified Dufour gland, an infinitesimal refinery loaded with volatile hydrocarbons that produced not just one but a dozen different compounds, all excreted through an orifice on the ant's abdomen. Clearly it was there for some purpose, but what?

Wally's role in the lab had to do with practical questions and methodology: How in the world could one take a sample of a trail laid down in droplets smaller than grains of pollen, smaller than single cells? For an ant, the microscopic scale of all this was natural. For clumsy human giants, it was next to impossible to detect, much less run tests on. *Next to* impossible. Which meant possible — just difficult.

Wally euthanized her six-legged subject by dropping her onto a piece of dry ice she had sitting in a petri dish, lifted her gingerly with her forceps, brought her into the microscope's field of focus, and sliced her little thorax open. Then she removed her Dufour gland and transferred it to the waiting test tube, where she pulverized it with a glass stirring rod and soaked the result in solvent.

If she did this enough times, she would get enough of the substance within to analyze. She did it for hours. She did it for days. She did it for weeks. Sometimes, as she froze and dissected another worker, Wally thought, *I am the god of the ants!* Well, maybe not quite. She certainly wasn't their creator, but she was their destroyer, their Shiva. And with the elixir they were working toward, she — or one of her advisors, really — might someday be the master of their actions as well.

Finally, she loaded her samples into the gas chromatograph and fired the machine up. She toiled alongside others who were doing much the same work, and together they did it for months, until they had identified every component and gotten the recipe precisely right. With work and money for equipment and time and patience, they finally concocted a copy of the substance: an ectohormone or "chemical releaser." That's what Dr. Pottmeisel was calling the chemical.

The whole team, including Dr. Pottmeisel and Dr. Somersby, assembled for the first test. A dozen ants were released into an observation tank while Dr. Pottmeisel laid down an S-shaped trail of the ectohormone with a pipette. The ants wandered aimlessly at first, then, where they encountered the trail, they waved their antennae. They backed up and walked away from the ectohormone trail, not merely ignoring it — disliking it, distrusting it. And then, gradually, the ants stopped caring one way or the other and wandered randomly.

Which was encouraging. It meant something to them. Quite possibly, Dr. Somersby theorized, they had isolated the scent emitted by a dying ant, just about to be frozen and eviscerated, a chemical that said, quite simply, *Flee!*

On the next round of trials, they discovered that volatility was the key. They laid out food and drew three trails leading up to it, at ten-minute intervals, then watched how the ants responded and clocked the time it took each ant to reach the food. The theory they developed had it that the ants laid down a blend of hormones to create their invisible trails, but that the chemicals evaporated swiftly, as a result of which the shortest and most followed trails would always be the strongest. This meant the ants had not only a method for finding their way to and from places but a built-in system for finding the most efficient route. The goal of the months of research, all that ant killing, had been to recreate the various mixtures of chemicals the ants used, and identify their purposes. And clearly, there were as many mixtures as there were ant behaviors. So, back to the bench they went, another season, another attempt. Another string of days when Wally was too bleary even to call Leo to ask him how his day was.

Wally and Leo fell into a pattern of weekly Friday night dates, but both of them were usually too weary to stay out all hours exploring the city's nightlife. Sometimes they just made spaghetti at the admiral's apartment. They had become a quiet, not-quite-engaged couple. Wally told herself — and Leo — that she adored him as much as ever, but she sometimes dreaded their obligatory Fridays. And she wasn't always sorry to get back to the lab on Saturday morning. She was more excited by the progress they were making than by Leo, who was simply there, who was what he was, who could be counted on.

It was funny, she sometimes thought, how she had gotten into ants way back when because she didn't like having to kill butterflies. She'd thought working with ants would be more observational — less bench-work, less death. But sometimes, she had discovered, we can only understand things by killing them. And it was worth it. They were getting somewhere with what Dr. Pottmeisel began calling a chemical theory of ant-trail optimization. It wasn't just numbers on paper. She was sure of it. Dr. Pottmeisel was sure of it. They were close, very close, to understanding so much. If her boyfriend was getting in the way, then it was the boyfriend, not the research, that must go.

One Friday, as they puttered in the

kitchen, Leo turned to her and said, "Wally, I think I'm losing you to your ants."

"Oh, Leo," she said, her stomach lurching with guilt. "That's ridiculous. We've both just been so busy."

"No, it's more. What's happening, Wally?" he asked. "I don't understand. Did something happen? Is there someone at your lab?"

Wally almost laughed aloud, thinking of the graduate students she worked with. If Leo thought she was married to her work, he should have seen them. They didn't even seem to have noticed that she was female, despite all the time she spent with them. But she knew Leo deserved a proper answer. She couldn't tell him the truth, that the thrill had worn off, without being cruel. But in all honesty, without that surge of pleasure she'd once gotten from just being around him, she wasn't sure having such a steady boyfriend was the right idea for a girl who was just twenty and had ambitions beyond being a wife.

"There isn't anyone but you, Leo, it's just I might need to be alone for a while."

"I was thinking the opposite — we need to get married now, so we can be with each other whenever we're not at work. It's just the being away from each other so much that's making it hard."

Wally thought of Loretta, who faced things straight on and brooked no evasion, no vaguery.

She took a breath and with tears of regret streaming silently down her cheeks, said, "No. I don't want to get married, Leo. Not anytime soon. It's not about you, I just don't want to get married right now. I'm not ready for that."

His beautiful mouth hung open, and she realized she had surprised him.

"Can we still see each other?"

"I don't know," she sighed.

"Listen, Wally, that's crazy. Couldn't we just slow down a little, if that would be better for you?"

"What about not seeing each other for a month or so?"

"Not see each other for a month? How about dinner again next Friday?"

"Just dinner," Wally said.

"Just dinner."

"And let's make it Friday a week, all right? I just need some time by myself."

"All right."

"So do we know where we stand?"

"You don't want to get married, but you will still have dinner with me on Fridays, sometimes, for now?"

"I guess." She laughed, in spite of herself.

The next day, Wally took the train down to Brooklyn Heights for her usual weekend with Gigi. She thought of Ham, as always, as she exited the station through the lobby of the Hotel St. George. She hadn't been swimming there in ages. Maybe she ought to take Leo sometime, she thought. He would like it. Swimming was always jolly, plus there was less likelihood he'd insist on talking about the future if they were in public. For that matter, she wondered why they never seemed to go out to hear music anymore. Perhaps she would devote a little time to planning their next date, make it something she actually looked forward to. She did love him, she thought, picturing his squared-off hip bones and smoky eyes and remembering the shock of being held in his muscular arms, back at his apartment, the first time — one of the better times they'd made love. It was just he'd gotten a bit too — reliable.

She walked through the door of her grandmother's house thinking about Leo, but there out of the yonder was Ham.

Ham.

He was there. In the brownstone. And even more weirdly, he was sweeping the hall.

352

Helping his mother, just as if he'd never left. His wavy hair was shorter than it used to be, but then again too long for a soldier. When had he gotten back? It didn't matter. She went to Ham and hugged him hard, too hard, possibly.

"You're back," she said.

"There you are, Wally," he said, looking at her with an enormous grin.

"There *I* am?" she said, laughing. "There *you* are. You're back!"

"I seem to be."

He had the same old crooked grin as ever, but straight off Wally thought she saw a change, a kind of hollowness in his eyes. What she said was "Put that broom down. For Christssake, Ham. That can wait. Let's go talk."

"All right. I was just helping out. Mama dropped a tray when she saw me come in. I gave her a shock."

"Well, you could have told us you were on your way home."

Before he could answer, Loretta and Gigi rushed into the room laughing.

"I told you he'd make it home in one piece, Loretta! I told you."

"Yes, ma'am, Miz Doc, you sure did. And I don't mind the least bit my being wrong, and your being right."

Wally looked at the three of them, from one to the other, thinking that her family was all there again, and then she stepped back and announced, to Gigi's raised eyebrows, that they must eat dinner together that night, in the dining room. All of them. They must celebrate.

"What are you talking about, Wally?" said Loretta. "Who's going to serve and clear?"

"Well, I'll help. We can put everything out on the sideboard, like a party, and you'll take your apron off and sit with us. And we'll open a bottle of wine."

"Well," said Gigi. "If you insist, we'd better make it two bottles."

"All right, then," said Loretta.

And so, awkwardly, they celebrated.

At dinner, though, Wally still thought there was something odd or absent about Ham, something hard to quantify. And it wasn't just him. Maybe it was the unusual arrangement, Walkers sitting down with Wallaces at the same table, but no one seemed able to talk.

For her part, Loretta knew something was wrong. It was unfathomable that her son would have failed to call and tell his mother that he was back, he was coming home. Had he been discharged dishonorably? His hair was long enough she knew it had been some time ago. All she knew for sure was that something or other was badly wrong.

Gigi was thinking it would have been easier to get him into school with a little lead time, but then she reasoned that perhaps it was better this way. Columbia was out, of course, but if she focused on getting him into Brooklyn College, she could make things happen right away and keep him in her sights, mentor him a little, open some of the same doors she'd once opened for Stella. Without discussion, she set her sights for him on Brooklyn College and Long Island College Medical School.

"How long has it been, Hamilton, since your discharge?" Gigi asked him, finally.

"A month."

There was a pause while all three women pondered that, wondering if it were true, waiting for him to say why he hadn't called or come home sooner.

"I traveled around a bit," he said. "Didn't want to disappoint you all by coming home in the state I was in when I got out. Let's just say I wasn't fit for society." He looked down.

"You couldn't have disappointed me, Son," Loretta said, putting her hand on his. "I love you no matter what."

"I know, Mama," he muttered.

"Well, you need to get busy, now that you're here," commanded Gigi. "And right away, too, Ham. If you want to be a doctor, there's work to do, and believe me, it won't help to brood on the horrors of war."

"What do you know about that, Miz Doc?"

"I lived through the Great War and the Second World War. Not to mention the Influenza. I've seen people who had trouble, when life resumed again, and people who carried on. Let's try and have you be one of the latter sort, shall we?"

He didn't respond.

"Now," she continued, "you are still *interested* in medicine?"

"Yes, ma'am. That I am."

"Well then, we'll get you started at Brooklyn College, and you can work with the Long Island College Hospital ambulance service while you study. Then we'll see about medical school. How does that suit you?"

"Let me think about it, Miz Doc. I just got home."

"If you don't want to wait an entire year, we need to enroll you now. And anyway, I thought you'd been home for a month. Why don't we talk again tomorrow, when you've rested?"

As for Wally, she barely spoke at dinner. She couldn't take her eyes off Ham. He was the same old Ham, and he was something else entirely. Seeing him after so much time was like seeing, at long last, a ghost — a ghost and nonetheless a man.

"Mallory," Wally said, "I don't know what to do about Leo. I'm not sure I want to see him. He's asked me to marry him, again, seriously this time. I tried to break up with him, but somehow he convinced me to go out to dinner with him again on Friday."

"You always have dinner with him on Fridays. He wants to get married and you don't. Just like always. What's news about that?"

"I don't know," said Wally miserably. The thing she really needed to talk to someone about was Ham, but even with Mallory, she didn't dare.

"Well, do you want me to come along on Friday and bring someone, to make it a double date?"

"No, I guess not."

In the end, Leo and Wally met at Chumley's, in the Village, alone, the following Friday, and there, amidst the sawdust and the smoke, she forgot, for a while, about Ham and his war and her ants. Watching

Leo's face as they listened to a poet read, she saw in him a mirror of her own impressions: a slight wince when the poet indulged in a too-sweet metaphor, a smile and a faraway look when the poet evoked the lost world of childhood through mud. After the reading was over and the poet had gone to join his friends at the end of the bar, Leo turned to Wally and asked her what she thought.

Such a simple question. When of course what mud had evoked for her was memories of Ham, her and Ham and the garden and the ants.

"They were good," she said. "The mud one especially. It reminds me of the day of my mother's funeral, which was a very rainy day. I wish I'd known my mother better, Leo. I wish you could have met her."

"What about that man who lived with you, during the war?"

"Mr. Niederman."

"You have all these ideas about him," he said, trying to be tactful about what Wally had told him she believed. "But you don't really know, right? Why don't you look him up, after all, and talk to him about her? Maybe you need to know more about her before you can —"

"What, commit?"

"Make certain decisions about your own life."

"I don't know."

"Just call up information and ask for Niederman."

"I don't know."

She thought about it, though.

Just as soon as she figured out what to ask him, she told herself, she would dial the operator and ask if they had a listing for a William Niederman in any of the towns encircling New Brunswick. She'd imagined doing this often enough that she knew them by heart, like a train conductor rattling off his stations: Highland Park, Edison, Milltown, North Brunswick, Franklin, Somerset, Piscataway. Maybe, in one of those towns, there was a man with the answers to all her questions. Maybe the lost part of her childhood was hidden away in plain sight, in suburban New Jersey.

Against her intentions, she went back to Leo's apartment that night. It was so easy between the two of them, if she let it be. They finished half a bottle of wine, and before she knew it, Wally was wriggling out of her sweater and skirt, and Leo was pulling off his jeans. He understood her. He knew how to make her relax, and then shiver and writhe and want to do things she hadn't thought she'd want to do. Did she love him forever? she wondered as he reached into her, making her gasp, and said her name over and over in her ear. Maybe. But somehow, even then, a stray thought crept into her mind: Ham. And by the time Leo lay sighing beside her, reaching for her hand, she was in another place and time entirely — not Leo's studio, not the present, but the future, in Ham's embrace.

29
THE TIGER BEETLE

"So how's old Somersby?" Ham asked the following morning when he walked into the kitchen, still damp from a shower.

Wally had left Leo's late the night before and taken a taxi home.

Leo had pleaded with her to stay over, but she'd told him Gigi was expecting her for brunch. It wasn't true. And she didn't tell him Ham had come home. She wasn't exactly sure why not, she just couldn't bring herself to say the words.

Ham's green fatigue pants and white T-shirt hung a little from his frame. He'd grown lean in the Army. As he stretched to scratch the back of his head, she glimpsed a sliver of his light brown stomach and forced herself to close her eyes. She envisioned him sleeping in those clothes on the little daybed, which must now have been far too small for him. It seemed wrong to Wally that this grown man still had to sleep in Lo-

retta's sitting room. There were three bedrooms going begging upstairs — more if you
counted the attic. Ham was a man now.
He'd fought for their country. She would
take the matter up with Gigi later.

"Do you want to go up and see him? He's
still my advisor for fieldwork, and he comes
in to the ant lab at the university from time
to time to observe certain experiments.
We're working on a group of newly isolated
chemical signals called ectohormones, or
the new word for them — *pheromones.*"

"Pheromones."

"They're secretions we think the ants may
be using to communicate. They secrete different chemicals in different situations. I've
come to learn that you can't say much
about communication with killed specimens. It's not about morphology."

"Too bad — I thought we'd figured out
ant communication years ago. Didn't we
think it would turn out to be RADAR or
something?"

"Well, you never know." Wally laughed.
"The pheromones are just a theory."

"All right, let's drop in on the old man.
I'd like to see him."

"It's a such a nice day. If Dr. Somersby
can see us on his lunch hour, we should
walk over the bridge and catch the train

362

from the other side. We haven't done that in a while."

"So your great-grandfather built this thing, huh?" Ham asked as they walked up the stairs to bridge's pedestrian path, not that he didn't already know it.

"He just helped. You know. He was just a stoneworker."

"And a criminal."

"No, he just married a girl gangster."

"Come on, your grandmother herself told me he worked for that gang, before he worked on the bridge."

"Only for a little while. I think they sort of shanghaied him."

"So I guess crime pays?"

"I guess it's possible for two very different people to find happiness together."

Wally had hardly touched Ham since he got home, since that first huge hug. She was afraid to, as if she might get a shock. Now, she turned and slipped her hand into his.

He took it.

It was a beautiful moment, but it didn't last.

When they were almost at the top of the Brooklyn Bridge, reveling in the fresh air, the view of the city, the strange familiarity of being together, a young greasy-faced kid sitting on a bench shouted, "Hey, nigaboo, get one of your own kind."

Wally looked at Ham. He had a dangerous expression on his face.

She thought about his years in Korea. He had killed men he'd never even spoken to.

"Don't answer him, Ham. Let's just keep walking."

"And you, little Sally, watchoo doing with that Negro? You can do better."

"Let's get out of here, Ham."

Wally hardly saw Ham step away from her, he moved so quickly, but she heard the sound of a soft thing being hit by a hard fist. "Thwack" was the way they wrote it in the comics, and now she knew why. The boy was on the ground, holding his head, but there wasn't any blood.

"I'ma call the cops on you, nigger."

"You ought to keep a civil tongue in your head," Ham said quietly to the heckler. "You don't know this lady or me, so just keep your opinions to yourself."

As they walked away, there was a rising sensation within Wally. Ham took her hand again, and pressed her fingers tight. They continued on silently, a strange favor having been done them. The ferrety heckler had pushed them over some edge. Down at the other side of the bridge, Ham paused and looked straight at her.

"What do you say, Wally Baker?" he asked. "That idiot thought you were my girlfriend. You want to make him right?"

She laughed. There was a giddy feeling, a thrill in her chest, and a bit of fear. The question was a joke. Wasn't it? Looking at Ham, she couldn't quite tell.

"I'll think about it," she said with a laugh, but she let him keep her hand.

Up at the museum, Wally wondered if Dr. Somersby noticed the new energy between them. Wally didn't know what to make of it, not yet.

They talked mostly about the insects of Korea. Ham had brought a battered, water-stained sketchbook full of drawings of ants and beetles, among other, more troubling images, which they skipped past quickly. The first half of the book was in colored pencils. The insects looked like jewels. Then came pages of writing and loose sketches, and then a very detailed picture of a trench full of bodies, just in graphite. Maybe he had lost the colored pencils. In the later pages, he had changed his attention to details of the landscape, the effects of the war. There were village scenes with no life in them, just exploded buildings next to others that had somehow gone untouched, their plank roofs all held down by neatly spaced stones.

Ham soon found the page he was looking for, a page scattered with beautiful green and multicolored beetles. Some were iridescent, which Ham had somehow captured with his pencils. The most beautiful ones had red and turquoise heads with scythe-like jaws, and black carapaces outlined in red, yellow, and green.

"The Asian tiger beetle," said Dr. Somersby. "Lovely."

"These guys were everywhere over there."

"But this one's very unusual," said Dr. Somersby, pointing to the bottom of the page, "the way its carapace —"

Ham scowled even as Wally and Dr. Somersby marveled at the rendering of the tiger beetle.

"No, it wasn't unusual. It's just a picture, right? I probably got the details wrong."

"I'm sure you didn't. I only wish you could have brought home a couple of specimens to share with us."

"I didn't exactly have a collecting kit with me."

"Of course not."

It pained Wally to hear Ham sound bitter in talking to their mentor and defensive about his drawing.

"You wrote me a letter about seeing a colony of fire ants building a raft," Wally said, trying to draw Ham out a bit. "Tell Dr. Somersby about that."

"Yes, please," said their mentor. "What amazing luck to see such a thing."

"Well, sort of," said Ham. "It had rained for three days, and there was flooding. We were looking for a way across a small river when we found a downed tree bridging it. We sent out a scout, this guy Morales, this kid from the Bronx. He played any instrument you could find, and when there wasn't one, he'd play spoons or tabletop. It turned out there was a sniper trained on the tree bridge. Morales went down. My job was to go out and see if I could help him, or set his dog tag if I couldn't, which meant likely getting shot at, too. So there I was crawling through the mud along the river. I felt them sting me before I saw them, but they weren't that aggressive because they were too busy trying to get out of there — just like we were. They were climbing up onto each other, holding on to each other's bodies with their jaws. It was a big mass of ants, almost like a ball, and slowly the ball got bigger and bigger, until finally it just went rolling and bouncing down the river."

"What about the guy who got shot?" Wally asked. "Morales. He was dead?"

"Yeah, he was dead when I got to him. What you have to do when someone dies on the battlefield is put the little notch of the dog tag between his front teeth, and set the backside against his lower teeth. Then you stand up and aim your boot at the tip of his chin and kick it shut. It goes *thunk,* like you kicked a door shut. Then it doesn't matter if the bugs and the animals come and strip him down to bone. The Army can identify the remains."

He said it with such detachment, it made Wally want to cry.

Dr. Somersby looked distressed as well. "Oh, son," he mumbled. That's just, just very hard."

"I didn't really like Morales. He gave me a lot of trouble. You know, he was the spic and I was the black, and both of us from the city. Instead of being friends, we kind of squared off somehow. There wasn't room for both of us. He died the same day I saw that Asian tiger there, in the book. When I bent down to set the tag, that's when I saw the beetle. I had this thought that Morales's spirit was in the beetle. It was beautiful, but it seemed so angry."

"What was it doing?" asked Dr. Somersby.

"I don't know. Walking along."

"They hunt alone, like tigers. That's the reason for the name, not the coloration."

"Yeah, like snipers. They hunt alone, too." Ham laughed, but it sounded hollow, the least amused laugh Wally had ever heard.

They took the C train back to Brooklyn, without touching each other. At home, he seemed to back off from her. Wally told herself it was just the presence of Loretta and Gigi that had changed things, but she almost felt that that trip uptown, when they'd held hands and he'd proposed a new arrangement for them, had never really happened.

All week, Wally avoided taking Leo's calls. She claimed to be sick, but in reality, the problem was she couldn't stop thinking about Ham, not Ham as her childhood friend but Ham as something more. His question lingered in her mind. The following weekend — her weekend off from Leo — she determined to find out if she was the only one who felt as she did, if she had been dreaming when she felt his attraction to her.

Loretta was at church and Gigi was pruning her bushes in the back when Wally

pushed open the door to the cook's apartment without knocking, just as if she'd done
it many times before. The truth was, she
was as unaccustomed to being in that space
in her grandmother's house as Ham was to
being upstairs. There had always been
certain unspoken boundaries.

She found Ham reclining on the daybed,
with its ivy-patterned coverlet and the two
little bolsters that matched. He was reading
an issue of *Captain America.*

"Hey," she said.

"You think there's ever going to be a black
superhero, Wally?" he said, dropping the
comic on the floor, not expressing any
surprise that she was there.

"Yeah, I think so," she said. "World War
Two gave us girls Wonder Woman. Maybe
it's your turn next."

"Maybe," he said, holding her gaze.

She approached the daybed and he stood
up. The second he touched her — just her
forearm — she knew he had just been being
careful. He wanted the same thing that she
did.

They breathed each other's breath, tasted
each other's lips and skin. Clothes were
shoved up and away. He reached her hip,
then further down, and she pressed herself
against him. It was only when it came to his

370

pants that they paused, looked at each other.

"Wally, what are we doing?" he whispered.

"I don't know."

"You want this?"

"Since you left," she said, just then realizing that was true. All the nights she'd thought of him, all the worry and anger she'd felt when he reenlisted were because she had been in love with him. She probably always had been.

"Me too."

She leaned in and smelled his neck.

"You ever had a boyfriend, Wally? Have you ever —"

"Yes," she said, cutting him off. "I have." Part of her was smiling to dispel any worry he might have, but another part cringed inwardly, knowing this was a terrible thing to do to Leo, to Ham, to herself. She had never imagined herself the kind of woman who would sleep around. And she wouldn't, she told herself. She would break it off with Leo. It had always been Ham. Ham was the one.

"And what about" — he looked around them — "*everything*?"

"You mean, our families?"

He nodded.

"It's a new era," she said. "They'll figure it out."

She closed her eyes and smiled as she felt his weight descend upon her.

Afterward, they still couldn't keep their hands off each other. They decided to get out of the house before they had to explain themselves.

They had the subway car to themselves for the whole last part of the trip to Coney Island, and they cozied up to each other and began to kiss. It was almost a disappointment when they had to disembark at Stillwell Avenue. They wandered the streets, paid a couple of dimes to gawk at a man who could stretch his skin with nails, then headed to the carousel.

"You want to ride it?" Ham asked.

"Don't you?"

"Naw, I want to watch you," he said with a grin. "Win me the brass ring."

And she did.

The boardwalk was hot, and they decided to get some food and take it to one of the shade pavilions.

"Hot dogs?"

"How about clams?" Wally said.

"And some lemonade and a funnel cake," he added.

They sat on a bench facing the ocean. The waves crashed. The breeze was warm. The gulls cried and swooped down, angling in for any dropped morsel. Wally wrung every sour drop from her lemon wedge, then jabbed the fried strips onto the notched tines of her tiny wooden fork and dredged them in sauce. She took a suck of cold lemonade from the paper straw. The air was hot. It had been a dizzying day.

"Can I have a piece of your funnel cake, Ham?"

"Sure," he said and ripped her off a large sugary chunk.

Wally was just about to chuck her red-checked paper clam bowl into a trash barrel and propose that they go down to the sand when someone yelled out: "You little slut! You disgrace your own mother."

It was a potbellied, sunburned old man.

Wally felt a surge of shame, then rage. She threw her empty paper bowl at him, and it bounced off his chest. The little fork clung briefly to his shirt, leaving a pink spot on the cloth, then fell to the boardwalk.

She could feel that Ham had gone rigid beside her, ready to pounce. She almost wanted him to fight the man — the way he had on the bridge. There was something about it that excited her as much as it scared her.

"Let it go. It's not worth it, Wally," he said,

leading her away.

She took a deep breath and went along.

"What you need, ma'am, is a good, strong white man to satisfy your unnatural urges," the potbelly called. "I'd be more than glad to comply."

Wally's and Ham's fingers found each other, and they turned and walked on, leaving the man staring after them.

"I think things are just worse now, worse than a couple years ago. It's as if there's no progress, no matter what people try to do," Wally said.

"I'd like to slit that cockroach's throat," Ham said.

"I'd like to smash his skull to jelly and run his brains through my gas chromatograph, see what the hell they're made of."

He smiled at the curiously academic sort of violence she'd imagined. While he was gone, she'd become a woman and nearly a biologist, but deep down she was still Wally, Wally the tomboy who was as likely as any guy to swing a punch or curse. He still knew her, even after the years apart, the things he'd seen.

"You know, Wally," he said, "it's not actually worse now. Not for me. It's just you didn't see it before. No one shouts 'nigger lover' at a little girl, but they always had their eyes on me. Now you're grown, walking down the boardwalk with a black man. You're that fat man's nightmare, Wally. He's terrified his daughter's going to do what you did — run off with a darky."

She laughed uncomfortably and gave him a little shove.

"Well, it's true."

"I wish it wasn't," she said.

"Well, it is. Let's go down by the water now. Let's take a swim."

Wally smiled slightly and looked away. "Okay, Ham. Let's do it."

30
THE HALF GRAPEFRUIT

She had written to Leo immediately upon getting home from Coney Island that day, but she knew a letter was inadequate. "I'm sorry. I was going to break it off, and you convinced me not to, but this time I really mean it, Leo. I'm not in love with you — not enough. I'm sorry, but I just can't be with you."

He called of course, but she didn't answer the phone, told her father and Loretta to say she wasn't home. He wrote to her. She didn't open his letters. She couldn't bear to.

The last few weeks of summer seemed to pass in a dream.

Weekdays up at Columbia, she observed and dissected ants, then analyzed their parts with the gas chromatograph. Saturdays, she did fieldwork with Dr. Somersby or visited museums or studied with Mallory. And every Sunday, which was the only time both Gigi and Loretta were reliably out of the house, she came together with Ham on the wildly twining vines of the ivy-covered daybed.

On the first of September, Ham moved into an apartment in Midwood that Gigi and Loretta had found so he could be closer to Brooklyn College. They were able to pull together the basics he would need from Gigi's attic: a single bed, a desk, a table and chairs. Waldo's codicil would cover his rent and living expenses.

The old furniture was to be delivered by Mr. Esposito, the grocer, and Abraham & Straus would deliver Gigi's housewarming gift: two brand-new captain's chairs with red leather seats and brass nails. Gigi sent Ham and Wally off in a taxi full of boxes to receive the furniture deliveries and get the apartment set up. From Loretta and Gigi's points of view, nothing seemed odd about the closeness that had developed between Ham and Wally in the weeks since he'd returned. The children were the oldest of friends. Anything beyond that simply went unimagined, and Ham and Wally made extremely sure not to do or say anything to challenge their assumptions.

That night, after they'd unpacked the cast-off dishes and spare pots and pans from Loretta's kitchen, Ham and Wally went shopping and bought noodles and tomatoes and cheese and wine and cooked the first meal they'd ever made together, just the two of them. After they ate, Wally began to clear the dishes, but Ham stopped her and led her over to the single bed.

"Don't you think we ought to wash up, put away some of your things?"

"No." He smiled.

She wasn't sure why she was nervous, all of a sudden. Something seemed different now, with them alone together in a place where there was no fear of interruption. It seemed like real life.

"I just want to unpack your duffel bag, so you can get the main things put away. And I want to see what a soldier has."

"No."

"Do you have any real clothes in there, or just fatigues, anyway?"

"Relax, Wally. Do you really want to unpack? I've got a better idea."

"No, I guess not," she said, letting herself flop backward on the bed. They spent a slow hour discovering its creaks.

That afternoon, Ham took the train back to Borough Hall with Wally.

"Are you going to come to the house?" Wally asked. "Because I think they're going to guess something before too long, if we don't watch it. They're going to see something."

"No, you're right," he answered. "I just wanted to see you home safe. But what if they did? What would it actually matter, Wally? Aren't we ever going to tell them?"

That was when Wally saw Leo. She wanted to turn and walk the other way, she wanted to evaporate, but it was too late. He'd seen her.

"Wally?" Leo called, approaching tentatively. She could see, even from that distance, that he hadn't given up. She had dismissed him cruelly, but he still loved her.

Walking toward them, Leo looked at Ham. First with puzzlement, then recognition, then a strained smile.

"Hi, Leo," Wally said. She didn't know how to go on.

"Wally, what happened? Why did you — Why wouldn't you talk to me? Are you . . . all right?" he asked, but his question trailed off. She could see his eyes dart quickly left, then right, his confusion morph into hurt.

"I'm sorry. I should have called you back," she said, but he didn't seem to be listening. He was too busy sizing up Ham.

"You must be Hamilton Walker," Leo said at last.

"Must be."

If Ham was confused — for Wally had never mentioned Leo — he didn't show it. But Wally noticed his posture shift slightly. He didn't know exactly who Leo was to him — an enemy or a fellow soldier, a superior or a subordinate — and it made him stand taller.

"Well, then," Leo said. "Welcome home."

"Thank you."

"I should introduce you," Wally stammered. "Ham, this is Leo; Leo, this is Ham."

"I'm a — uh — friend of Wally's," Leo said.

"It's nice to meet you," said Ham, sliding his hand into Wally's, staking his claim. She wished he hadn't, but she took it in hers automatically.

"Well," Leo said, and she saw all his plans change — for the afternoon, for the future.

Wally had been very bad to him, she knew. She hadn't meant to. She really had loved him — and madly, for a while — but never as much as she did Ham. It wouldn't have been honest, she told herself, to stay with a man she didn't love anymore.

"I'm sorry, Leo."

"Me too."

"Good-bye, then."

"Good-bye."

As Wally and Ham turned away from Leo and headed for Columbia Heights, their hands fell apart. He was silent for a while. Finally, as they neared the Wallace house, he asked quietly, "Was that what I think it was?"

"What did you think it was?" she asked.

"Was that your *boy*friend?"

She remained silent. She didn't know how to explain the timing of it all.

"Who was that, Wally?"

"That was Leo. He's a painter. I was seeing him, before you got home."

"He's still in love with you."

She didn't answer.

"Isn't he?"

"What does it matter? I'm not in love with him. I haven't seen him for a month, not since before you came home. I was kind of cooling off with him, and then when you came home I just . . . I wrote him a letter, and then I just didn't call him back anymore, after we —"

"You mean you were his girlfriend till right when I came back?"

She didn't answer.

"And you wrote him a Dear John letter, even though he was right in the city?"

"I didn't know what to say to him."

"Why didn't you tell me about him?"

She looked away.

"You were keeping your options open."

"That's not it. I'd told him all about you, before."

"What did you tell him?"

"I don't know, Ham, about when we were kids."

"Because there wasn't anything to tell, unless you described how the son of your maid used to get paid to be your friend."

"What?"

"I don't know, Wally," he said, backing up and looming tall. "Why don't you just go be with the white boy? He's more your type."

"Why are you being like this? What was I supposed to do, stay a little girl the whole time you were gone, waiting for you to come back from war?"

But Ham didn't answer her, he just turned and walked away.

He got back on the subway and rode it out to Flatbush Avenue, still fuming about Wally's boyfriend. He could see in her eyes that Leo was more than just a guy she'd dated. She was genuinely torn, or at the very least guilty. Wally had made him so happy, but now he was more unhappy than he could believe. The way she looked at that man, Leo, made him question what the two of them had been doing. All of a sudden, Ham felt almost depraved. She was practically his sister, after all. It wasn't right.

He bought some beer at the deli on Nostrand and walked home. When he got inside, he slammed the door behind him and muttered, *"Dammit! Damn her!"* He opened a bottle of beer and then went to his duffel bag. In the middle, inside his worn left boot, he found a bundle carefully wrapped in an old sock.

He hadn't touched it for weeks now.

It called to him sometimes, and sometimes he was afraid of it, but the last month had been easier. He hadn't been listening to any Siren calls but Wally's. Wally, he'd thought, was good for him. He knew the small brown glass bottle of morphine wasn't. Now he didn't care. He unfurled the wrapping and found the bottle, a couple of glass syringes, and a bag containing dozens of preloaded ampoules of morphine.

Over there, he'd used as much as he wanted to, as much as he needed to, to make it through the day. When he first got injured, it didn't take much of the stuff to turn pain to relief, even happiness. Then his leg was better, and he was happy to quit it. He was glad to be able to take a shit again, to think again. But then there were other injuries, smaller ones, and a hellish case of trench foot. He'd slipped back into the medic's bag to find an answer, again and again, till he needed it just to get through the day.

How many men had he given it to, in the field, tagging them with the time of the injection? How many times had he watched their agony rise up and away from them like steam? It was just the same with himself, but then, gradually, the amounts he needed to feel good increased. No matter. It was easy to get, for a medic in Korea. He wondered how long it would be before he found a way to buy it here, or a doctor who would write him a prescription.

A quarter grain, he thought, pulling the ring off the syrette, and pressing the ampoule into his thigh. He liked the small sting of the needle. His heart surged in anticipation as he squeezed. *To ease unbearable pain.*

Rejoice! he thought, with all his being, and in just a few beats, his breath was happy.

His lungs were happy.

His skin was happy.

His very atoms were happy.

His eyes blurred.

His lips buzzed.

Rejoice!

Before that moment, he'd been angry, hungry, hurt, and irremediably unhappy. Now, with the small help of that chemical, he was fine, all of him, even his mind. His mind floated free. He drifted into the realm of joy as his eyes rolled back into the darkness of their sockets.

After God knew how long, he stirred and rubbed the injection site, reawakening the pinch that meant release, relief, and he thought about Twombley. Of all the men he'd fought alongside, Twombley was the only one he could imagine having kept up with, after the war. If only he'd been a medic then, instead of a fellow victim, he could have given Twombley the relief he needed, the full sweet rush of the junk hitting his brain, the blurriness, the clarity, the smoothness throughout his body, every cell. When the drug first hit, nothing was *that* bad. Not dying, like Twombley had been, not even being lied to by the love of your life. He was angry with her, jealous of the artist, but then it dawned on him that she'd rejected the white boy, after all. She'd chosen Ham. She'd said so. Everything was going to be all right.

A quarter grain, he thought, lying back on the blue ticking of his still unmade bed; *it sounds so small, but it's so large.*

■ ■ ■ ■

The next day, Ham stopped by the house, as expected. Because Loretta and Gigi were there, Wally and Ham spoke as if nothing exceptional had passed between them. Wally was desperate to catch him alone, or just to catch his eye, but Ham avoided any possibility of that.

"Why don't you invite Leo for supper this weekend, Wally?" Gigi suggested. "I haven't seen him in a month, I don't think. I suppose you've heard all about the fabulous Leo, Ham?"

"Actually, I've met him."

"Oh?" said Loretta. "When'd you meet him? I was just thinking he hadn't been around much."

"On the street the other day."

"There's something I didn't tell anyone," Wally began, not at all sure she wanted to speak. "I broke it off with Leo a few weeks ago."

"Oh, honey," said Loretta, looking puzzled. "Did you really?"

"But why?" asked Gigi.

"I don't really want to talk about it."

"Excuse me," said Ham and turned to go to the cook's apartment.

"Just a moment, Hamilton," said Gigi. "Before you go, I wanted to say that I'd like to continue our dining together. It was a grand idea of Wally's, I think. What would you two say to a regular evening, say Sunday, when Wally is here already?"

"I'll be in Midwood, Miz Doc," said Ham. "I don't think —"

"Nonsense. You'll take the train home. How long is the trip?"

"Thirty-five minutes."

"Well, that's not even as far as Wally comes. So it's settled. You'll come home on Sunday nights for a family supper, and you'll both give us all your report on your schooling."

"All right, Gigi," said Wally.

"Yes, ma'am," said Ham, somewhat to all of their surprise.

Soldiers, Gigi thought, were among the frailest people she had ever seen. Stella'd had it too, that soldier-like fragility — tough but on a precipice. She certainly had seen death and suffered repeated shocks, as Gigi supposed most veterans had. One thing Gigi knew: People like that, with shadows lurking in the backs of their minds, didn't do well with idle time. She was determined to make sure Hamilton Walker didn't have any.

Getting Ham into college had been the

first step, an easy one, since she knew the dean of freshmen. The next was to keep him interested in his studies and interested in medicine, and to make sure he didn't drift off the way so many returning veterans were doing. To that end, she secured him a job as an ambulance driver, a perfect position for an Army medic, if there was one, and if she did say so herself. He would find the usual urban emergency a simple thing and take even the occasional trauma case in stride. Ham seemed glad to have it. Working things out for Ham was important to Gigi because of Waldo, but it also made her feel better about never having permitted him in the parlors as a boy, not having raised Loretta's wages as often as perhaps she ought.

A few nights after their next family dinner, which was somehow even more awkward than the first one had been, Wally went to Ham. She didn't call, just took the train way out to Midwood and knocked on the door. She was afraid he might not be there, or worse, that he might not let her in.

But he was there, and he opened the door. They stepped toward each other almost reflexively, then both pulled back.

"Wally."

"Hi, Ham."

"I'm mad at you, Wally Baker."

"Don't be," she said. She looked around and saw how neat the apartment was. The bed was made tight as a drum. The military was good for some things, she thought.

"Ham, I wasn't ever lying to you. I told you I'd had a boyfriend, and I did break up with him — though I admit I didn't handle it very well."

"No."

"So, that's it? Just because Leo is still hung up on me, you're not interested anymore. You don't even know him. He's like a puppy. He's been asking me to marry him since the first day we met."

"Wally, it's not just that. I've been thinking — I don't think it's right what we've been doing. You're almost like my sister."

"Your sister?" she said with a kind of revulsion, but as soon as he'd said it, she knew what he meant. It was true. He'd been with her all along, every day, and all the best and worst moments of her life. She loved him, but maybe she wasn't really in love with him, after all. Maybe it was all an enormous mistake. And then she was crying, and he was holding her, comforting her, but not caressing her.

"I'm not sorry we did what we did, I'm not," she said. "But you're right. We have to stop it."

"Yeah, I'm not sorry, either, unless it's hurt you."

"I don't know," she said, stepping away from him and sitting down at his dinette. "I'm okay, but I feel badly about Leo. I dropped him without any thought. I think I may have ruined something good."

"Is that skinny white guy really your type?" He laughed.

"Come on, Ham. You can't have it both ways."

"I know. It's just —"

"I'll be busier with classes anyway, I guess, now the semester's started."

"What are you taking?"

"Biochem, scientific German, art history, and a lab section. Plus an independent study for the ant lab."

"You want to know what I'm going to be taking, Wally?" he asked. "Listen to this: biology, history of philosophy, the World Wars, and calculus."

"That's great," she said.

"Plus your grandmother's got me all tied up with her ambulance corps. I won't even have weekends free to catch up on my reading. Maybe next semester I'll start on some electives."

"You're a real college boy now."

"I guess you would know. I can't believe you're ahead of me now. You're going to graduate a year before me."

"But I won't be finished. I'll just be going to graduate school after that."

It felt good to be talking to Ham like this, though she was still taking in all they'd said. She went into the bathroom to wash herself up, splash water on her face, and try not to cry at the thought that she couldn't be in love with Ham Walker, because something like that, it just wasn't allowed. She was looking for a bottle of aspirin for her splitting headache when she opened the medicine cabinet, but what she found was unfamiliar. His kit. The tourniquet, morphine, and syringe. She came out pale and livid with the brown bottle in her hand.

"Ham, you're going to kill yourself, you fool."

"What?" he said, turning, and when he saw what she had he grew angry and lunged at her, trying to grab the bottle. "That's none of your damn business. What were you snooping in the cabinet for?"

Wally felt a falling sensation, maybe fear, as she backed away from him and moved the bottle behind her back.

"So you take it? You take this stuff?"

"What do you think? You found it in my

bathroom, didn't you?"

"Why? Why are you doing this to your-self?"

"You wouldn't understand. And you don't have to understand. It's my business."

There was no way he could tell Wally about the visions he still had from Korea. Twombley. Morales. The wounded GI he had pulled from a pile of dead bodies, mag-gots dripping from the gunshot wound to his arm. Three dead soldiers lying beside a path, naked but for their dog tags and the dozens of spear holes that punctured their flesh. He didn't tell her how he woke, many nights, at 3:00 A.M., seized with a terror of being abandoned by his platoon behind enemy lines.

"But, Ham, I care about you. This is bad stuff."

"I can manage just fine, Wally."

"I'm not giving this back to you."

"That's mine," he said. "Not to mention I have more."

She made for the door, and he blocked her, grabbing her wrist and prying the bottle from her hand. It bounced against the wooden floorboards but didn't break, then rolled beneath the bed.

Both their eyes followed the sound.

"Fine." She wasn't going to crawl around

392

on her knees beneath his bed looking for it, only to have him overpower her.

"Now why don't you go," he said evenly, letting go of her arm.

So she went.

Wally worried, worried and pined, she knew not for whom, whether Ham, Leo, or herself. All she knew was she had found two men she loved and lost them both. She tried going out to Chumley's with Mallory a few times, but it just wasn't the same. Instead, she poured herself into her work at the lab, and in early December, they finally isolated a pheromone that worked. The ants actually followed the trail. There was going to be another paper, a really important one this time, with her name on it somewhere — twentieth, perhaps, but still the name Baker, B. would be somewhere on the list of authors.

And then came the Saturday morning just before Christmas when Wally and Ham were both back in Brooklyn for the holiday. Wally came down to the kitchen in her pajamas for breakfast. When she heard Ham coming out from the back room, she suddenly wished she had dressed. They'd seen each other at Sunday dinners, but though they'd acted polite, they hadn't exchanged a meaningful word since she'd found his morphine.

Loretta was making pancake batter when Wally entered the kitchen around seven. The coffeepot was steaming.

"Oh," said Loretta. "I thought you were your grandmother. She hasn't come down yet."

"But where is she?" asked Wally. "I didn't hear her upstairs. You're sure she hasn't come down?"

Wally went to see why Gigi wasn't up, and there she was, lying on the carpet, facing away, on her side.

"Gigi!" Wally called, her voice shrill and afraid.

"Loretta!"

It was her heart, said Dr. Evans, who came along with the ambulancemen and stayed after they had left. "The heart's what gets most of us, you know." He was an old friend of Gigi's, though a generation younger — Wally's mother's age, or the age she would have been, had she lived.

At noon, when everything was said and certain, the grapefruit half was still there, drying up in its glass dish on its blue willow underplate, five or six dutiful fruitflies hovering above.

In the murky time between death and

394

burial, Wally crept up to Gigi's room often, to look around, to touch the things on the dresser, the brush with loose gray hairs caught in its bristles. Once, she lay down on Gigi's bed, trying to find her grandmother's particular scent, but then she remembered she and Loretta had already flipped the mattress and put fresh sheets on.

"Why did we have to flip the mattress?" she asked Loretta later. "It wasn't soiled. What's that for?"

"Because that's what you do, that's why," Loretta said. "Some things you just do, no point asking why."

The night before the funeral, Wally wasn't sure she would ever fall asleep. She thought not of her grandmother, of her mother, of Leo, but of Ham and his tranquillity. Was he using it, still? She felt afraid that he would die, that Loretta would die. Of course, she could hear the small sounds that told her Loretta and Ham were in the basement, very much alive. She tried to tell herself that everything was just like it used to be, but it wasn't. She was terribly alone.

She wished Ham were with her, or Leo. She wished her mother were still alive, or Gigi. Just someone to call her family, so she wasn't so alone. She felt a twitch in her gut

There seemed to be a faint draft, though the door and the window were closed. Was she alone?

"Gigi," she cried out. "Gigi!"

She clutched her blankets as a falling person might clutch the turf on the edge of a cliff. Her eyes opened wide.

Here I am, she thought, sitting bolt upright in bed.

Awake.

Alone.

Then she felt it again, that strange fluttering in her stomach.

31
SCRAPBOOKING

Loretta flipped down the steps on the kitchen stool and climbed to reach the highest pantry shelf, where the big cookbooks were and, beside them, the scrapbooks. Her latest one was thick and heavy — almost full. She had been filling up scrapbooks at the rate of one every three or four years ever since she began at the Wallace house, but in the month since Gigi Wallace had died, she hadn't added a thing. Now, somehow, she felt ready.

Her paste pot was in the utility drawer along with the scissors, the screwdriver, the hammer, some tea tins full of nails and cup hooks, a dish of rubber bands, several dull pencils, a red china marker, a roll of tape, an errant canning lid, and a church key that more properly belonged in the kitchen-utensil drawer. She gathered what she needed, opened her clipping folder, and sat down at the table to begin the page that would document the death of Gigi Wallace and the state of the world at the time she had died. She'd saved articles from the newspapers, the latest from Indochina and a picture of a lynching in Alabama. There were clippings of movie stars, too, of course, the death notice of Gigi that had run in two national papers, and the glowing obituary published by the neighborhood weekly gazette. Loretta left room around the items she pasted in to write a short narrative of the day Gigi died, and the funeral.

As she worked, Loretta envisioned the layout of the first scrapbook she'd ever pasted up. It was just a simple bound notebook, with snapshots and clippings glued over the lined paper. It was tucked away in a sealed box because she had never wanted Ham to find it and start asking questions. There was a picture of Loretta and Washington with Hamilton and Ham's mother, Nellie, when Nellie was pregnant. There was Ham as a newborn baby in Nellie's arms, then older in Loretta's, and another of him being pushed in a stroller through the garden at Columbia Heights by a young Stella. She'd also included the inauguration of Franklin D. Roosevelt, an article about the terrible exploits of Bonnie and Clyde, an obituary of John Dillinger, and the headline that proclaimed the end of Prohibition. As Ham grew older, news of conflict in Europe took increasing space in the scrapbook, but Ham's childhood was the thread that connected the events of the outer world. That's what a child's life ought to be, she thought: the main event. The pictures of Ham were taken by Waldo or Stella with the Wallaces' Kodak. The Wallaces slipped in, too, frequently enough, and the entire last page of that first book had to do with Stella's engagement to Billy Galt: a handwritten invitation to the engagement party, a picture of Ham with the caption "Ham will be the ring bearer!" and even a list of wedding gifts that Loretta had somewhat anomalously jotted down on the inside back cover: the dozen silver goblets sent by one of Billy's aunts from Minnesota, a silver stuffing spoon, eight crystal water glasses, a wine coaster. She'd meant to paste something more meaningful over top of that, eventually, but in the end, it remained, with each item crossed out by Loretta in pencil when she sent it back to the giver with a note advising of the accident and the cancellation of the wedding. Loretta had pasted Billy Galt's obituary in where she'd originally expected the engagement announcement to go. But that was then. This was now. Why were the death pages the most memorable? she wondered. Why couldn't people fix their minds as strongly on happy times and regular days?

She turned to the items in her current folder. They had sent a dog, of all things, into space. That would have to go in, somewhere on the periphery. The next clipping was the key one: "Georgeanna Harris Wallace, M.D., 77, women's physician and maven of Brooklyn society, survived by her granddaughter, Wallace Baker, also of Brooklyn," it began. *And don't forget her maid,* thought Loretta, and then laughed at her own audacity. Obituaries were curious things, she thought: too short to be meaningful to anyone who knew their subjects, too long to be of much interest to strangers. As she trimmed the edges with her scissors, she recalled mounting Stella's death notice, years before, opposite the V-J Day headline from the *Times*. There was nothing so definitive to pair Miz Doc's notice with — it had been just another day. All death notices are about the same length, Loretta thought, regardless of how long one has lived or how much one has accomplished. She spread a rectangle of glue and positioned Georgeanna Harris Wallace smack in the center of a page.

"The lord is my shepherd; I shall not want," she wrote beneath it. "Yea, though I walk through the valley of the shadow of death, I will fear no evil. . . . My cup runneth over. Surely goodness and mercy shall follow me all the days of my life." Same thing she wrote on every death page.

She pictured Stella's page, created so many years before, and the moment when Miz Doc had walked into the kitchen, wearing her light blue gabardine. Loretta despised that suit. It took a stain if it even got close anything oily, and it was murder to iron. She'd spent more hours slaving over that one piece of clothing, over the years, than she cared to tot up. Loretta had slammed the book shut, not wanting Miz Doc to see. She had included something Miz Doc would not have wanted her to.

"Loretta," Gigi Wallace had said to her, a few days before, just the day after it had happened, "you must swear something to me."

"Yes'm," Loretta had said. She always said *yes'm* to Miz Doc.

"You're not to tell Wally."

"Not to tell her what?"

"Loretta, this is not some joke, I mean it."

"I wouldn't joke, Miz Doc. But not tell her what?"

"That Stella took her own life, of course."

Loretta blinked. She'd never thought she'd hear anyone, least of all Miz Doc, speak that fact aloud. There were so many ways a person could tell a story about what had happened. She was baking a cake and there was a momentary bobble in the gas, letting the oven go out. Or it was her heart. In Loretta's estimation, no one ever had to say *she took her own life,* not out loud at any rate, not while Wally was a child. Loretta didn't know what she'd been planning to say to Wally, but it certainly wasn't that.

"I'm sure not going to say it, but I can't help what she saw. One day, she'll understand more about the world and put things together. It will be good for her to know what happened. She can read the note then."

"No, don't you see? She didn't understand, Loretta. Certainly not about the gas. And I don't want her ever to understand it. Do you hear? You told me yourself she didn't see the note, so she doesn't know about that, does she? It's up to us to shape what she remembers. To make sure what she remembers about her mother is something — tolerable."

"Children take in a lot, Miz Doc," Loretta said. The two women gazed at each other in a kind of standoff. "So you're not planning to give it to her then, not ever?"

"Of course not. It's not something she should have to read. As far as Wally is concerned, Stella died of natural causes. And that's it."

Loretta took a breath, looked down and then back up and straight into Gigi's eyes. "I think the letter is important. The last words of a mother to her daughter. We can't —"

"Well, it's too late. I burned it in the fireplace last night."

What Loretta would have given for a last note from her mama, whatever it might have said. That someone could destroy such a thing appalled her.

"Loretta," Gigi said, seeing Loretta's disapproval. "There are many reasons she can't ever know. I need you with me on this. *Promise me.*"

Loretta bowed her head. What choice did she have?

"Yes, ma'am, Miz Doc, I swear it," Loretta said. But then she'd gone and transcribed it — or all she remembered of it — into her scrapbook so she could make her own choice, when the time came. There, amidst the record of turmoil of those days — not just Stella's death but the telegram

403

announcing Washington Walker's loss over the Sea of Japan and the bombing of Hiroshima — there stood, written out in Loretta's loopy handwriting, the only existing copy of Stella's final letter to her daughter.

What troubled Loretta now wasn't that she had written out the letter, or what she remembered of it; it was that she had kept it hidden from Wally for so long, that one and the other one, to Bill Niederman. Now that Miz Doc was gone, it was time to let Wally know what she knew, but Loretta still didn't have the whole truth. There had been one more piece of the puzzle — a telegram that had come for Stella, but all that was left of it was the empty Western Union envelope and a pile of ash with one perforated corner of telegram paper left intact, sitting in the white enamel sink. So Stella had lit a match, Loretta had thought, at the time. She'd had a match, and she'd lit a match, and there hadn't been an explosion, meaning it was only after she burned the telegram that she turned the gas back on.

When a woman dies, worlds die with her. All Stella's exploits — her jokes, her sorrows, and her quarrels — gone. All her memories of other people, gone on before. And whatever that telegram had said that sent her into despair. There was so much that Wally could never know about her mother. There were other, knowable things that Wally had been prevented from knowing because that was the way Miz Doc wanted it. What strength did the oath she'd extracted from Loretta still hold?

Gigi Wallace's was a grand funeral with all the pomp and eulogies that an upstanding lady physician of Brooklyn Heights could have hoped for. As she sat in a pew beside her father and listened to the words of the Book of Revelation — "Death will be no more; mourning and crying and pain will be no more, for the first things have passed away" — Wally wondered what her own mother's service had been like.

With no one but Loretta to depend on, and Loretta busy putting on the funeral reception, Wally clung to her father's side, but she was terribly at sea that whole day. She smiled sadly so many times her jaw ached. She shook so many hands she had the urge to go and wash her own. All she wanted to do was weep alone in her room, but it just wasn't possible.

Then, as she struggled toward the powder room, to steal a minute alone, Leo approached her. She was surprised to see him.

They hadn't spoken since that time on the street.

"Wally," he said and clasped her hand, and this time she didn't need to smile. She let herself cry. He didn't take her in his arms — they were far from that being possible — but from the way he asked her what had happened and listened to her answer, she felt as if he did.

"You know," he said sadly but smiling slightly, "I was always rather terrified of your grandmother. I was more relieved to find out she liked me than I was to find out you did, I think."

"She did like you. She was cross with me for messing things up."

"Me too," he said.

"I'm sorry, Leo."

"Me too."

Somehow, when he was gone, she'd found she was able to bear the rest of the afternoon. He had seen her aloneness and somehow, quietly, kindly, without their having reconciled, been willing to relieve it.

Two days later, he came by the Wallace house unexpectedly.

"How did you even know I'd be here?"

"I just kind of figured you would be, for a few days at least."

It seemed like an overture to something more, just his coming there. And he let her talk — about her family, her grandmother, her mother, her mother's death.

"I remember more about when she died, all of a sudden," Wally told him. "Something came back to me. Somehow seeing Gigi lying there on the floor reminded me of the most horrible sight: my mother keeled over on the floor with a pool of black liquid around her."

"Blood?" he asked.

"I don't know. I don't know. No one ever said she had been killed, though I used to imagine it. I don't know where that image comes from, but it keeps flashing before me."

"Maybe you need to ask Loretta a little more about what she remembers, what she knows," he suggested. "She might tell you things — now — that she couldn't before."

"Do you think?"

"Maybe," he said. "And speaking of Loretta, how is Ham?"

"I'm not too sure. I think he's doing well at school."

"But aren't you —" he asked.

"We're not, you know, seeing each other or anything."

"I thought you were. I kept wondering

where he was all this time."

"Not anymore. We had been, but it wasn't right. We grew up together."

"Wally?" he asked, taking a risk now, reaching for her hand. "Would you consider going out with me again sometime, just to Chumley's or something?"

"Yeah, Leo, I would. I'd really like that."

32
DEAR WALLY

"Loretta?" Wally called. "Sorry I'm late! I had to stop by Daddy's to get some things for the weekend. Leo and I are going out to the movies later."

"Are you now? So that's back on?" Loretta frowned.

"Maybe."

Loretta was in the kitchen, standing at the stove, tending to a pot of stock. She was glad Wally was still getting on with her father, and glad she was still splitting her time between the two residences, but there was worry and melancholy, too. The Wallace house couldn't possibly remain the Wallace house for very long, and as for Wally, Loretta wasn't at all sure what she was going to do next with her life — she was about to face some awfully large decisions.

"Well, dinner's almost ready. Ham'll be over any minute."

"What?"

"Well, it's like this. I've been thinking you two have some things to talk out, and it's about time I got you together."

"What do you mean?"

"Nine minutes, and noodles are cooked. Nine months, and a baby comes out. Nothing to be done about the timing of certain things, Wally, and no time to lose on this one."

The blood left Wally's cheeks.

She was late. And she'd felt that fluttering more and more as the weeks passed, try as she might to ignore it. How could Loretta know it before she did? She didn't think Loretta had even known about her and Ham.

"Ham used to say to me, *I can't wait, Mama!* How many times?" mused Loretta. "Just about regular things, dinner, baseball season, growing up. Then other times, he'd just dawdle and procrastinate. And now, you two. First, you couldn't wait. Now, you're putting off things that need tending to. Reason I called you both here, Wally, is to give you a talking-to. You don't have a lot of time to make your minds up."

Loretta couldn't pinpoint the moment when she'd realized something was brewing between Ham and Wally. At first, it was simply unimaginable, but not long after

Ham returned, she'd sensed a magnetism between the children that had frightened her. Her worry increased when Wally quit bringing Leo around. She hadn't guessed they'd gotten quite so carried away until the past week or two, when despite their apparent estrangement, Wally had begun to blossom in a way Loretta couldn't help but notice. She was going to get herself expelled if she didn't do something fast.

"But, Loretta," Wally said. "Oh, Loretta —"

She couldn't form her thoughts into words. It was such a different conversation than Wally had anticipated. She'd been planning to talk to Loretta about Leo, how she might be getting back together with Leo. Not that terrible mistake between her and Ham. Not what Loretta seemed to be suggesting: that she was having a baby. And she could not possibly be having Leo's baby, Wally thought to herself, wishing she were wrong.

"It's time to figure things out, what you're gonna do."

"Loretta, I didn't even realize it," she said.

"I guess you didn't, but to me it's plain as day."

"How —" Wally said, but she couldn't go on.

"You have the look, just exactly like your mother looked, and Miz Doc Wallace before that. And I guessed as much about you and Ham."

Wally felt her face going red, the way she'd felt as a kid, when she was caught reading comics off the rack by Mr. Merganser.

"What about Ham, does he know already?"

"Not yet."

"What am I going to do?" Wally looked at her feet, feeling like the harlot that man at Coney Island had accused her of being.

"Sugar, there's only two things you can do."

One look at Wally's face and Loretta knew: Wally was going to have the child. But would she keep it? As for how Ham would take the news, she couldn't guess. He'd been so unsteady since he came home, so distant.

"Loretta, Ham and I aren't seeing each other anymore —"

"I noticed, but that doesn't change your situation."

Loretta couldn't fathom it, Ham and Wally, together, Ham and Wally even thinking that way about each other. They were both like children to her. It made her uncomfortable, to say the least, but that didn't mean she could ignore reality.

The kitchen timer went off.

"Dinner'll be ready soon," Loretta said. "Now why don't you go wash up?"

Noodles were far more reliable than people, she thought, pouring off the water as Wally left the room. And so were timers, just as long as there was someone there to hear them and respond to their alarm.

The Bakers' kitchen timer had gone off just as Loretta and Wally had entered the apartment on V-J afternoon. Then came a thud and a clatter. At first, before they went to the kitchen, Loretta had thought it was the oven door slamming shut, but in fact it was the weight of Stella's body tipping her chair, the chair hitting the tiled floor, the coffee cup breaking. The sight of Stella lying in that pool of spilled black coffee was as harrowing as if it had been blood. Loretta figured that the gas might have been flowing for as much as a full hour, what with the timer. The oven was set to 275 degrees — just right for a two-hour cake, cold start, all except for two things: The match had never been lit and Stella had already baked her cake. There it sat, on the table.

Sometimes, when she thought about it, Loretta still wanted to shout, What in damnation, Stella, what in *damnation* was that oven doing on? What were you thinking, you fool girl, Stella Wallace? Then she just sighed. What was the point? She'd never spoken to Stella that way in life. She wished she had, but the chance was long past.

She wasn't going to let anything go unsaid, this time. She hadn't seen the end coming, with Stella. She had held her tongue, though she'd known well enough that Stella was going to have a rough time of it, one way or another, dealing with Bill Niederman's baby. She had been waiting for Stella to come to her. And look what had happened. That was why now, with Wally, she wasn't going to leave a single thing to chance, much less Wally's life dangling from the thread of a half hour's delay.

The noodles sat steaming in the colander. She poured them into a bowl, lopped off a good quarter stick of butter, and tossed in a pinch of salt and a grind of pepper. The chops were sizzling in the pan. The new boy at Esposito's had cut them nicely, eighth inch of fat all around, and thin. The butcher paper they came in still sat slack and bloody on the plate, and she wadded it up and threw it in the garbage. The okra stood washed and chopped in the bowl, waiting to take a quick trip past the frying pan, just a sizzle of oil, salt, and vinegar and a grind or two of pepper. Wally liked it when the seeds were still crunchy and the stickiness hadn't come out. Loretta and Ham, they liked it gooey, so she would leave theirs in the pan till the last. She looked around her, toward the front hall, wondering where Ham was, whether he knew anything, if he would even come.

There were things she needed to say to the two of them, Ham and Wally, together. It was time. There was a baby's life at stake. Her grandchild. Loretta had always believed a good meal could ease a person's mind, perhaps even help to change it. Noodles and pork chops and a dose of honesty were what she planned to serve to Ham and Wally that night.

What would Ham say, when he learned he was going to be a father? What was Wally going to do when she learned how her mother had died and that she had been with child? Would it bring them back together? She didn't even know what she herself wanted — a baby, for sure, but a marriage? Between those two?

She knew how hard it would be for Wally to have a Negro child. It had been hard for Nellie Grun, Ham's mama. Loretta had no illusions that Nellie had ever really meant to come back to her mixed-race baby. If she had the baby, Wally could expect to face constant curiosity, and judgment and scandal.

Loretta poured herself the last cup of coffee from the morning pot, put up a new one straightaway, then went to the icebox and took out the square glass bottle of cream. She shook it, popped the lid, and poured a dollop in her cup, then watched the whiteness sink down and rise again before it was lost in the paper-bag brownness of the coffee.

She got out a Ball jar of homemade applesauce and poured it in a bowl. Ham could put away a large plate of pork chops with buttered noodles and applesauce. Wally too.

Loretta set the table for three — Wally at the head. Wally was the mistress of the house, now. She seemed just the same as when she was a child, and yet she wasn't the least bit what anyone — say Waldo, or her mother, or even Loretta — would have predicted. What she was, Loretta thought, was a kind of glue. With the baby she was carrying, she had the power to join two families that had been living side by side for decades now without anyone thinking of merging them. In her belly, in that baby, if only Loretta could make sure they kept it, there was part of Ham, and that was as close as she was ever going to get to some of her being passed down in the world.

Who are we to one another tonight? she wondered. *Who will we be next month, next year?* If they didn't keep the baby, would she stay? If they did, would Loretta still be the maid?

Would she work for Wally, just the way she had for Miz Doc Wallace?

"Do you want to keep waiting?" Wally asked. Dinner had been ready for a quarter hour, and they were still sitting at the kitchen table, waiting for Ham. "I'm ravenous."

"I guess I'll just make him a plate and set it in the oven."

"Loretta, what am I supposed to do? I'm not in love with Ham. Neither of us is —" She paused. "I'm in love with Leo."

"Love is a whole separate business from babies, Wally."

"But that's ridiculous, of course it isn't!"

That was when the front door slammed and Ham walked in.

"Hiya, Mama. Hi, Wally," Ham said. "I didn't know you were coming. I thought it was just going to be the Walker family tonight."

417

"I'd still call it a family meeting," said Loretta.

Wally tried to give Ham a look that might warn him what was coming, but there wasn't any way to convey it. He looked back at her puzzled and said, "What?"

Wally shrugged and looked away.

"All right, you two," Loretta said, once they had started eating. "You've got yourselves into trouble."

"What is this, Mama, dinner or a land mine?"

"Wally, you better go on and tell him."

"I might be —" She paused to breathe, to swallow, to look at the floor.

"— pregnant," said Loretta, at last.

"Pregnant?"

"Yes."

"Why didn't you tell me?" Ham said, his fork dropping to his plate with a clatter. "What'd you have to get Mama in on it for?"

"I didn't tell her," Wally said. "She knew before I did."

For a few minutes it was silent but for the clinking of silver on china. Finally, Loretta fixed her gaze on her son.

"What do you have to say, Hamilton?"

"Well," Ham said. "I guess there's two choices. I know which one I'd take."

Wally began to cry into her napkin.

"Oh no, uh-uh," said Loretta. "Let's not get started off this way. There's some background information I want you both to think on before you all go down any particular road. The first think has to do with Ham's mama. Did you ever show Wally that picture I gave you, Son?"

"I saw it," said Wally. "She was beautiful."

"So what's your point, Mama? Just because I'm half white I ought to have a child with a white woman, too?"

"Ham, don't you be an ornery fool."

"Wally and me, we don't want to be together. It was . . . a mistake. We can't raise a child."

Wally gulped and wiped her face.

"Wally," said Loretta. "I want to tell you something about your mama. Maybe it would help you figure out what to do now, if you knew the whole story."

"You mean if I knew more about what happened to her? Are there things you haven't told me?"

"There are."

"Like what? What do you mean? Why didn't anyone tell me before?"

"It starts with Mr. Bill Niederman. Your mother and him were in love."

"I already guessed that much."

"And they were going to have a baby."

419

"What?"

"Darling," Loretta said, "there's some letters I have that have been waiting too long to be delivered. There's some things you need to understand about what happened to your mama at the end, what she thought and felt, and how she died."

For all those years, it had been almost as if Wally hadn't entered the kitchen that afternoon — as if she'd never seen her mother lying there. But as soon as Loretta said it, Wally remembered what she had seen.

She had a sudden vision of pushing the door open and seeing her mother facedown on the floor in a puddle of darkness, her legs askew, her shoe dislodged. There had been a pen and some papers on the table.

"What happened, exactly, Loretta? Did she take her own life?"

"She left the gas on, sugar, unlit, and it poisoned her."

After a long moment in which Wally stared blinking blindly at the greasy plate before her, Loretta stood and put her hand on Wally's shoulder. "Now come on, String Bean, there's something I need to show you."

Leaving Ham to ruminate over the prospect of fatherhood, Loretta led Wally to the pantry, where a cardboard shoe box of robin's egg blue sat on the counter. It was worn at the edges and printed all over with figures in bright yellow, red, and white: babies, elephants, geese, cats, balloons, children's blocks. A ribbon had been wound around it, a long time ago, it seemed. Some chemical in the ink or the cardboard of the box had made the threads go crispy and turned the satin brown.

"Do you have my mother's suicide note, Loretta? Is that what's in there?"

"Not a suicide note exactly, but a letter to you, and another one to Mr. Niederman."

"Loretta." Wally's voice was shaky. "I've always wanted to know what happened to her. How many times have I asked you about it? Why didn't anyone tell me? How could you keep my own mother's letter to me hidden away for so long?"

"Miz Doc made me swear not to tell you about it. She burnt the letter, but I had already read it, and I wrote down what it said, you see, at least what I could remember. You see, your Gigi didn't want you knowing how your mama died. Didn't want you remembering her that way, brooding on it, or God forbid, ever doing like your mama done."

Loretta took out a thick scrapbook from the box and flipped the pages till she came to one bordered in black ink. She handed the book to Wally, and as Wally read, she heard her mother's voice, that beautiful contralto, ringing in her ears.

I love you, my darling. I know you will grow up beautiful and strong and so smart, Wally. I've made a decision today that you may be angry about, but I feel I am right. I feel it is the only way. May you forgive me if it casts shadows over you, but please know, my darling child, that you are my firstborn, my first love, and I will always love you.

Wally found herself wiping her cheeks, almost shaking with tears, but she was still desperate for more information, something that would give sense to this new certainty: that her mother had taken her own life — had taken herself away from Wally forever — on purpose.

"What about the other letter?" she said quietly, at last. "The letter to Mr. Niederman."

Loretta turned to the front of the scrapbook and pulled out a blue envelope with an unfranked stamp on the front.

Wally saw the old bloodstain. "What's that spot?"

"A bit of blood, I think," Loretta said, just looking at her, steadfast in her certainty that she was doing the right thing. "I think she cut herself trying to pull it back out of the mail chute, after she'd sent it. Same thing happened to me when I got it out. But my hands were smaller."

Wally touched the bloodstain — a part of her mother's body, she thought.

"But why did she —"

"Read it."

Trembling, Wally slid her index finger under the flap and opened the envelope.

"Dear Bill," she read.

I would rather have told you this in person, but, well, it's a strange time, and all of a sudden, you have left. You have gone home. I don't know when you'll be back, but I have news, news I don't want to send by telegram or say over the telephone lines. Here it is, then, my love, my news: There has been an accident, a wonderful disaster: We are going to have a child.

It didn't read like a suicide note, Wally thought. What was this use of the future tense?

This is going to be complicated, to say the

least. It's nothing we'd have planned, God no, but we love one another, you and I, and even if that love is challenged, I know we will both love our child. The rest is going to be painful, uncomfortable, embarrassing, and possibly quite expensive. To have a child out of wedlock, it bucks propriety — and worse. I know Rudy and Louise are going to be hurt, probably Wally and your boys, too. But love, but life — mustn't they trump all the rest? Love and life, Bill. Remember those two, when you ask yourself how you got into this nightmare. I've been in a turmoil since I suspected it, but I feel redeemed all of a sudden. This awful world we've made — the horror your good mind helped to create — that isn't the end. Death and war happen, but nonetheless, there will be more babies, more joy, somehow. A child is better than an atom bomb — and stronger. It's the antidote. Isn't it obvious? Our lives may become more complex, but they'll be better.

"Loretta?" Wally said, looking up when she'd finished. "Did Gigi ever read this?"

"She never knew it existed. I never gave it to her. It wasn't addressed to her, after all."

"It's strange. She doesn't sound like a

woman about to kill herself."

"I know."

"But, Loretta, how does this make sense? If she was going to kill herself, why make plans for the future?"

"I don't know, but I blame myself, Wally. She was prone to ups and downs, sorrows and worries. Why did she try to take the letter out of the chute? Maybe something told her that dream couldn't be. Sometime around when she wrote those letters, she called me. She asked me to bring you home. Maybe she was afraid of what she might do. She needed me — and you — to keep her tethered to this earth, and we didn't come. I just wish to the good Lord we hadn't been late."

"Late?"

"We were thirty minutes later than she'd asked me to come. I had dinner to get on, and Ham had run off. We were late."

"You think that's when it happened?"

"I do."

"Something happened then, to make her despair?"

"Maybe just her own thoughts, her fear of bringing a child not her husband's into this world. And then there's the telegram I found burnt in the sink. Nothing left but

425

scraps and ashes. We'll never know what it said."

"A telegram."

"The reason I'm showing you this tonight, Wally, it's because I don't want you to go down her path. I don't want you to despair over this child. You can lose it if you must, or you can have it, whether you marry Ham or not, and whatever you do, you won't be alone. I'll be there every day of my life to help raise this child, if you have it. It's part of you, part of Ham, part of me."

Wally looked down. It was so much to think about. Her mother's suicide, the decision she had to make. It almost angered her, the way Loretta had arranged to deliver all this news at once, but it was so clear that Loretta was overflowing with worry and love, and doing anything she could to help.

"But I don't want a baby, Loretta. I'm not ready."

"Let me help you."

"Ham and I — that'll never work, you know."

"You don't have to marry to have a child, you know, if you're dead set against it. Your mother was going to do it, after all."

"I need some time to think about it. Let me take the letter. I think I'm going to deliver it."

33
Answers

The next day, Wally looked up the number for Rutgers, asked for Professor Niederman, and was connected to the Math Department.

"He's in class," said the secretary. "Can I take message?"

"Could you please tell him that Wallace Baker called, from Brooklyn?"

"All right. That's Miss Baker from Brooklyn College?"

"*Wallace* Baker. And not from Brooklyn College, just Brooklyn. Just Wallace Baker from Brooklyn. He'll know," she said and gave her number.

Just two hours after she'd left her message, the telephone rang. So many years since they'd talked, but his voice was the same. She wondered if her mother's voice would have sounded the same, if she could hear it again, after all that time.

"Is this Wally? *Wally Baker?*"

His voice was as sonorous and familiar as a radio news announcer's. She remembered suddenly how much she had loved him. Then a sharp anger coursed through her. He had abandoned her.

"Hello? Wally?"

She said nothing.

She had placed the call. She had rehearsed what she would say innumerable times. She had not, however, expected this rush of emotion. She coughed, managed a hoarse "This is she."

"How wonderful to get your call. *Wallace Baker from Brooklyn.* I'm glad to hear your voice after so very long. I'm so glad you called."

She didn't return his warmth. "I would like to speak with you, Mr. Niederman, about my mother."

He exhaled slowly. "Yes," he said, "of course. You've decided to settle some old questions."

"I do have questions. I need to know what happened, Mr. Niederman."

"What *happened*? What do you mean?"

What did his face look like, now? she wondered. She couldn't picture him old. "I need to know why she died and why you never came back, for starters," she blurted. "How could you do that to a child you were close to, just vanish at a time of . . . *crisis?*"

Wally cringed inwardly. It wasn't what she'd planned to lead with.

"Oh my goodness, Wally," he said at last. "There's a lot to talk about. And it's been waiting a long time to be said. Why don't we meet?"

"Yes," she said, not at all sure she was up to seeing him or hearing what he had to say. "Yes, let's meet somewhere to talk."

"Good. I'd like that, Wally. I look forward to hearing everything about you. It's hard for me to picture you all grown, you know, except that you always looked like your mother."

Wally said nothing.

"May I ask what made you track me down, now, after so long? Has anything happened?"

"We can talk when we meet," she said coldly. "When would you be able to come into town?"

"Hang on, now, Wally. I can hear that you're angry. Let me just say this to start. You asked why you didn't see me again after your mother's death. It's pretty simple: I went home. I had to. Your father was coming home. I had no right or reason to be involved with you anymore. It was terrible for me."

429

"I don't want to hear this on the telephone," she said, but he just kept talking. It seemed almost as if he were the one who had called her.

"Maybe you've found out some things, Wally. I guess you must have, but either way, I'll tell you: I was in very much in love with your mother, Wally . . ."

This time she said nothing. She closed her eyes. The phone call had gotten totally out of her control.

"And as a result," he went on, "I had a very guilty conscience about . . . so many things. I wasn't sure how much your father knew, since he'd been away the whole time, but people knew, and I realized he would not want to see me again. I understood that. I was an interloper. I wanted to spend time with you, but your family needed to rally around, you and your father, the way families do, when a loved one dies."

She wanted to scream, but she could hardly breathe, much less speak. Why had she decided to call him, again? What in the world had she hoped for from this conversation? She didn't know anymore.

"I said I can't discuss this on the telephone," she said again, with difficulty.

"I understand, Wally. I'm sorry. I just needed to — to get that out in the open. I'll be glad to come out and see you. I don't have any classes tomorrow. I haven't been back to Brooklyn Heights for so many years."

"No, not Brooklyn." She hadn't thought that far ahead, but she knew she wanted their meeting to be on neutral territory. "Let's meet at the Times Square Horn and Hardart, two o'clock tomorrow."

She chose the Automat because it was bright and anonymous. And because he wouldn't be able to buy her coffee. She would come early and armed with her own nickels, just to be sure of that.

He agreed. And then, without a good-bye, before she had a chance to cry or otherwise further embarrass herself, she hung up.

Wally's trip uptown on the subway the next day felt like an eternity. She kept smoothing her hair, checking her slip, polishing her glasses, worrying her cuticles, scrutinizing her reflection in the dark window across from her. And why had she worn such a conservative blouse and skirt to go meet him, as if she were interviewing for a position as a typist somewhere? She wished she'd worn blue jeans.

She arrived at the Automat early, got herself coffee and a rice pudding from behind a little glass door, and was about to sit down to wait when she saw Mr. Niederman across the room. He'd been earlier yet. His hair was silver now, but his face was the same, his eyebrows still dark. He did not seem to see her. Maybe he didn't recognize her.

"Mr. Niederman?" she said, approaching him. "Is that you?"

He rose up and turned toward her, smiling warmly. So her mother had died carrying this man's child. Her mother had been making love to this man, probably every night after tucking Wally in bed. She wanted to be disgusted, but Wally could see how her mother had fallen for him. She realized when his dark eyes found hers and his full lips parted to say her name that she'd been a little in love with him herself, as a girl. Her heart began to race.

What do you know about how my mother died? she wanted to ask. *Why did she do it?* But it didn't come out. Instead she found herself shaking his hand, asking him politely how he was, how his family was, sitting down. He told her his wife had died of lung cancer several years before, and she offered her condolences.

"It was terrible," he said and looked down at his lap, but all Wally could think was that, however she died, Mrs. Niederman had somehow won.

"Mr. Niederman," she began.

"Won't you please call me Bill?" he said.

"All right then, Bill," she began, but he cut her off.

"What are you doing now, Wally? Have you finished school?"

"You have to understand, Mr. Niederman. My grandmother just died. There are certain things that we are suddenly speaking about in my house that have been very closely held for many years. I'm not interested in small talk."

"Wally, I want to get one thing clear. I was in love with your mother. We were in love with each other. It was a difficult situation, with both of us already married, but it wasn't casual."

"I know that. I also know something I don't think you did: She was pregnant when she died."

He looked stunned.

"It can't be. But — How do you know that? Did she leave a diary?"

"No, actually I learned it from a letter my mother wrote. I saw it for the first time just this week."

"My God," he said, and a mask of sorrow descended on his features. Wally wondered if he really would have left his wife for her mother, if he'd known. What would her life have been like then?

"You know, Mr. Niederman, when I was younger, after you disappeared, I thought maybe you'd been murdered alongside her, or you had vanished for reasons to do with national intelligence. For a time, I also suspected you of killing her. Now, I think it was a different kind of murder."

"I'm not sure I follow you. Stella died of a heart attack. There was no murder involved."

"No, Mr. Niederman, she gassed herself."

"*Gassed herself?* But why, if she was preg—" He looked stricken. "Why didn't she tell me?"

"Well, she did. The letter was to you. The thing that doesn't fit is that she never mailed it."

"You have a letter from Stella to me? Do you have it with you?"

"Did you send her a telegram, that day?" Wally asked, ignoring him.

"Yes," he said slowly. "I did."

"And did you send her a message that could have broken her, made her not want to live?"

"No, that's not the way it happened! I hardly remember what I said, just I love

434

you, and that I would be staying in New Jersey that week. Do you have that, too, then?"

"No. She burned it."

"What about the letter from Stella to me? Do you have it?"

"Yes, but why should I let you read it?"

"They are your mother's last words to me. I loved her. She loved me. You simply must."

She reached into her handbag and pulled out the blue envelope, set it on the table between them.

When he turned it over and saw the address, in her hand, and the unfranked postage stamp, he paused for a long time. It seemed to Wally he was praying, or maybe just remembering something. Then he slid out the folded sheet of paper, densely covered with her mother's script.

As he read, Mr. Niederman's breathing slowed, almost stopped, it seemed, and then he erupted into sobs.

"I didn't know," he said, covering his face with his large hands, "I didn't know."

"Would you have done it?"

"What?"

"Acknowledged the baby."

"I hope I would have been so brave. It's all so long ago, now. I was a different person with Stella."

"So, this is my question, Mr. Niederman. What happened between this letter and the suicide note she left me?"

"I don't know."

"Because the way I see it, yours must have been written first. Or she wouldn't be dead."

"Yes," he said quietly.

"What did you really say in that telegram?"

"I've always regretted the way I put it. Ever since I learned of her death, I've hoped she never got it."

"What did you say?"

"I broke things off somewhat casually. I hadn't the courage to do it to her face. I told her I was going back to my family. I think I remember the exact words, if you must know."

"Go on."

"What a war we had," he said slowly and certainly, as if the words had been engraved in his mind all that time. "I'll miss it. I'm sorry not to tell you directly, but I won't be coming back to Pierrepont Street. My family needs me now."

"You bastard, it was you. You killed her."

"Wally, please, I'm so sorry — Oh, Stella —" he whispered.

"My mother was dreaming of a wild unconventional life, of risking everything

436

and breaking all the social conventions to bear your love child. And you broke her heart, Mr. Niederman. I guess everyone was right all along. It wasn't the gas. It was her heart."

His eyes were rheumy now, filled with tears.

"I didn't know. I never thought — I loved her so much more than Louise, but I was married, and so was she. We both had families. Rudy would be coming home. I was doing what I thought was right. Oh, Wally, I'm so sorry."

"At least it makes sense now, why she tried to pull the letter out of the mail chute. Why she despaired. At least I understand," Wally said. It wasn't forgiveness, but it was all she could offer. Or almost all.

"You know, Bill," she said, "you made her happy for a while. And me. I was a lonely kid, and you were kind to me. You did the best you could." And then she touched the letter on the table in front of him, as if saying good-bye to it. "Why don't you keep this?"

He nodded.

With that, Wally rose, leaving him sitting there, an old man filled with regrets. There was nothing more to say.

34
GOOD NEWS

Sometime during her conversation with Mr. Niederman, Wally had made a decision. Perhaps it was when she saw his anguish at having lost a child he hadn't known existed, or when she thought of her mother's letter to him and her courage, her fearlessness about doing something so unconventional, but at some point she'd realized she had to keep this child. It would be a mess, she knew, but it would be her mess. She was going to do it.

She walked out of the Automat to Grand Central Station, where she called Leo. There was a lot she had to talk to him about. When he didn't answer, she decided to take a chance. She took the subway downtown and walked over to Jane Street. There was no answer when she rang the bell, so she went and bought herself a paper cup of coffee and sat on the stoop and waited.

An hour later, he came home, burdened

with a large sack of folded laundry.

"Wally?"

"Hi, Leo."

"What are you doing here? Did something happen? I thought we weren't going out till later?"

"I just needed to talk to you. I met Mr. Niederman, Leo."

"So, you did it," he said, suddenly interested, setting his laundry down on the steps. "And?"

"It was him."

"*What?* He *killed* her?"

"Well, he might as well have. He sent her some sort of a telegram, breaking it off with her."

"Breaking it off in writing? That sounds a little too familiar."

Wally winced. She hadn't made the connection.

"You're right," she admitted. "But in her case it's a little worse. She had just found out she was pregnant."

"Oh, that's terrible. He knew she was pregnant and he dumped her?" He sat down beside her and began to put his arm around her.

"Actually, he didn't know. He was pretty crushed to hear about the baby. I don't think he could have imagined how badly she would take things."

"Wally," Leo said, quietly. "Do you want to come in?"

Wally nodded. "Yeah, I do."

Inside, Wally told Leo everything Loretta had told her about the day her mother died. They opened a bottle of wine and talked about what it might have been like for Wally's mother, if she'd had a child out of wedlock. What it would have been like for Wally, growing up.

"I probably would have hated that baby," she said.

"And Niederman. You would have despised him if he was your stepfather."

"I don't know. He never had to work very hard to win me over."

"You think he ever told his wife about your mother?"

"No way. And she's dead now."

When they'd exhausted the subject of her mother, Wally moved on to another, easier topic.

"So, can I tell you about what we're working on at the lab, now?"

"Sure, it's been so long. I'm sure I must be way behind on the thrilling events of the ant lab."

"Aw, come on," she said, "it's interesting," but she didn't mind being teased by him.

He really had always been curious to hear about her studies. "So, we've isolated a group of molecules called terpenes, and they're highly volatile. When an ant lays its trail, it lays down terpenes, but they evaporate so quickly that only the most frequently traveled trails persist. That means the most efficient and the most productive routes are reinforced, making them the strongest smelling and most attractive to even more ants."

"Wow," he said. "So you figured out why ants go in a line."

"Oh shut up." She laughed.

"I've just gotten good news myself," he ventured. "In the mail today. I'm going to have a one-man show at the West Broadway Gallery."

"Oh, Leo, that's so good."

They had been talking for hours when she finally got up the courage to talk about the real news she had to share with him.

"Leo?"

"Yeah, Wally?"

"I want to tell you again how sorry I am about what happened when Ham came back," she ventured. "I was just —"

"What?" he said, all of a sudden the injured party again. "You were what?"

She wished she didn't have to go back

over that time, but there was some ground-work that had to be laid.

"I wasn't ready to get married. You were pushing me too hard. I couldn't figure out how to say no. And then Ham came home, and I just fell back into my childhood infatuation with him. It was a mistake. I'm sorry it happened. I wish we could have . . . just taken it slower somehow."

"Why are we going back to this? I know you slept with him. Didn't you?"

She wanted to say it was none of his business, but it was.

"I did."

"How could you have done that?"

"I'm sorry."

"And how could you just break up with me in a letter, like we hardly knew one another?"

"I guess I was afraid. I was afraid I couldn't do it if you were there in front of me."

"I know," he said, remembering that they'd already come through this once. Her relationship with Ham was over.

Leo hadn't focused on how beautiful Wally was that day. It was just good being with her. Now he looked at her and saw her wide open, at a momentary loss for words, and he was floored by her, her beauty, her

442

honesty, and by his near loss of her. Her slightly almond-shaped eyes were magnified behind her silver glasses — shiny and almost brimming over.

"But now there is something else I need to tell you. I'm —"

"What?" he asked.

"I'm having his baby."

Leo blinked and looked down at her hand as if he'd missed something.

"I'm pregnant, Leo, and it happened when I was with him."

"Oh, Wally," he said, leaning slightly away from her. And after a long time, "So, you're having it?"

"I am."

"What does Ham think?"

"He just assumed I'd — get rid of it."

Leo squinted a little, not sure what Ham's attitude meant for Wally. Was she going to stay with him, then? Was Ham sticking by her?

"I understand if you don't want to be with me, given everything, but, Leo — I still love you, Leo."

He could hardly fathom what she was saying, or the idea of Wally being left alone. What fool would leave her?

"So you're not going to get back with him, even though he's the baby's father?"

"How can I? I'm in love with you."

"What about Ham?"

"He'll be in the child's life, I think. We're going to be friends again, eventually, I'm pretty sure."

"Wally?"

"Yeah?"

He imagined what Wally and Ham's baby would look like, so different from the baby he would have had with her. He thought about her grandparents' house on Columbia Heights and those two families, the Walkers and the Wallaces, and what it would be like to be thrust between them. Then he thought about a life lived without this woman, what a waste it would be. He pulled his hands through his hair and then shoved them in his pockets and then finally he held them out to Wally and drew her close to him.

"I want you, Wally."

"And a baby?"

"In fact, I like babies."

"You do?" she stammered. "You wouldn't be angry all the time?"

"I'm not the angry sort," he said.

"I know," she said. "I like that about you."

He reached for her, touched her stomach with its new slight tautness, and kissed her.

"Leo?" she said, a minute or two later.

"Shhh —"

"I just want you to know, I know my options, Leo. I know I could get rid of this baby. I'm choosing not to. You don't have to sign up, just to take care of me."

"That's not why I'm signing up. It's because I love you, Wally Baker. I have for a long time."

"Me too, Leo. I just didn't really know it, till it was too late."

"It's not too late," Leo said, kissing her again.

"I'm so glad," she said.

They lay face to face and kissed and talked and even laughed until the blue haze of the sky faded to gray and the ships in the harbor began to blast their horns in the looming darkness. Wally had never felt so lucky, so loved, in all her life.

35
BEATRICE

"Loretta? Is Ham still coming?" Wally said, the contractions coming faster now.

"Yes," Loretta said. "I called him."

"When?"

"I don't know, sugar, a while ago."

"No, I mean when is he *coming*?"

"He'll get here when he gets here. I guess he's on the train."

"This baby's not going to wait for the train, Loretta," said Wally. She and Ham had agreed that he would be there when the baby was born, agreed that he would not disappear like his own father had. It was important to both of them.

"It's all right, sugar. Leo's here. I'm here. And this part you do alone, anyhow. Ham'll be here by the time they have the baby ready to meet people. Meantime, you need to get up and move, Wally."

"Okay."

"Now, walk. Don't think. Don't worry.

It'll all be over soon. You won't even remember this part or who was here."

"There's a bedtime story you used to tell me, Loretta. I want it to be the first thing I tell the baby."

"What story's that?"

"Once upon a time, when the world was young . . ."

"Oh, that one."

"I can't really remember how it goes, Loretta."

"So, practice it on me."

"Once, when the world was young," Wally began, but then a grappling hook ripped through her core. When she'd caught her breath, her lower lip tasted metallic and chewed on.

"Loretta, I feel another one — it's only been five minutes. I think it's time to go."

The next time Wally's eyes could focus, she was flat in bed, drenched in sweat, and there was something sweet and cold running between her lips and down her chin. Tea. Somehow, Loretta had gotten her there, and then she must have gone away and come back again without Wally even noticing because there was a tall glass of tea on the dresser with beads of condensation clinging to the glass. Now Loretta brought the glass to her mouth. The coldness felt

good against her lips, good in her gullet.
She slurped. A couple of minutes later came
another pang, and she spat up a little bitter
brown water — nothing like the tea — into
a basin that Loretta miraculously had ready.

"Don't drink so fast, Wally. Tiny sips. As
soon as you can walk again, we're going to
go."

"Can you tell Leo?"

"I already told him. He's getting your
bag."

"And have you called Daddy?"

"He's meeting us there."

"And we'll just leave Ham a note on the
door?"

"Exactly."

Loretta rose and went to the telephone
table and dialed the livery service. Next she
called the maternity ward, whose number
she had known by heart for decades, to
warn them Wally was coming. Finally, she
called to Leo, who was downstairs pacing in
the dining room, and he came to help Wally
to the car.

"Leo?" Wally said.

"You're going to be fine, Wally," he said,
smiling.

Wally laughed. "Just double-checking."

A short time after Wally went into the

lying-in ward, Ham arrived in the waiting room.

"Hello, Admiral Baker," he said, and then a little stiffly, "Hello, Leo."

"Hello, Ham."

"Hello, son."

"How's she doing?"

"We don't know anything yet," said Leo.

"Excuse me, gentlemen, is there a Mr. Baker here?" asked a nurse to the room at large a few minutes later.

Admiral Baker, Ham, and Leo all stood up.

"I'm her father," said Admiral Baker.

"I'm the father," said Ham.

"I'm the boyfriend," said Leo.

The nurse looked back and forth between Leo and Ham, at first confused, then appalled.

"Well I'll be a son of a gun," said a man in a business suit sitting beside another expectant father. "Did you hear that?"

In a way, the absurdity of the moment helped to bond them together, and it was all the three men could do to keep from laughing out loud as she took their names and then turned on her heel and left.

They sat in silence and waited while other women's husbands and fathers were informed of joyous news and smoked a half a dozen cigars in celebration. But still, no one came for them. Through each of their minds, the same worries ran: a child born awry, Wally bleeding freely on some table somewhere deep within the hospital while surgeons struggled to save her. They waited and paced and blindly turned the pages of the newspapers that littered the waiting-room tables.

In the hours of labor, Loretta was there, by Wally's side. Nurses came and went, dispensing pain medications and clean, damp towels, but to Wally, it seemed she was alone. Alone, until there, in her isolation, she saw the image of her mother, Stella Wallace, the Silver Wonder, wavery through the ether of time, as if Wally were peering into a barrel of water. Her face was cold but lit by the sun, fractured with shadows and ripples. She was so beautiful, there, just beneath the surface, iridescent with tiny bubbles. There was a faint underglaze of blue.

Wally stilled her mind and took a breath. Refocused her eyes. She was in the kitchen of the Baker apartment on Pierrepont Street. There was a common black sugar ant on the outside ledge of the window, one of those small ones. Then there were two of them, then three, then four, a line of them, and they clustered briefly, waving their antennae. The ants' sisters had told them of a bountiful meal — a scattering of spilled sugar and flour, smudges of butter and chocolate and egg. The counter beyond the window had not been wiped since Stella had begun her cake. The ants wanted into the kitchen to get to that batter, to bring it home, but the way was blocked. The window had been shut. Inside, there were other ants trapped, cut off from the nest. If ants deal in hope, these ants would long since have lost it by the time Loretta came in, but when Loretta came in and saw what she saw, the window was suddenly opened and the ants set free. Some wandered randomly, vainly seeking the faded trail that had linked them to their nest, and were eventually picked off by a passing grackle. The luckier ones crossed more recently laid paths of sisters who still had their bearings, and the good whiff of terpenoids guided them home.

The ants lived or died according to the luck of their wanderings and the half-lives of the scent trails they laid. If they lived, they lived so their hive might live on beyond them. If they died, they didn't appear to mind — so long as their colony survived. In this, if nothing else, Wally thought, we are not like ants. We mind when we die.

Sometimes, when she worked at the ant lab, Wally thought about the vinegar that Loretta had always used to obliterate ant trails. It didn't just wipe away terpenes, it overwhelmed them, making it impossible for ants to reestablish their way. Loretta had always known things that Wally had had to seek higher education to figure out. How did Loretta stand there so calmly, so reassuringly, bathing Wally with damp towels, and patiently waiting for the baby that would be her grandchild as well as Miz Doc Georgeanna Wallace's great-grandchild? She was so sure of herself and so sure of Wally, though neither of them had ever borne a child.

Meanwhile, every time the pain came, Wally drifted away, back home, to her mother, where everything was bluish white, like the pattern of the everyday dishes of the Wallace house, the blue willow, like the blue of Stella's face. Lovers fled across the bridge, water flowed beneath it, the wind rustled the leaves on the branches, the birds took flight. Where was the red? The life? The blood? The oxygen? Gone. Her mother was drowning in a vapor of odorless methane.

Ignited, gas had such amazing power, the power to move and expand air, to bond molecules, to transform. Hot from cold, stars from nothing, cake from batter. Unlit, it had other powers, less renowned. It could pass through a mucous membrane and bond to a mammal's hemoglobin better, more tightly, than oxygen. Hot turned cold, a star plummeted, a mother was reduced to a collection of fluids and cells.

The telegram, that cold and hasty telegram, had purloined her hope. What if she truly had only been flirting with annihilation, knowing Wally and Loretta would be there soon to force her to pull herself together? Would that be any better? Was it worse if it was Wally and Loretta's fault, or if she'd really meant to go through with it?

Now, in Wally's mind, they arrived in time. Wally found the room oddly close and left the door ajar, threw the window open, letting out ants and ushering in clear air.

Wally shut off the gas and plunged her arms into the barrel of bracing blue water and dragged her mother's body out of it, onto the patio, where the breeze fed her brain.

"Mother?" Wally called, and Stella roused. She cradled her mother in her arms. She comforted her. *It's all right, it's all right. It's all right,* she told her. It's all right, she whispered into an ear, a cold blue elegant whelk, a tiny warm pink nautilus, it's all right to

453

have this baby.

And with that and a final, terrible push, Wally was released from her labor. The baby was released into the world. She cried out as she was caught in Loretta's hands. And the moment Wally heard her voice, she named her: Beatrice, after her great-grandmother, Beatrice, the immigrant, the girl-gangster, the doctor, the woman who had wrested respectability from an illicit life. Beatrice, the name she'd always carried but never used for herself. It was perfect.

What would Wally have lost, if she kept her mother? It seemed certain she wouldn't be the mother of Beatrice, this daughter, the tiny being who was suddenly clutching, clutching and sucking, twining Wally's hair in her damp little fists. She was born, and immediately she needed Wally. Wrinkled and misshapen though she was, Wally saw only beauty.

Would Wally give up that life, Beatrice's, if only she could go back in time and save Stella's?

No.

It seemed to Wally as she held her baby that just yesterday she was a child herself, a bespectacled nine-year-old girl out marching in the street with patriotic zeal, banging her pot, unwitting of her mother's imminent death. For all the years since the Victory in Japan, Wally had been in mourning. Now, the first day of the life of her daughter, Beatrice, she realized what was done was done. She must let her mother go.

"Once," Wally whispered, "when the world was young, our planet had no people on it, just plants and stones and mountains and rivers. The Earth was beautiful, but the Great Maker wasn't satisfied. The warm parts were too hot, the snowy places too cold. Nothing ever changed. So the Maker hung the Earth from string and suspended it in a clay pot, which she set on a ledge just near enough to the Sun to keep it warm. I'll let this one set awhile, the Maker thought, and then went on and created countless other worlds. In fact, the Maker all but forgot about the Earth, until one day a spirit child — a daughter of the Maker, from another, more finished and perfect world — sneaked out of her proper place to go exploring. Each world she found seemed too perfect and complete to touch or interfere with, until finally she came upon the great clay jar where the Maker had set our Earth to spin. Down, down, down she went, into the shade of the pot, riding on the silken thread of a mechanical spider of her own devising. She was determined to find something that was new and to do something that would make her mark. As night fell, she realized she hadn't considered how difficult it would be to ascend again. When she tried, the thread broke, and the mechanical spider fell clattering through the stars, where it lodged and became our moon. *Mother,* called the spirit child, but the Maker did not hear her. And so, the spirit child got to work, doing what she'd seen the Maker do so many times: She chipped holes in the pot to let more sunlight in. She invented all the forms of animal life, one by one, with all their wonder and imperfection. And though it was not flawless, like the Maker's worlds, the spirit child had started something beautiful in motion, and still it spins from its thread, and you and I are part of it."

In her arms, Beatrice lay limp and heavy, damp and warm, and then, as Wally began to drowse, she came alive, blinked, nuzzled.

"Wally," said Ham. "Let me hold her. Pass her to me."

"How long have I had her?"

"A while," he said.

"Good," she said.

"I'm waiting, too," said Leo.

"And me," said Loretta.

The admiral just stood back and smiled.

"Well, you all have to wait. You can't have her yet."

The child began bleating, and Wally held her to her breast, and after a while she quieted, and slept, and they fell back to breathing as one. Beatrice dreamed what dreams a newborn child can dream, and Wally dreamed not of her mother or the past, but of her daughter and the wide-open future.

ACKNOWLEDGMENTS

I am grateful to the following institutions and individuals for their invaluable support of me while I was writing this book: the Corporation of Yaddo, the Brooklyn Historical Society, the Getty Foundation, the Schomberg Center of the New York Public Library, the New School, *A Public Space,* Powderkeg, Proteus Gowanus, the St. George Tower Yahoo Group, Andrea Chapin, Candace Wait, Elaina Richardson, Robert Polito, Luis Jaramillo, Helen Schulman, Laura Cronk, Brigid Hughes, Bob Tomlinson, Deborah Schwartz, Kate Fermoile, Liz Call, Julie May, Sadie Sullivan, Mary-Beth Hughes, Daphne Klein, Tammy Pittman, Sascha Chavchavadze, Holly Morris, Sharon Lerner, Sheri Holman, Al Attara, Kate Medina, Leigh Feldman, Jean Garnett, Anna Pitoniak, Derrill Hagood, Lindsey Schwoeri, Millicent Bennett, Evan Camfeld, Susan Brown, Ingrid Powell,

Howard Cohn, Ann Gaffney, Bronson Bin-
ger, Emily Boro, Gil Boro, Alex Boro, and
Lucy and Willa Gaffneyboro.

ABOUT THE AUTHOR

Elizabeth Gaffney is the author of *Metropolis*. She is the editor at large of the literary magazine *A Public Space* and teaches fiction at The New School. Her stories have appeared in literary magazines such as *The Virginia Quarterly Review* and the *North American Review*, and she has been a resident artist at Yaddo, the MacDowell Colony and the Blue Mountain Center. She lives in Brooklyn with her husband, the neurologist Alex Boro, and their daughters.

The employees of Thorndike Press hope you have enjoyed this Large Print book. All our Thorndike, Wheeler, and Kennebec Large Print titles are designed for easy reading, and all our books are made to last. Other Thorndike Press Large Print books are available at your library, through selected bookstores, or directly from us.

For information about titles, please call:
  (800) 223-1244

or visit our Web site at:
  http://gale.cengage.com/thorndike

To share your comments, please write:
  Publisher
  Thorndike Press
  10 Water St., Suite 310
  Waterville, ME 04901